NOBLE NETWORK GUNNER

A PROTECTIVE HERO NOVEL

NOBLE NETWORK
BOOK ONE

JODI JAMES

JAMES VENTURE PRESS

To my dearest husband, thank you for being my protector. Your strength, love, and integrity soars leaps and bounds. I'm blessed to have you in my corner. Thank you for giving me my happily- ever-after, you are the heart of all my stories and everything good. I love you so, very, much. You are my hero.

CHAPTER

ONE

One guard tapped at the door, then bolted in.

"Psst...get down. Someone is coming."

CJ cowered, her teeth chattering. She glanced at the firefighter crawling to the furthest wall. There had been plenty of close calls, but this had been one of the most dangerous situations to date. Other than running from people trying to kill her at every turn.

Silence filled the dilapidated cabin. No one dared breathe. They could hear voices and footsteps outside the structure. If these were the guys chasing them, they'd just been busted. And no way out. If it was the bad guys for hire involved with the motorcycle club Denver's Devils' Delinquents, they were in deep doodoo.

If anyone was saying anything, CJ couldn't hear a sound, only the thundering of her own heartbeat. She looked around, but couldn't see another exit. *We're trapped.*

One of her protectors inched his way to the window as the other crawled to the only other room in the cabin. Voices drew closer. One of her guardians flattened himself against her,

1

wedging himself between her and the front door. She was lucky to have such able-bodied guards keeping her safe, but another level entirely with Gunner. All of them had been together for several years with rotations and additional guards often woven through. Gunner was the only constant—he often took extra shifts, opting not to rotate out.

The bloodied firefighter sported a mountainous bump and laceration on his head. He had been in the wrong place at the wrong time, the innocent in all this mess. *Why did he get anywhere near me and my bad juju?* He eyed his hands and looked at the guards' weapons, probably wishing he had one of his own. *Don't we all.* "What's your name?" CJ whispered and gave him a jab.

"Jackson Honeycutt. You can call me Jax."

"Okay, Jax."

"You can run, but you can't hide, my little pretty. I know you're in there," someone spat venomously outside. "Get your asses out here or we will torch you. Either way, someone won't see tomorrow."

CJ's hair raised on the back of her neck. Fear shot through her. Something unnerving and familiar that sliced deep. She had heard the malevolent tone before and, with everything in her, she believed they were the reason she was in protective custody. They were *why* she strived intently to put most of them behind bars, finally making a dent in getting the drugs off the street so innocent children wouldn't die anymore. CJ had to see this final trial through to the end.

She had to shake off the feeling. Now was not the time to panic. She locked sights on her bodyguards as they signaled one another in their unspoken language. They'd protect her.

Yes, they will protect me.

She swallowed hard and shook her head. CJ had witnessed it over the years and usually could gauge their next move. Each of them had a military background and was put to the test more than she cared to admit. They excelled at numerous combat skills. They always had a plan, and would fight to the death to protect her and succeed in their mission. They could get a metric shitload done in seconds. Her faith in them was tested, but never disheartened.

One of them took off at a sprint to another window. A shot rang out, busting the glass and spraying shards all over the space. Jax, stretched flat and locked his limbs around the leg of the table, yanked it with his good hand and sat up in swift move, flipping it on its side as a barrier in front of them.

Another pop sounded, hitting Tiny, her biggest protector. He staggered backwards, trying to right himself, before he dropped to the floor in a tank-size heap. Jax slid across the floor, pulling Tiny with a grunt behind the table. She scrambled to aid him in his attempt. Watching it all unfold went from waves of hyper-speed to slow motion. Jax examined her guard and shoved her hands over his wound. "Apply pressure," he said as he did what he could one handed.

Sweat beaded above her upper lip, goosebumps prickled up her spine. The stagnant air lingered and she tugged at her constrictive hoodie. CJ had the sensation of being underwater. Every intake of air echoed, her pulse boomed in her ears so loud she thought she'd go deaf. Tiny was hit in the shoulder and scarlet splattered from the front to the back of his white dress shirt. Shrapnel whizzed overhead, lodging in one wall. She hoped the bullet had missed vital organs, thankful she dodged it too. *I couldn't live with myself if something ever happened to any of these men who protected me after one of the biggest mistakes in my life. I can't fathom ever forgiving myself.*

The hottie firefighter, Jax, was in his zone. He yanked one of the curtains down and fumbled to rip it, instead wadding it into a ball. CJ sniffed the air and memories flooded her. The way her dad smelled when he came home from a shift at the firehouse, the campfires with her family.

She was jarred back and shouted "Fire!" The bad guys were making good on their threat.

A noise erupted from outside. "You can stay in there, but it's gonna get hot. Woman, if I were you, I'd come out. You've been opening your pie-hole long enough. You're going to die anyway, you bitch."

Gunner had his usual peeved demeanor when anyone messed with her. He aimed a gun at the voices through another boarded window.

CJ tightened her jaw, trying to stop her teeth from chattering. Bile rose in her throat. Waves of fear shot through her. Why did she think she could testify against one of the biggest drug lords on the west coast and the Denver Devils Delinquents bike club?

"I'm not about to walk through fire just to get shot, you weenie heads," CJ screamed out.

She felt everyone's watchful gaze, including Tiny's bulging eyes from his sockets. "What?" She gave them a stare. "I'm not."

Tiny grimaced and whispered, "Weenie heads?"

"It was the first thing that came to mind."

He held his shoulder and laughed. "You're something else with your old slang and unique words."

CJ's foot was swelling from the spring earlier. Jax hadn't had a chance to slip an ace bandage over it after he'd removed her shoe, so he slipped it in his pocket and tried to put her shoe on. She winced in pain, ripping at the laces to loosen them. But was nothing compared to Tiny's injury.

A clear, high shrill came from Hawke, signaling Gunner. They locked eyes and Hawke gave his head a jerk to his left. A split-second later her favorite protector took a flying leap and slid across the floor to an extended space behind the kitchen. CJ's mouth gaped open at Gunner's impressive move. She held pressure on Tiny's wound, hoping her attempt would help stop the bleeding. She craned her neck, inspecting what they were doing. Jax waved the air to circulate the plumes of billowing smoke. She coughed and hoped they had an exit plan, and fast.

Jax inched his way to the corner near the cot and yanked the other part of the curtain. He ripped the fabric between his teeth, tearing it into large strips. He grabbed one of the half-emptied water bottles, pouring out the liquid, soaking the cloth.

"What can I do?" CJ asked as she grabbed it from him.

"Put your hoodie on. Any more smoke fills this place, I want you to wrap this around your face, covering your nose and mouth." He handed her a waterlogged stretch of material. He aided Tiny with his wrap. "It won't help much, but it's all we got. Do you understand?"

Smoke rolled under the door and through the broken window as she gasped for air. "It won't be long before breathing becomes difficult," Jax stated, and his point was taken.

Who is he kidding? They'd all die if they didn't get out of there soon, succumbing to toxic fumes; she knew that much from her father and brother. Firefighting was a family business she'd hoped to pursue before she blew it all on her first crush. A tragic lapse in judgement.

The explosive sound of gunfire reverberated from all directions, from the guards and the familiar voices outside. CJ flinched at the noise. She shrunk to escape the bullets, hurling herself over Tiny who was unconscious now. He'd lost a lot of blood. Her adrenaline spiked and she wanted to flee.

"I need to stop the bleeding." The firefighter squinted, looking through the haze. "Where's the kit?"

"We have a first aid kit over there." She pointed to the duffel bag.

Before he barely had the words exit his mouth, CJ had limped across the floor and dragged the bag, as big as she was. Unzipping it, she handed him the satchel of sutures, antiseptics, and drugs.

"You're speedy."

"I would have been faster if I didn't have a bad sprain on the wiggly doodads connected to my shin." He gaped at her. "What?" she gave him an equally epic eye-popping stare. "Through the years I've learned to think fast. What else do you need?" She coughed. "It's stifling in here." She tugged at the neck of her shirt and pushed her hair away from her sweaty forehead.

"Psst..." CJ followed the sound and caught sight of Gunner as he whispered. "You good?"

She nodded, pulling the saturated cloth over her mouth again and squinting through the haze. Cinders of ash and sparks fell through the ceiling. "I'm ready to roll, on your cue."

"Soon." Gunner's gaze shift and he whistled to the firefighter, directing him to move the injured Tiny closer in his direction.

Hawke reloaded and continued his explosive assault, sending rounds of bullets through the window, dodging and weaving away from the thunderous return fire. He got on all fours and scampered away.

I am not about to stay rooted in this spot by my lonesome. Do something...

Gunner was methodically pulling away floorboards. CJ crawled over Tiny and helped Gunner with the planks. "There's a hidey-hole here," she said in surprise.

"Yup. We don't go anywhere without an exit strategy. You realize this by now, don't you?" Gunner cocked a brow.

"Why do you think I feel so safe with you? You are amaze-balls, my number one hero." She rubbed her nose back and forth with a shaky hand. "I knew I liked you for some reason. Maybe I'll keep you." *Here I am scared to death, yet somehow focusing on my silver lining. Gunner.*

CJ had never noticed Gunner get flustered or cave under pressure, but this time was different. It was there in a flash—something changed in his hazel gaze as she inspected him. His smooth bravado stammered a little. A softening of sorts. It pierced her soul. He had been the best part of the past few years in the witness protection program. If it hadn't been for him, she didn't know if she could've made it through the other trials and living life undercover. He brought a different level to the mix.

"Hey! If you two are finished with the terms of endearment, we need to high tail it. Now is best." Hawke grumbled over his shoulder.

Jax followed with, "We're minutes away from a flash over. We'll be ash."

"What do you think I'm doing here?" Gunner retaliated. And just like that, the soft edge of Gunner changed to the fierce warrior he was. "We gotta go."

"Say no more." CJ crab-crawled across the floor to retrieve the duffel bag. She knew the drill. They'd had to leave at a moment's notice after their cover was blown, but the weapons and med kit in the duffel bag saved them between places. Where they went, the bags did too.

"Don't let her out of your sight, Captain America, if you know what's good for you. We're leaving in two." Gunner removed the rest of the floorboards, strapped on his extra weapons, and jumped into the pit. He waved CJ in as he lifted his neck rag over his nose and mouth. The smoke was dense and huge chunks of the ceiling were torpedoing down. Cinders found their way through CJ's clothing and burned her skin. She went this way and that before leaping into Gunner's waiting arms.

Jax followed behind, dragging Tiny by his legs. A barrage of gunshots went pop, pop, pop. The sound was ear-splitting. Hawke was still behind, firing at the stalkers, until he yelled, "Incoming!" Hawke was known for his over-zealous moves. She thought he'd be perfect as a stunt double in Hollywood with his charismatic looks and dramatic personality. They bounded under the floorboards and hit earth.

CJ peered through the darkness and noticed Jax wincing in pain. She crawled through the trench of high-grade rubber tarps covered with tree limbs and leaves. They powered further as the smoke dissipated and breathing became easier. She heard Hawke at the rear say, "Move it. Won't be long before the leaves and our covering go up in smoke, but I have a little surprise waiting for our uninvited trespassers." He lit something and CJ heard a hissing sound, like a sparkler on steroids. "Bust a move, kiddies. Unless you want to be a part of the fireworks display."

CJ was yanked forward by Gunner, who was hauling ass at warp speed. Not a minute or two later, an explosion erupting the ground. Everything shook beneath them and she lost her balance. CJ's ears rang as she wiped her mouth and spit debris, swearing she'd eaten a mud pie. The temperature dropped, her skin cooled, and a sensation of descending made her feel like she was about to do a somersault. Her bodyguards knew what they were doing and, like every scenario to date, this was another well-thought-out escape plan. Good thing they were dedicated to their mission, or she'd be dead.

An unnerving stillness cloaked her. There were no sounds from the shooters and the roar of the fire had been replaced by dampness on her skin. The smell of moist rock and soil invaded her nose. They trudged through knee high water, Gunner aiding her when she slipped too far behind a multitude of rocks and boulders.

The darkness allowed her time to think. Beams of light soothed her, shining through holes in what she believed a cavern. They finally stood up from the trench, they pushed forward into an old coal mining shaft. Gunner and Hawke uncovered a mountainous heap under a large tarp. Each handed helmets with headlamps in haste, Gunner rigging the tarp and two wooden dowels to carry provisions and their injured comrade. Lanterns were lit for their descent. A trail of blood streaming from Tiny, who floated in and out of consciousness. For the moment he was his cranky, peeved self, not mincing words. The f-word was his favorite cuss word for his pain.

"Hey, I think we need to stop so I can look at the bullet wound better," the firefighter said as he grabbed the back of Gunner's shirt. Gunner looked at the man's hand, then his face. His lips were in a flat line.

"Oops. My bad." Jax said as if the proximity had burned him.

"Keep going," Hawke said. "We're almost there. Then you and I can give him medical aid. Right now, our priority is getting CJ far away from those vile asswipes."

CJ turned to Tiny. "I'm sorry. This is all my fault."

He grabbed her hand. "What? This? It's nothing." His brows puckered and he faked a smile.

They stopped at a circular area with a high opening. Hawke opened a map as Gunner held on to CJ. "You look pale. I got you. There's nothing to be frightened of."

"Right, just another day in paradise. Thanks. This darn foot is not helping matters." She moved closer, clutching him in a death grip. She tried to mask her fear, but who was she kidding?

"We can stop so you can rest," Gunner said.

His gaze filled with concern and his harsh lines softened again—a rarity until recently, catching her off guard in a pleasant way. "Nonsense." She wiped her forehead with the back of her hand. "Where are we?" Her words came out in a rush.

The firefighter grabbed the pack sitting nearby and tended to Tiny. Hawke passed water around, and Gunner dug through the bag for drugs to ease his partner's injury. He handed him a couple of pills, and Tiny gulped them fast. Hawke eyeballed a vial, loaded the syringe, and administered a heavier dose of antibiotic. "I'll leave the stitching up to you, Honeycutt. Usually its Tiny's forte, though we can do it in a pinch."

"What do you need? This bag is like a mini urgent care. We don't need hospitals this way. It's safer for us, and if we need more, our boss can arrange it. We have everything at our disposal," Gunner said and handed him a packet. "Use this to slow the blood flow so you can do what you need to. We don't have much time. I'll assist."

He inspected the package. "You have it all." Honeycutt's eyes widened. "I'd say."

CJ was transfixed as firefighter Honeycutt stitched up Tiny. Her stomach rolled in waves at all the blood. She spun around, almost losing her balance on her sore ankle, and threw up.

Maybe following her father's footsteps was not in the cards after all.

Gunner stopped what he was doing, looked at her, and rifled through his own backpack.

She lifted a finger and swung back and forth to stop his attempt. "No thanks." She ran her hand along her stomach. "I'll barf again."

"No argument." His deep voice boomed in her ears. "You need your strength; we don't know what's ahead of us. Here." He shoved the electrolyte drink and a protein bar in her hand. His eyes flashed when she complied. "Try the liquid first. It will help your stomach, since you're probably dehydrated. Eat the bar, when you feel up to it."

"Thank you, G, I mean Gunner." She smiled and dropped her head. Calling him Gunner was more endearing than G.

In the beginning, the only thing she had known about any of her protectors was their code names. G, Hawke, Tiny, Ry, Luca, and so on—it was very impersonal. Their weapons were intimidating, and they had taught her to protect herself.

After being with her handlers this long, she even recognized their familiar footfalls. Gunner was stealth like a hungry mountain lion. Waiting. Watching. Nothing got by him. He barely formed a sentence, let alone a word to her, for the first few years. They were her loneliest. He'd protected her but kept his distance. His walls were impenetrable, which made her want to break them down. His energy that spoke volumes without a syllable.

Something in his eyes, like he understood loss and heartbreak. She was drawn to him like a moth to a flame. An invisible thread. When he moved, he soared like the wind. He could be on one end of the house, the next moment beside her before she knew it. But when he meant business, each step was like an anvil. Each stride had purpose.

Hawke, on the other hand, he was an assessor, studying everything and everyone's actions ad motives. His look alone could give you chills. He was massive, scarred, and inked up. Like them all, he had intention in every movement, every look, his steps quick and fast. He was one of best to have at your side when your life mattered. The stories they told gave her chills; most of them were alive because of his quick action.

Ryker had an easiness to his saunter, like his jokester personality. His smile could light up a room, which was off-putting because he was completely unexpected. When needed, he was lightning, agile, fast and went in for the kill. He'd mastered all weapons, but martial arts were his jam. His body was the most lethal.

Luca and Ryker were two peas in a pod. Pranksters. They reminded her of her brothers. Luca was the risk-taker, a genius with online stuff. He had many facets to him, including being linguist in the military, which was usually reserved for the top brains. He was a story spinner and got bored fast, so he was always wearing many hats. He had the kindest spirit. Axel, Tiny, Jett, and a few others had rotated through, but these four were her extended family, because they wanted to be her guards.

That was a lifetime ago. She'd lived many places and testified at two trials, with the third in the wings. CJ longed for her family, but since she was in hiding, she craved connection, and these men had become her family.

In the witness protection, we played the roles we're assigned. Their connections had become more solid. Everything was all by the rule book—they didn't know CJ and she didn't trust them—but over the past five years, things had shifted.

The stakes got higher with every case. Tiny, Ryker, and Luca usually had replacements for as much as six months when they went on some secret assignment. Hawke was around more, but Gunner was her constant. These situations were dangerous. Liking Gunner had been unexpected and beyond a simple connection for her. She'd rather keep her feelings close and protected. *I'm broken already.* No family, no lives in danger. CJ held herself responsible for getting people killed. *I shouldn't have gotten mixed up with the triple Ds.*

Her guards were respectful and professional. To date, there had been no canoodling outside a role they portrayed, though one kiss had changed everything. It might have been for duty, but one could wish with Gunner.

Oh...a girl could wish.

"Let's pack it up and move forward. We need to find a spot to call and get the extraction team up here," Gunner said. He snapped his fingers at CJ. "You solid? What did I teach you? Keep alert." He tapped his temple.

She jumped and saluted him, pulled her hair away from her face. "Ready. Keep alert, keep alive." *So much for a daydream.*

Each of them, including CJ, shouldered Tiny's weight. Sometimes they were at a crawl and other times they were lowering him into tiny crevices with the tarp. He was in and out of it most of the time, sweating profusely, weak from the loss of blood. They needed to hurry.

CJ pressed her hand on the injured man's forehead. "He's burning up." She poured more water on a cloth and ran it along his forehead and neck. "I don't think the antibiotics are working. We need to get him to a hospital." She jumped as gunfire echoed through the cavern, the sound amplified against the rocks.

Gunner and Hawke stilled, listening intently. Both guards were laser focused, rod straight in their stance.

"Where did the shots come from? Are they behind us?" CJ whipped around.

Hawke and Gunner fanned out.

"I hear something back there...or is it coming from here?" Gunner pointed in one direction, then the other. "The sounds are bouncing off the rocks."

Gunner and Hawke took off at a fast jog to where they thought the shots came from. CJ inched her way closer to Jax, looking this way and that.

Honeycutt pulled on CJ's jacket to get her attention. "How do you think they found you? They either knew where you were going, or they followed your trail." He leaned in and whispered. "I thought your bodyguards were good. Do you trust them?"

"Trust them?" She puffed out a little air and hissed. "They've gotten me away from worse jams than this," CJ said with a matter-of-fact smirk, a hand on her hip. "Don't even go there, big guy. My guards have saved my life on more than one occasion. Look what they did today." She played with the plastic cap on her drink. "They saved your tail from getting killed at the courthouse and then just now. I trust them with my life." She rested against a huge boulder. "You should too. Wasn't it the gunfire had you flying into our van? I wouldn't be here today if it wasn't for them, and that's a fact. They've done everything they can to keep me hidden until I'm required to testify, but each time more threats come in droves. The people I'm testifying against have connections everywhere. The drug lords, the dealer, the bike club. This next hearing is with the head of the drug distribution and his sidekick. Barry Ryder and James Devland have already made several attempts on my life. I barely got away from them when I was a teen and I've been running since. But you probably know this." She swung around as she heard heavy footsteps pounding though the puddles.

"I think I know who you're talking about. They've caused pain and havoc to everyone I know, including me."

"You don't owe him anything. He doesn't deserve any of your explanations." Gunner laid a soft hand on her elbow. "Come on. We need to move fast." Gunner swooped her up and CJ teetered. She gave him a smile and wrapped her arms around his shoulders. His warmth comforted her away from the dreary dampness of the tunnels. "Don't want your ankle to get worse." He winked and gave her a glimpse of his pearly whites.

CJ clung tight to her savior, who never broke a sweat. He weaved, ducked, and snaked through the tunnels of the mine shaft. She peered at Jax. The fire guy gawked at her again.

"Geez, I'm trying my best to right the wrongs of my past. I guess he hasn't forgiven me." She hated being under the microscope.

"Who cares?" Gunner said with a snap.

I do. I care.

They hit daylight again at the mouth of the cave-like entrance. Gunner sat CJ on a nearby rock.

Hawke pulled at the arm of Gunner's shirt. "Come here."

The two men were hovered in a corner, whispering. CJ inspected their back-and-forth exchange. A muscle in Gunner's jaw ticked and he gripped his shoulder harness, tugging on it. His brows slashed over his intense stare at his comrade. Gunner shook his head and Hawke stepped forward with a yes. Their conversation was getting heated, but the two of them usually hashed out the best plan of action.

Her protectors joined them again, Gunner's line of sight was everywhere but upon her. He raked his fingers through his hair and shifted from foot to foot, all the while never engaging one glance. This was one time she could read a room, and the pulse ticking in her neck made her wish she hadn't. Something was changing and, if her radar served her correctly, Gunner wasn't a fan. He was wearing the look he usually did when he either didn't want to comply or was gauging an exit strategy. Both were plausible.

"What are we doing now?" CJ asked.

Hawke attempted a step in her direction, but Gunner stopped him. He inched closer and raised his gaze.

Her heart pounded against her sternum. She took a long swig of her drink to coat her parched palette. "You're giving me the willies." She jutted her chin upward. "I have a feeling I will not like this, but what else is new?"

Gunner inched closer and reached for her hand. "The three of you are in no shape to travel and we need to get help." He ran the pad of his thumb over the back of her hand. "I—I hate this. If there was another solution I'd stay, but it's our best option." He swallowed hard and trudged off to Jax.

"Leave us here?" Her voice echoed louder than she expected. "With him and Tiny?" She pointed at the firefighter. "We're all sitting ducks with our injuries."

"We don't have a choice. You trust me, right?" He inched closer and whispered, "You still have your burner, right?"

She nodded. "I do, but..." Images of what could happen flashed through her mind. "Yes." She padded her pocket.

"Honeycutt, we need you to stay behind and look after our mate. He needs your medical care. I know you still have a head splitter, but you're our only option. CJ can't travel with her foot. We have the best chance locating the extraction team and getting transportation here pronto." He shook his head. "Tell me now if you're not up for it and I'll send Hawke alone." His voice was almost a growl.

"Go. Tell me what to do."

"I'm putting all my faith in you." He pointed a finger into Honeycutt's chest. "I never leave a post unless I have a damn urgent reason. My professional responsibility over the years has been by CJ's side. If anything happens to her, I swear I will hold you personally responsible."

Tiny tried to sit up and piped in, "Stick with the worst case exit we already planned for. I'm here. I have a weapon. I'll protect her."

Gunner crouched to the ground and whispered to his wounded partner. "You have a bullet hole in you, and you're barely conscious. I'm saying you'll need someone to watch your six."

"I know better than argue. Get moving and hurry." Tiny's shoulders slumped and he winced.

Hawke hung up his radio call with the extraction team. "G, we need to move out. They're miles away and we need to break ground." Hawke yanked at his shirt. "First things first. Get these three set up for success. Into the hidey-hole."

"Weren't we just in one?" CJ said, looking at Hawke.

"It's compromised. Who knows if they're already inside? We couldn't tell where the shots were coming from, but they were close." Hawk pointed. "We have another one."

CJ stepped outside and shaded her face against the sun. "Where?"

"Exactly. If you can't see it, no one else will."

Gunner grabbed his binoculars and surveyed the area. "Clear." Hawke took the lead, gauging the landscape. They directed CJ and Jax to follow. Moving to higher ground, they had an advantage, seeing everything from a panoramic view.

"Is it just me, or did you plan this all out?" Honeycutt said.

"We didn't do this alone. There is a lot at stake, with no room for error. We didn't just happen upon this place. Being hijacked by gunfire after a meeting with the District Attorney and your jump into the van wasn't a part of the plan, but we improvised and went to plan B. Then plan C. Or is this D?"

"Being in the middle of this drama and the waylay of

bullets was not on my agenda either, so I guess we're even," Jax sneered.

"We'll see how well you take care of CJ and Tiny," Gunner popped. "If we're not back and you get surrounded...see the grouping of boulders over there?" Gunner pointed. "It's an old bear den. There should be room enough for the three of you to hide. Excluding any bears."

CJ's head whipped around to where he pointed. "Bears?" Her bottom lip trembled at the thought.

"Don't worry, CJ. I'll find you. I promise." Gunner said.

Hawke tossed Jax the med bag. "You might need this. There's food and water. Best take care of our cargo."

Gunner stepped close to Honeycutt. "You may not realize this yet, but she's good people." He took another step; this time they were toe to toe. "Anything happens to her and I will hunt you for life."

"Gotcha." Jax nodded, then they took off through the trees. "Shit. They're fast."

CJ bit at her nails and caught sight of Gunner turning around. He crossed his heart, and she gave him a thumbs up.

"Guess you didn't expect this outcome either?"

"What?" She didn't want to turn away from Gunner, but did. "Not in the slightest." When she turned back, they were gone. "I'm used to following them, but Tiny isn't good. I'm afraid it's up to us." She reached over to feel the guard's forehead again. "He's still got a fever and he's out more than he's awake." CJ winced, jerking in pain from her swollen ankle.

Jax rustled through the contents of the bag. "He needs more antibiotics, and we should tape up your ankle in the event we need to hit the ground running."

"We were busy with our tagalongs. First the bullets, then the blaze." She craned her neck around and again, fiddling with her fingers. "Hmmm..."

"What are you thinking about?"

"My sister. Her name is Blaze. She hated her name as much as I hated mine."

"I take it your name isn't CJ?"

"You got that right, but let's leave the conversation for another time and place."

"The fire has spread. We need to keep an eye for a change in the wind's direction. This is fire season, and the conditions aren't favorable. Look at the trees over there—they're candling." He pointed to the area near the smoldering cabin. "And there's debris burning. The last time we had conditions like this was from a campfire, another time a cigarette. Disastrous for Colorado."

"I remember. Candling? I've heard the term before, but it's been forever. What does it mean?"

"Burning from the bottom of a single tree or cluster to the top." Jax snapped a twig and threw it.

"Oh yes. I learned a lot from my dad and brother."

"Your family is in the fire service? From Solemn Creed?"

Tiny coughed uncontrollably, breaking up their conversation.

"We need to get him away from the smoke. It's getting worse. At this elevation, he's probably having a hard time breathing. His coughing might gain attention."

CJ patted him on the arm and gave Tiny a sip of water. "Shhh. You rest, buddy. Go to sleep." All sorts of scenarios spun in her mind as she circulated the air above Tiny. *Anything can happen.* "You're right. I'd feel better if we weren't here, exposed. What if Tiny coughs and they hear us? Should we take cover?" CJ looked to Jax for guidance.

CHAPTER

THREE

J ax craned his neck around to the rock caves the guards mentioned earlier. "Our only option is over there." He hitched a thumb across the way. "We have this tarp. It's not made to stop, drop, and roll, but it will come in handy."

"I'm ready if you are. Load me up." She waved a hand to get him to hurry.

Jax handed CJ the duffel and tarp. "If you can hobble a little longer, I'll haul your guard." He grabbed Tiny under the arms and lost his footing. Righting himself, he began the journey, grunting in pain.

"Are you sure you're, okay?" she asked as she hobbled to keep up.

"Dandy. I'll follow. Can't have you lagging. You sure you can handle everything?"

"Don't worry about me. You're the one with Tiny. I'll do my best limp action."

"Your guards would kill me if something happened to you."

"Doesn't look like you're doing much better. Your head's

bleeding again and you're going in the cave first. If there are bears in there and they have the munchies, they'll eat you first and be full before they can get to me."

CJ AND JAX swatted fiery ash as they took off as fast as they could to the old bear den. They stopped at the opening. "Go on." She inched into the crevice while Jax maneuvered the wounded guard into the cover.

"We have company. They're hunting and we're the prey."

"You're not talking about bears, are you?"

He put a finger over his lips and pointed.

CJ crouched, yanked him into the cave, and pointed off into the distance. "Look. I think that's them." She squinted through the haze, trying to recognize the face from the familiar voice she'd heard earlier.

Jax nudged her. "Exactly what I was talking about, having company and all. Those are your stalkers, right?"

"Unfortunately. Everyone's a stalker these days. I'm assuming they come in all shapes and sizes. I just don't know anymore." She gave a nervous laugh. "They don't look like they are hunting caribou."

"We need help. Wish I had my phone," Jax said.

CJ patted her pocket. "I have one. It's a burner phone."

"You've had a phone all along and you said nothing?"

"I've been kind of busy, you know. I use it only in dire situations. Gunner slipped me one so I could send phantom texts to someone. Made me feel better, over the years, but until recently they didn't even know it was from me. A girl must protect herself. I wasn't sure if I can trust you. Anyhoo, Hawke and Gunner said they wouldn't be long."

"We don't know how much time they'll be gone. I could

have had someone called by now." They cowered near the opening.

"Squeeze in. Let's get all the way inside." He nudged her a little further. "Look for something to block the entrance."

"Like what? It's a little cramped in here. We can't even stand."

"We can use some of these basketball-sized boulders. I'll need your help."

She crawled over on her hands and knees and used her good foot to push them, but at this rate, she'd be old and gray before they got anywhere near the entrance.

He shifted Tiny off the tarp. "We can use this to cover at the opening and prevent the smoke from coming in."

CJ and Jax crawled around playing a game of twister over body parts. "I'm getting claustrophobic." She curled into herself and prayed to the gods Gunner and Hawke would hurry. "Now what? They should have taken Tiny with them."

"Yeah, I'm not so sure they should have left him here with us. I need your phone."

CJ hesitated, then handed him her phone. "Who are you calling?"

"I'm doing what most people do in an emergency; I'm just not usually on this side of it. We're going to need all the help we can get if we're getting through this alive."

"I want it returned."

Jax dialed 911. The dispatcher answered the line. "My name is Jackson Honeycutt. I'm a first responder. I'm trapped near Rocky Mountain National Park with an injured man and woman, one's been shot. Smoke's getting heavy here," he said, then coughed.

Tiny trembled uncontrollably and CJ rubbed his head, trying to sooth him. "Tell them to hurry." She waved some of the smoke through a crevice.

"I need you to locate Roberts with Solemn Creed Dispatch Team. It's urgent." Jax looked at CJ, holding the phone so she could hear.

The voice on the other end of the line said, "Jackson, stay on the line. I'm contacting them."

Jax coughed again into his elbow and lifted the wet rag over CJ's mouth and nose.

"We've located her. It should be just a moment; she's in the emergency mobile unit in the field."

"Hurry." Jax gagged. CJ handed him a bottle of water and waved some of the smoke away, listening intently as he waited on the phone.

"Is that you?" Jax said as he gasped, clearing his lungs. His breathing was heavier than before.

CJ squinted and got a better look. "You're looking a little pasty."

He took a swig of water and answered the person on the line. "Yes, it's me." He coughed again and held his head. "Listen to me carefully. I haven't been kidnapped. They're the good guys. Someone is chasing us. We were in a cabin and they torched it. Tell the search team to turn away. The fire's spreading," Jax said louder than a whisper.

CJ's pulse raced through her veins and her heart thumped against her chest. Were they going to burn alive? The firefighter was not looking good at all. They were all going to die.

"Listen. The guys who torched a cabin shot at us, and they're not far away. We're hiding. Two of the men with us went for help, but I have a badly injured man with us who's been shot, and the woman can't go far with her sprained ankle" He coughed and gasped again. He rubbed his eyes and shook his head.

"Geez. I swear you don't look any better than Tiny," CJ mumbled. "You okay?"

He shook his head yes, then from side to side. His eyes were red-rimmed and his head wound was trickling crimson

"Let me take care of you." She dabbed at his head, but he swatted her away. "Don't be such a tough guy."

"We're near the first responder training facility. It's just southeast of us. We're injured." He tucked his head in his shirt. He garbled, "But I'm good."

"Don't listen to him." CJ whispered into the phone as she gave Jax her best seriously, you're fooling no one squint. "You're not okay. Stop being such a tough guy and give me my phone back." She grabbed the phone without much of a fight. "We're near an abandoned shaft. This macho man got us to a safer place, but he's suffering from a head injury, and we can't hang in there much longer." Her words tumbled out in a frenzy.

"Who are you?" the person asked on the other end of the phone.

"They call me CJ. I can tell you this much. I'm being protected as a witness and a hell of a lot of bad dudes are hunting us. My handlers fought them off until one of them got shot. The other two went for help. If you don't get us lickety-split, we will be cinder." No truer words were spoken. "Do you get what I'm saying, sister? You best hurry."

The person on the line asked if Jackson was conscious.

"Not exactly. He doesn't look so hot and I'm getting woozy myself. Hey, wait I hear the airplanes overhead."

"CJ. We deployed law enforcement and firefighters near your location. Is there any way you can see outside of your cover?"

"I can't see a thing in here. Give me a minute. I'd have to crawl over this male meat sandwich to get to the opening."

The person on the other end of the line gasped and shouted. "Cin?" Her name rang in her ears.

"Yes, ma'am." CJ jolted. Only one person called her Cin. "Hey, wait a minute. You sound familiar." The voice pulled at her heartstrings.

Silence encompassed the line. "My name is Andrea Roberts."

CJ gasped. "My mom's maiden name is Roberts."

The responder on the line sounded distraught. "My mom's too. Was your father a Johnson?"

What the... "You got it, Sissy!"

"Pissy!" the woman cried. "Cinder?" The line went dead.

CJ slapped a hand over her mouth at the rebuttal; no one had ever called her the nickname but her sister Blaze.

"Wake up!" CJ slapped the firefighter. "She said the fire service was nearby." She smacked him again. "Focus!" She poured water down his throat. "Drink this. Stat."

He gulped half of it and poured the rest of the water on the cloth around his neck.

She got in his face. "You tell me to cover my face and you don't cover yours. Silly man."

"Were you able to tell them our location?"

"I did what I could when you went all lights out on me."

"I did not." He moved his head fast and pinched the bridge of his nose.

"Did too."

"The reception wasn't good on the call, so I pulled the rag away."

"Excuses, excuses, I heard just fine. You conked big time." She put her nose to her watch. "You've been unconscious for about fifteen minutes." She nodded. "I haven't heard anything in a while. Maybe the heathens ran off when they heard the sirens? It sounds like the sirens are closer."

"I was lights out?" Jax rubbed his head.

"Like a baby. I swear." She raised her hands as a solemn oath. "What did you say your girlfriend's name was?"

"Andrea Roberts. She's a 911 dispatcher for emergency services."

"I figured she worked for them, since you asked for her there. I guess we have a lot more in common than this cave and our lives intersecting years ago."

"I don't understand. What are you getting at?"

"Doesn't surprise me. I almost didn't realize it myself, but she did. I think she knew exactly who the person she was talking to this minute." *No one else would know what male meat sandwich means since we made it up years ago. Lickity-split was one of dad's 'go to' words.* "Sisterly vibes. She always knew stuff; a sixth sense."

"I'm confused. Are you delusional? The smoke and lack of oxygen must be getting to you."

"Not in the slightest."

They both jerked, startled by nearby yelling. Jax crawled slowly, having to right himself as he swayed to the cave opening. He tumbled back from the rocks as they were being pulled away. "Fire and Rescue."

Best verbal cue they had ever heard.

CJ clasped her hands. "Thank God. Take him first." She pointed to her bodyguard.

The first responders hauled the guard away, covering him with the heat resistant wrap and put a portable breathing apparatus on him. "He looks like a baked potato," she chuckled. "Take this big guy next." She hitched a thumb in his direction. "He needs assistance more than I do."

The emergency crew tended to Jax, who needed his own oxygen. He caused a fuss slapping them with an "I'm fine."

"Listen to them." CJ suspected Jax had a girl to get to. She smirked. "Got a live one, Sissy," she chuckled.

"You're next, spud," Jax razzed.

CJ caught sight of her bodyguards, just feet away. She inhaled deep, knowing with them by her side she had lived another day.

Jax eyeballed the guards; Hawke grabbed the duffel. Gunner nodded.

Before CJ knew it, they had swooped in and carried her off. She looked back as they held her mid-air, whisking her away. She blew Jax a kiss for keeping her safe. The way he'd talked to her sister on the phone, she knew he was smitten. Today may be over, but it was not goodbye. Mr. Honeycutt was family now. CJ suspected their paths would cross again.

CHAPTER

FOUR

*S*olemn Creed, Colorado
Five months later
CJ wrung her hands together over and over.
Another day waiting for a trial. *Is this ever going to end?*

She looked around the courtroom from the gallery, leaning around her handlers to get a better looksee at the few people she recognized. Hawke and Gunner were two mammoth bookends, one to the left, the other to the right. Rarely did she see them all dressed up, except for hearings, meetings with the D.A., and trials like this one. She was not complaining one iota.

Ryker was standing behind them, near the door. She turned and he smiled. His blond faux hawk was downscaled especially for the day. Luca was outside in the hallway, from what she had heard, checking for suspicious activity. But she suspected his dark eyes, olive skin, and slicked back hair were making all the ladies and gents' swoon. Entirely too comical seeing the effect he had on everyone. The walk-into-walls-gorgeous reaction, she had witnessed by the bushels over the years. He did nothing for her. He was more like a brother.

All her handlers had an intense presence about them, but no one should ever mistake their good looks. They were lethal, and she couldn't have been prouder of them. It was a long haul getting to this day. A few times, she didn't think she would. She ran a hand along her green pencil skirt, then to the soft scooped-necked pistachio sweater the lawyer had chosen for her. Her unruly red hair was smoothed into a French twist. The way Gunner was looking at her, he either saw an alien, or she scared him in some way with what she was wearing. There were times she thought he was looking at her, but when she turned in his direction, he'd dart his gaze away.

"Do I look funny?" she asked.

He squirmed in his seat. "Nope. Why would you say such a thing?"

"I don't know."

He leaned in and whispered. "I think you are the most beautiful woman in this courtroom."

"Then why are you looking at me like you saw an aberration?"

He cleared his throat. "Not used to seeing you this dolled up. It's distracting."

"Sorry." She picked at her nails.

"Don't be."

His response warmed her and pleasant, feeling like a woman again. Preparing for this trial had aged her more than the other ones. The years were stretching to eternities, and she was over it. The closer she got to the end, a multitude of back-peddling ensued, but she was not about to slow her roll.

She hid behind her protectors as the two guys by the defense lawyer started throwing manic evil eye darts in her direction. Memories flooded her system of their brutality. Any time they turned and threw her some shade it was like an elevator door closing. Her guards drew in, retracted, and blocked the view. So many people were there, several she recognized, a few fresh faces, and glimpses from the past, creating waves of emotion and a gut-wrenching dread. If she'd only known then what she knew now. Faces and names she imprinted into her core. The Winslows for one, the Honeycutts, Evan Parker were her priority to right the wrongs of her poor decisions. Yes, not entirely her fault, but CJ had played a big part in the death of Evan's brother and Connor and Cade's parents, though she'd had no choice. It took her an eternity to realize she had been as much of a victim as they were, but she'd had to live with her decisions. Those who'd died had no choice. Her skin crawled, looking at the two men who started it all, who had held her captive when she was in her late teens.

CJ shivered and Gunner leaned in. She found comfort with a mere touch. She felt safe. He was the constant in her life, but she knew better than to think she was anything more than a job for him. He was getting paid to protect her.

His warm breath prickled over her skin. "How are you doing?" He squeezed her a little tighter. His eyes were deep pools of golden honey today.

Hawke nudged her from her right and gave Gunner a knowing stare. "Focus." He pointed to a group entering the courtroom. CJ's heart panged at seeing her family for the first time. Pent up years of emotion riveted her. A wail escaped and she shook uncontrollably, turning heads. Her mom and dad stopped dead in their tracks as her mother reached out with a gasp. The pain she had caused them was unbearable. Years aged her parents and CJ blamed herself. Her older brothers, Roman and Brady, gave her a quick nod. But seeing Andrea sitting next to Jax gave her strength. They were connected in a way she couldn't explain; it had always been that way. Her sister nodded and her familiar eyes gave CJ unwavering support. She could do this.

CJ's attention on her family was interrupted by a vulgar comment. Her gaze shifted to the two men sporting their flaming orange onesies. They had changed everyone's lives. She could barely look them in the eyes for fear of getting violently ill. Barry Ryder, the head of the triple D's operation and his second in command, James Devland—both were vile excuses for men. All equally guilty of killing innocent children by peddling drugs for the almighty dollar and the other a wife-beating ex-husband. Such innocent lives affected. Children lost. Ellie had barely gotten away from Devland, but now she was in a better place, CJ had heard, with new husband Connor Winslow and a mother to twins. He tried to swivel around, but her own family blocked his view.

The dingle-hoppers looked rougher around the edges from prison life, in handcuffs and leg shackles, shuffling to their seats, giving everyone in the gallery the creepy stare. They had tried time and time again to kill her off over the years because she had the ammunition to take down their entire operation with what little she had witnessed. Same for her bad decision —ex-boyfriend Trent aka Taz—who had drawn her into this mess. CJ had witnessed it and tried to escape, but her attempts were stunted until she herself got away before it was too late. A decade of hiding and trials was worth it to see justice take place, but this one had lasted almost three years. Nothing like a *Groundhog Day* marathon. CJ hoped all of this would be worth it in the end. Her life would never be the same. She'd always have to look over her shoulder. *What life?* This would have to be her penance.

A verdict given: guilty on all counts. Today was the sentencing. The day they all patiently awaited. Something deep in her soul knew this would probably never end. Would she ever find her happily ever after? *Probably not.*

The judge addressed the courtroom and the two men waited for their sentencing. Now was the time for family and friends to deliver their victim witness statements. Barry Ryder, the leader of all the wrongdoing, stood up and yelled. "I don't have to listen to any of your sob stories, you morons. Just rip the fucking bandage off and send us on our merry little way." He eyed someone in the gallery, gave him a quick nod, and several onlookers jumped over the railing, trying to disarm the bailiff. James Devland wrestled another guard for his keys to his handcuffs. Chaos ensued. Terrified screams echoed the walls from friends and family. All the men were placing themselves in front of their loved ones as a barrier. She could barely see a testosterone-infused tackle. A tumble, rumble, and a major throw down, one worthy of the World Wrestling Federation. She'd never seen so many limbs flail.

Everything happened in the blink of an eye. One minute order, the next a sea of destruction. She was sitting there, and the next moment yanked with her three handlers, using themselves as a shield. Someone directed half of the onlookers away from danger.

Is my family okay?

Connor Winslow and Jeffrey Richards, Ellie's brother, stood protectively, acting as a wall for their loved ones. Evan Parker guided some of them to follow the rest of family and friends into the hallway.

"CJ, you okay?" Gunner snapped. She leaned around their massive bodies to see what was going on. Jax, Cade, and two other guys all barreled forward. Evan and Jax tackled the two onlookers. Cade flung himself, doing a superman soar at Barry Ryder, and pummeled him to the floor.

"Yes!" she smacked her hand. "Got them."

She'd heard Cade and Ryder had a history. *I guess payback is a bee-yotch.*

"How do you like those apples? Daddy dearest, don't you ever pull your shit around me and my family again, you weak piece of pond scum," Cade yelled. Another agent karate chopped James Devland and freed the guard from his grasp.

Evan Parker kneeled on one guy's back, making him eat the floor, and surveyed the chaos. Another frenzied shuffle, but this time it was Gunner, Hawke, and Ryker pushing her into the judge's chambers. CJ could barely catch her breath, and she was certain she was moving lickity-split, but her feet never once hit the floor. She was used to being whisked away as she attempted to air pedal with her feet.

The door slammed behind her as Gunner had her flattened against the furthest wall. Hawke grabbed an umbrella and the coatrack it hung on from a nearby corner, a threat to anyone who got past Ryker on the other side of the door. Every day, she was in awe of the dedication of her handlers and how they would sacrifice their own lives for her. They were the only bright light in this dismal nightmare.

Gunner was her beacon. He had been the only constant in the last decade. Sure, handlers had come and gone, like Tiny, Axel, Ryker, Luca and more, but Gunner had been there from day one. He was only gone once for six days, four hours, and thirty-six minutes. Gunner towered over her. If her heart hadn't been throttling out of her chest so wildly, she thought her shell of a body would crumble. She'd have another secret fantasy invade her cranium.

A tap at the door startled her wayward daydream as Ryker peeked his head inside. "All clear. Everyone copacetic in here? The buttheads are subdued; it's safe to return. The judge is heading in and they're getting this show on the road." The door swung wide and two uniformed guards waved them on, along with Luca.

CJ took each step with trepidation. She put her hand over her face, not wanting to make eye contact with the two men who would be heading to the clink soon enough. Her legs did the weebly-wobbly thing until she plopped herself down. *How will I ever make it through the victim witness statements?* This was the first time and the last time she would be in the same room with everyone. Most of her statements had been done via satellite while she was in an undisclosed location.

Eyes were glued on the honorable Judge Judith Downs as she entered the courtroom. She straightened her robes, smoothing a hand over the black fabric. She cleared her throat once and slid her glasses higher up her nose. Her lips were in a flat line. "District Attorney, you may call our witness for today's special session."

"Thank you, Your Honor." She turned and nodded, allowing Connor and Cade Winslow to go first at the mic, followed by Evan Parker, Lina Ortez, and Ellie Richards. CJ wiped her eyes during the statements. The air was thick with dread and so much love. She felt it as she gained strength from her own family when they had their turn at the podium, speaking on her behalf and of their own personal losses.

Her mother stepped to the microphone, escorted by her sister, and they directed their gazes to hers. "I've never been prouder than I am today of my daughter. As I look upon this grown woman, I am saddened by the years we missed, but grateful she is here. We didn't know she was alive and all because these poor excuses for DNA hunted her." Her mother shook and Andrea ran her hand along her back. She turned to the two men in shackles and pointed. "I blame them. You are cowards. You've lied to, stolen from, and dealt drugs to innocent children. My daughter is one of them who unfortunately got in your path. You deserve the harshest hand of the law for the lives you have affected." Her mother faced her again. "CJ, your father, and I love you and will forever be the proudest parents. Your siblings gather around you, and if you ever need them, they will move heaven and earth to protect you. Find strength in my words, my dearest daughter, and don't you ever forget." She dabbed at her tears with a tissue. "I don't know what the future holds, but you will always be my little girl, always have a home, and you will always have our unwavering support. We love you, sweetie. You are braver than all of us in this courtroom." She blew CJ a kiss. She caught it in the air and held it to her chest.

CJ sobbed uncontrollably, still clutching her chest. Every syllable would be forever etched into her soul, and she would mourn for them in her heart for the rest of her life. The District Attorney turned her gaze towards CJ, who took a deep breath. How could she have the strength to get through her own statement when she was a blubbering mess?

"Your honor, we advised her not to, but CJ was determined to speak. May I approach the stand? Though she has already done her just prudence as a witness, her safety is our utmost judicial duty. Can I ask her security staff to be able to approach as well?" Everyone gasped and several of CJ's family cheered. One of her brothers gave a loud whistle and the other followed suit.

"Quiet in the courtroom, please." The judge rapped her gavel on her podium.

Her father the fire chief gave CJ a thumbs up. "You got this, sweetie." Pride filled his voice, and his CJ blew him a kiss on her way to the stand. She felt naked as everyone's eyes were on her.

"Quiet, or I'll have to ask hecklers to leave," the judge called out as CJ took her seat up front. Everyone else had given their statements at the mic, but no way she would get anywhere near the two men in coveralls who had threatened and almost had her killed.

The district attorney was calm, focused. "CJ, could you please address the court and state your full name?

Okay, here it goes. This is what CJ asked the District Attorney to begin with. *I have faced a heck of a lot more than stating my name. Pops was so proud of my given name.* It had been years since she heard her own name and even longer since she had gone by it. Everywhere she traveled, she was someone else. Today something simple and empowering was having someone ask her name.

"Take all the time you need." The D.A. nodded.

CJ pulled her shoulders back and raised her chin high. She blew her father a kiss. "My name is Cinder Ashley Johnson, like cinder and ash. I get it, but no one better say anything." Her lip lifted at the side. She ran her hands along her thighs. "My given name is Cinder Ashley Johnson. My father named me." Tears filled her eyes as she looked into familiar faces. "Today, I'm prouder than I've ever been of the name I was given. Everything has been stripped away from me. Most days, I'm someone else, and I have no connection or backstory. But today I do. Today my name is my sword and I know exactly who I am and why I am here." She picked at her nails and held in what was about to be another epic blubber fest. Her gaze went to Gunner, and he nodded, mouthing the words. "You got this." And he winked.

CJ wiped away a tear and observed her family, who were studying Gunner. She tucked a stray hair behind her ear. "I'm lucky today because I can see my family for the first time in a decade. I'd like to begin by saying I'm sorry, Daddy. I didn't mean to disappoint you." Tears welled in her eyes and her breath hitched. She had waited so long to say the words.

Her father stood as he shook his head and stretched his hand to her. "You didn't, baby girl. I've never been prouder."

She had never wanted more than to run into his arms. She turned to the judge. "I'm sorry. I think I'm ready to tell you my story."

The judge nodded. "Take all the time you need."

"Thank you, your honor. My story began when I had just turned sixteen. I liked someone who took me along a path of destruction I could have never imagined. The process was slow and could have taken years. I was naïve, I made mistakes, but in no way did I ever imagine hurting someone in the process. They did, and I got caught in their crosshairs. I never imagined my life without my family. If I could do it all over again, I wouldn't have been so eager to grow up. Barry Ryder and James Devland took everything from me. They forced me against my will, and I fought to get away for myself, but today as I bear witness, I am fighting for those who have no voice. I'm doing this for Fire Chief Thomas Winslow and his wife Beth and Adam Parker. I'm fighting for Connor and Cade Winslow who lost their parents, Evan Parker who lost his brother. Ellie, Lina, Janet, Journey, and Jackson Honeycutt. I will continue to honor them, and every innocent victim affected by the violence and drugs. But mostly I'm fighting for my loved ones who spent years thinking I was dead while I was making amends for my sins. My fight will probably never be over, but I promise with every fiber of my being I will try to right the wrong. I'll never have my old life and that's my cross to bear. I accept my destiny. I ask for forgiveness from those I have harmed and take full responsibility for my actions. I thank the court system, my keepers, and the witness protection alliance for giving me an opportunity to regain some kind of self-worth."

CJ gazed around the courtroom. *I've done what I came for.*

She locked eyes with the two men awaiting their sentencing. "I can't imagine I'm the only person whose world you have turned upside down and inside out, but I suspect you have zero remorse for your actions, or you wouldn't have continued wreaking havoc to this day."

"Shut up, bitch." Barry Ryder yelled.

She stood and clutched onto the wooden podium in front of her. "I have the power today and I have waited a long time to speak, so you will listen." Her voice trembled and pitched another octave.

Applause erupted in the court room.

She took her seat and took a sip of water. "I hope you rot in jail for the remainder of your life. It's the very best I can do, and the nicest way I can say it."

"Shut up, you cunt. You will pay," Barry spewed. One guard pushed him into his seat and another stepped forward.

Gunner walked toward him, Hawke close behind. Luca and Ryker intercepted them with an iron grip. Gunner closed his eyes and inhaled. "Watch it." His stare was intense as he pointed in their direction.

The judge's gavel pounded.

CJ leaned forward and braced her arms on the podium again. "I. Already. Have. Paid. Catastrophically." Emotions she had stuffed inside bubbled to the surface. She trembled at the enormity of everything. She steadied herself for a moment before taking the first step. CJ stood tall and rolled her shoulders back, finding her way to her protectors. The two guys on trial watched her every move.

Hawke pointed at them. "Turn your sockets away or it will be the last thing you will see."

"Yeah, whatever!" Barry Ryder sneered.

Gunner retraced his steps this time and pivoted. "Try us.

While he's doing so, I'll make damn sure you will be licking your ass up close and personal."

CJ gasped and placed a hand on her neck. "Yikes." She winced. "Can't explain the visual I'm getting right now." A tidal wave of emotion and a tsunami of nausea assaulted her. Her time in Solemn Creed was ending. Soon she would have to say goodbye to her loved ones. Her heart ached with sorrow. *I don't think I can take much more.*

Gunner saw it in her eyes, the artic blues that shielded her vulnerable, warm spirit. He heard it in her words as they broke, and as she fought for every ounce of strength within her. She was at her breaking point. CJ was stronger than anyone he had ever met. She had set out to right a wrong and took down an empire. One woman, ten years in hiding, three trials, and a collapse of drugs infiltrating the streets. A mighty, strawberry-haired, petite flower had once again kicked major ass. She'd earned his respect years ago, but today all he wanted to do was hold her and tell her how proud he was, and she could have the life she wished for. But he couldn't. Wishing he could take all her woes away, all he could do was stay close in proximity and let her know she was not alone. Someone else could help shoulder the pain. He wanted it to be him.

"Once they get rid of Devland and Ryder, we can find a quiet place for you to see your family."

"I'd like that." She leaned closer. "First, I want a front-row seat as I watch them get hauled off to prison." She ran her hands along her arms.

Gunner looked around the courtroom. No one had left their seats in the gallery. She was not the only one who wanted this saga to end. He nodded to his battle buddy, Jeffrey Richards, who was sitting with his family. He watched for the nod from Cade Winslow and the DEA team for the okay to move to a new location. Hawke and the rest of the crew were a united front around CJ. Time to end this shitshow and move on. He could feel the anticipation in the surroundings, but the deep-seated sorrow on CJ and her family's faces that had the ability to unravel him. She'd waited a decade to be in the same room with them. It was important. All of them needed it. He did too. The love her father had for her was apparent even across the room, making Gunner think of his own with distaste. If his father had showed him and his brother this kind of emotion, they'd had an entirely different outcome. He swooshed the thought away and locked it down. Today was CJ's rite of passage.

DREAD ENCAPSULATED CJ, cloaking her in an earth-shattering gloom. The moments ticked by slowly. A quick goodbye from her family and she'd be thrust into her next façade in the witness protection program. Would she ever be able to live life on her terms again? Where would she be next? What role would she play? Her bodyguards whisked her out of the room, down a flight of stairs, through a tunnel, and into some dimly lit hall all while she was covered in a shroud. Cade and his crew at the DEA had arranged a private area worthy of royalty, but she didn't feel all that regal.

Time was ticking, and she didn't have long by the way

Gunner was checking his watch. The secret language Hawke, Luca, Ryker, and Gunner communicated without a syllable. Time to disappear again even though there were no more trials for her to testify in. Barry Ryder still dangled his power from behind bars and his followers had been present—the uproar in the courtroom was proof. Waiting until the dust settled was the safest plan of action. Her parents, two brothers and sister would follow close behind.

This was the hardest part of it all, was seeing her family and knowing she would have to say everything she could for a possible lifetime apart. She would fill the space with kisses and hugs to sustain her through the lonely nights ahead. CJ paced the room, quietly waiting. The room was no bigger than a walk-in closet, but ample enough. There would be no space between the love they shared.

"You know, you look a lot like your mom and your sister."

CJ jumped and glanced at Gunner. He fought for words. Why was he so angry? CJ didn't need his anger. She needed tenderness, but he couldn't break the barriers he'd fought so hard to shore. Not right now, maybe never when it came to her. She had been sobbing while they'd left the courthouse and seeing her in so much pain tore at his soul. Emotion like this could get both of them and the team killed.

CJ replied, "I used to think so. It's hard for me to see it objectively since I don't recognize the person I see in the mirror anymore. I may still know my name, but I am not her anymore."

"I recognize the same person who came to us for help a decade ago. She's still in there. Somehow, you have to find her again."

"I sometimes wonder." She peered through the window again into the blackness. "How long have we been driving?"

"Awhile. You slept for the first three hours."

CJ swiveled her head in his direction again. "I did. Hmmm. How much longer?"

"We'll stop in about an hour. We need to pick up another vehicle and get our new papers, and some of us have other assignments." He chewed at his thumbnail.

"Who's in charge now?" CJ rubbed the sleep from her eyes. "Gunner? Will they give you a new assignment?"

If he only knew. He'd asked to stay on through the next rotation, but his boss had all the control. "Don't know. None of us do."

"But...but you've always been here." CJ flipped around, her eyes wide.

He hoped she didn't notice; he figured she didn't see him most of these years. "That I have, but it's not the norm."

"What about Luca and Hawke?"

"None of us have the answers. But this is what we signed up for." He scrubbed his face and repositioned himself. His knees were a permanent fixture in the back of Hawke's driver's seat.

Gunner didn't know the outcome, or if the top notches would bend to his pleas. He didn't want another job. He wanted CJ in any capacity she would have him. After the kiss they'd had seven years ago, when they'd had to act like they were married at one of the safe houses as an unexpected car rolled by. CJ had been in the dirt planting flowers, totally oblivious. He flung himself midair and toppled in front of her, not distinguishing if there was a threat. The proximity had him kissing her instead of drawing his weapon, hoping his move had given the passersby the hint to move along. The kiss only lasted half a minute, tops. One certain thing was she didn't fight it. Turned out the car had had some teeny boppers in it, and they'd yelled, "Get a room."

Their kiss changed his trajectory and stuck with him over the years. His job was to watch her, her surroundings, and keep her safe. After a decade together, Gunner had memorized every nuance that made her CJ. He could lay awake and watch her forever, but the glimpses she gave him after the kiss that fueled his desire. They had an undercurrent—the guys razzed him for it—but he was locked in with her.

"What are you thinking about?"

He stretched his neck from side to side. "Ah, nothing." He diverted his gaze to the blackness.

"Whatever, G." She patted his leg.

"What do you mean?"

CJ chuckled and leaned closer. "Big guy, you are a lot easier to read than you used to be."

"How so?" His brows furrowed and he twisted in his seat, anchoring his fist under his chin.

"Why would I dare tell you?" She winked. "I see more than you think I do." She gave him a wry smile.

With just a wink and a smile, his temperature elevated. He shifted again and pushed the down button on the window. "You do, do you?"

"Uh hum," she hummed deep in her throat, followed by a very confident, "Indeed." She gave him a push.

He raised his hands high to fend off her uncoordinated jabs. He loved the sparkle in her eyes after the trials, like the weight had evaporated and the stress had washed away. She joked around a little more, her usual ritual. He couldn't imagine the pain she must feel deep into every nook and cranny of her DNA.

Neither of them had any idea what the future held for them, or if they would see each after they got her to her new location. But he couldn't fathom a life without her. They'd warned him he would get too close. He'd originally taken this job like the others through the years, but they were a permanent fixture in the Noble Network, more jobs were coming their way. Most of them were just puppeteers with many shades of grey. Some jobs were simple security, some sanctioned, and others government hires like CJ's. Most of their earlier experience was recon in the service and after, doing odd jobs in the early days for fellow military buddies, including Jeffrey Richards and his sister Ellie. They were never in one place very long, and the team timed out or rotated through. The only constant had been CJ in this last decade.

"Eyes sharp," Hawke ordered. "CJ, keep low. We're not taking any chances."

She slid onto the floorboard of the SUV.

Gunner put his night vision goggles on and surveyed the landscape, whipping around in his seat, making sure they weren't being followed.

"We're making a stop for Z's, our new orders, and a new ride." Ryker eyed the screen on his phone. "Take a left and it's only a few miles through some of this terrain." Every half a mile, they slowed their roll and listened quietly. Then started at a snail's pace over the gravel road.

"First right, coming up here in two meters."

"There's no road. You sure?" Hawke asked.

"Not my first time reading coordinates, Boo."

"Just checking, Ry. It's black as shit. Gunner, you see anything?"

"Nada."

The SUV teetered and bumped along the road another mile.

"There is it at 1:00, a rickety old barn."

"It's about time. I think this thing needs new shocks. I'm

going to need a back crack adjustment," CJ said from her position.

"Yeah, an attitude adjustment tike."

"Geez, Ryker, tell me how you really feel." CJ elbowed the seat in front of her. "I swear a girl could get a complex if she didn't think you truly loved her." She laughed, coughing through her chuckles as the dust sifted through the interior of the SUV.

If she only knew... Gunner thought to himself.

They pulled around a large, weathered barn.

"Stay here for a minute while we look around." Gunner locked the vehicle doors as he got out. Hawke and Ryker went around the front. Gunner pulled out his Glock and talked into his earpiece to the other two. Both the front and rear barn doors slid open simultaneously. They checked the loft inside, the interior of the black Humvee, and the corner. Gunner took off at a jog and opened the vehicle, followed by Ryker, while Hawke closed the front barn door. Ryker cranked the engine and reversed the SUV inside behind the other vehicle. They opened the hatch and lifted a huge army green duffel and propped up half a dozen weapons, including traps and wires to keep the perimeter safe.

"Is anyone else hungry? I swear my stomach is eating itself," CJ said as she wrung her hands and flitted about.

The guys' heads whipped around. "Food after. I swear, for an itty-bitty one, you have an epic appetite." Ryker laughed.

"A girl must eat. All this stuff is very taxing. I'm a stress eater, but my metabolism hasn't got the memo yet." CJ rambled. "I swear, I'd be a lot thicker and have a lot more junk in my trunk if I didn't burn it all off with nervous energy."

"You still eat less than Gunner. Trust me, we always have plenty of rations," Luca added.

"Rations meaning double stuffed Oreos, Twizzlers, and circus peanuts," CJ said.

"Those things are disgusting," Ryker said, as he faked gagging.

"Don't knock it until you've tried it." Gunner rummaged through a bag and ripped open a tray of Oreos.

"I don't mind if I do, but don't you have any protein?" CJ snagged three Oreos and took a bite of one, took a few steps back, peered into the bag, then took the circus peanuts.

"Save some for me," Gunner grumbled, and swallowed the rest of his cookie. "We should have all the food and supplies we need." Gunner wiped crumbs from his mouth and took a long swig from his water bottle. "You will not starve tonight. I mean —have you ever?" He lowered his head and gauged CJ's reaction.

She tapped her chin. "There's been a few close calls, but no." She cocked a brow and her lips raised in a wry smile. "Starvation is not the thing I've almost died from." She fidgeted with the lace of the green high-top sneakers he'd bought for her after her yellow ones had been bloodied from Tiny's injuries in the mountains of Colorado.

"Thank you for my new shoes. What do you call them again?"

"Anytime. Glad you like your *Gofasters*, since they make you go faster." Yes, green was her color and now his favorite too, but only on her.

Gunner's spine went rod straight, his teeth snapping together. If he had his way, she'd never again know an ounce of fear again for the rest of her life. How could he keep her safe if he got transferred?

He raked his fingers through his hair. Who would watch over her? Who would get to see her as a smile tilted her lips, how the sun glistened off the warm golden tones of her fiery hair and the shimmer of her light blue eyes? Who would watch over her in the middle of the night as she had full- blown conversations in her slumber or guide her to bed as she sleep-walked? Would they understand she hated liver and onions with a passion, and just the words alone would make her rosy complexion go green? That she could eat boneless hot wings with French fries and a side of ranch every single day and never tire of them? Would they figure out she covered her pain with a weird sense of humor?

Cinder Ashley Johnson was a free-spirited songbird who had no other choice than to become caged. Hunted.

He still saw her light when most couldn't and assumed otherwise. Gunner fought the urge every day. He once thought he could handle the job with no attachment, but he'd give it all up. His career for a life on the run with her, however it looked when the dust settled. If she only knew she was not what she thought: a disappointment, not worthy of a life because she'd made a mistake as a teen, barely a woman. She was pure strength down to the little crooked pinky toe which she'd broken a time or two on the run. He was powerless; if she only knew the depth her presence had on every molecule of his being. Why could he spend time in the military fighting enemies and not be able to fight his feelings for her?

Gunner dug a fist into his chest. Their time was drawing near. How would he function without knowing she was safe? Happy? Something just didn't feel right in his gut. *What had the general been talking about? What other threats?*

SIX

"Hey you." She cleared her throat. "Gunner." Her voice echoed. Gunner was a million miles away. Everyone twitched, turning at the sound of her voice. Geez. There were times she felt naked in the colossal midst of the Manwiches surrounding her.

I wonder if they can see it. Meaning the rhino in the room. How she pined for him. Gunner, not by his looks or his size, but the feeling she always choked on when they were together. They had to, especially Hawke; the looks he gave them both were suspicious. Serious as a heart attack, but all of them were her keepers and she wouldn't have lived to tell her story if it hadn't been for their bravery. Two of them had been injured, one seriously because people wanted her dead. Hawke was always suspicious of everyone. He never let his guard down; his walls were impenetrable.

Gunner used to be the same, but had wavered through the years. More than once, she could see it in people's eyes when they caught a glimpse of Hawke. His size and the tattoos on his neck. He could intimidate because he looked like a fictional predator. She was never so glad to have them all on her side. Ryker and Luca reminded her of her brothers. They had been her family over the years, but her heart missed her own.

CJ brushed away a tear at the thought. Through the years, she'd cried herself to sleep. Seeing them had made it even more painful.

She hadn't noticed, but Gunner had scooted closer. She jumped when he whispered in her ear. Goosebumps prickled her skin.

"Don't go there," he said in his deep baritone.

"Where?"

"Where you always go."

"How can I not? I let my family down, and I'll never see them again."

He leaned back and crossed one leg over the other. "By making a minor mistake in your youth. Ryder and his asswipes took advantage of you. I saw your family's faces in the courtroom and after. I saw a family who was proud. They support and love you." He pointed a finger. "You. They're proud of you, so am I." He gave a quick nod. "Miracles happen. Maybe one day you'll see them again." He shrugged his shoulders. "My money's on you." He slipped a piece of licorice in his mouth.

"I'm not holding out for it. Look at my track record. Dare I dream? No way! Survival is the only thing I have time for. The system is rigged against people like me. But it's impossible not to dream, to wish. To hope."

He pointed the Twizzler at her. "Cinder, you are living proof the system is not jacked. Look what you've done. Hope, at times, is all we got. I'm proud of you and if you're not strong enough to realize it yet, I'll carry you until you do."

She shifted, propping herself on her knees, so they were eye to eye. "How did you get so intuitive?"

He shrugged. "With you, it's an easy thing."

She swept a wayward hair off his forehead. "Thank you."

He bit his bottom lip. "Anytime. Remember, I got you. You're not going to fall on my watch."

CJ's heart was almost leaping out of her chest. She could feel the tap of her pulse at the base of her throat. This was the most beautiful thing anyone had ever said to her. She wanted to grab him and kiss him silly for what he'd said.

"Heads up. We've had some grub and our bellies aren't barking. Let's do this, and go over the directions to the new location," Hawke barked.

Ryker spread the map on the hood of the vehicle and gave a quick whistle.

"Boss says once we're there, we get our new orders. Rumor has it we're splitting the team up for a while. We need fresh eyes."

CJ and Gunner spun their gazes at one another. Her bottom lip quivered.

"No need to worry, CJ." Gunner got up from the floor, patting off his black cargo pants and shifting his shoulder holster, securing his gun. He extended a hand and helped her from her sitting position. "I'm sure we have a long ride ahead. You'll be sick of us and itching for some newbies."

She gave him a scowl and bit her inner cheek. "Not on your life. I just got you trained. I've spent a decade perfecting everything. You're a commodity."

"Ha! You might be right." He shook his head to the left, then the right. "We're still too close to the west coast, and we need to stay away from heavier populated areas on our route, like always." He crossed his arms over his chest, his stance rock solid, but his eyes were soft. "Are you up for another trip across the country?"

CJ nodded. "Do I have a choice?"

"You always have a choice, but you can't opt out of the program. It's still too soon after the trial. We need to let the dust settle." He brushed a piece of straw off her arm. "You're done with all the court stuff. Now you can focus on other things."

"Not sure I know how."

"I have faith." He tapped her nose. "Complete faith you will amaze yourself. You're a firecracker." He made a swishy boom noise and splayed his hands wide.

She could feel her cheeks heat. CJ pressed her palms to her face, hoping to cool the fire under her skin. "I'm glad someone has faith in me." How did Gunner always understand the right thing to say?

Hawke waved the men forward, and she stepped away, taking a tour around the barn. All the bodyguards huddled around the map, whispering. Gunner craned his thick, corded neck. CJ could feel his eyes on her, and he winked.

He retreated his gaze to the map again, but she continued watching the show. How Gunner's black cargo pants fit him in all the right places. His scuffed-up size 12, military grade boots —he always wore a concealed knife in them. A solid black t-shirt covered what she'd had several glimpses over the years: firm abs, a light dusting of dark chest hair, bulging biceps, broad shoulders, pecs prominent for days.

His hair was a lot longer than it had been when they first met. He usually had it pulled back, but she loved it less restrained. Black as the night. He'd only cut it short once a few years ago when he had been gone from her side for what seemed like an eternity. He'd never divulged where he was when he disappeared, nor did she ever ask.

Feelings for Gunner bubbled to the surface, even with CJ knowing full well absence strengthened her feelings. She was lost. A complete basket case. He was her haven, and she didn't work without his nearness. She'd badgered Hawke daily, asking where Gunner had gone and when he'd return. The guy was tight-lipped, an armored tank, and wouldn't give in to her no matter how she tried. They were brothers and a code no one could penetrate.

Gunner had returned different in so many ways. More approachable, more engaged, he even engaged in more eye contact, but then would stare off into the distance. From that day forward, she had been a puddle of goo around him. So much easier to hide when they prepared for trials and moved around, but during the quiet nights and solo days she struggled with the façade.

Most people probably got all tongue-tied in situations like this, but nooo, not her. She could out-talk anyone; she could literally yammer on for a century about anything and everything. If he was bored, you would never know it. He squirmed a little bit when she'd go off on a tangent about some of the romance novels she and her sister would read in their teens, or anything female related. She often did it deliberately, just to get him tearing off into another room holding his ears and yelling, *enough!*

Hawke's phone rang and he hit his earpiece. He waved a finger in the air and spun it around. All four men dispersed and dodged around the barn, throwing things into the vehicle, checking their ammo, securing their earpieces. Luca took off, his feet a thunderous pounding on the ground, to swing the barn door aside and take off at a run into vehicle they arrived in. Hawke threw their garbage into a bag and tossed it into the vehicle.

Gunner stomped to her and grabbed her by the arm. "We gotta go. Someone's coming. Luca's trying to head them off. Ryker, you got everything?"

"Damn straight." Ryker grabbed for his rifle and propped it

up, looked through the spotting scope, then threw a duffle into and rolled into the rear of the SUV. Hawke tromped around to the driver's seat, slipped the key into the ignition, and cracked the back passenger window. Gunner opened the door and maneuvered CJ in. "Get down on the floorboard and don't move. We're heading out." He covered her with a heavy wool blanket. "You know the drill—hands over your head. Stay low." He slipped a bottle of water and a collapsible police baton beside her.

HAWKE OPENED the north entrance to the barn and ran around to the driver's seat. Gunner took his weapon from his holster and grabbed another from the compartment between the driver and passenger seats. He used the controls and moved the seat as low as he could, tugged his leather gloves on, flung his sunglasses on, and flipped his ball cap around. Hawke clicked his seat belt on and revved the engine. He called on the radio to Luca. "What do you see?"

"A van's barreling down the dirt road. Get moving. I'll meet you at the first stop after I take this party on a joyride."

"Be careful, my man. See you in a bit. I'm calling the boss for backup. They're not far."

"Aye, Aye, mate. See you on the flip side."

Hawke yanked the gear in drive and stepped on the gas. The tires spun, spraying dirt and debris. Hawke and Luca were the best drivers on the team. Ryker and Gunner had been weapons specialists in the service. The SUV chassis howled as Hawke increased the speed over the bumpy terrain. Gunner heard CJ grumble something inaudible from the back. There were a few times they were airborne. When they bounced off the ditches they all took a jarring.

"Hold tight." Gunner squeezed her under the cover. CJ flew like a rag doll to the ceiling of the rig with a yelp and clocked him with her Converse. "Hang onto something," Gunner shouted. They dodged and weaved old oaks and weeping willows. Hawke overcorrected, swinging to the left, then the right, before hitting a gravel road, only to see they were headed straight for a wire fence and a shit ton of cows. They spun off to the east, fishtailing. "Where am I heading? I'm all turned around." Hawke's deep voice echoed through the cabin.

Gunner's focus locked his sight on the route and swung his arm to the right. "Over here, just past the heifers." A shot rang out, hitting the side view mirror, and a round of bullets from Ryker blasted bullets from the third-row area of the vehicle. "Disabled the tires, but there's more coming. Luca has a van on him."

"Where in the hell, did they come from? We covered our tracks!" Gunner's phone buzzed, and he wrestled to pull it from his front pocket. He eyed the screen. "It's Richards!"

"Kind of busy. What? A leak from where? Somewhere from the courthouse, they might have dropped a tracker on us. Shit! Thanks man. You are? See ya."

"A tracker? How in the hell? This ride's been wiped. I checked it myself. Must have been the other vehicle we were in, or it's on one of us. As soon we're in the clear, we will get rid of it."

"They've been following us for hours. Guess they were lying in wait to get more on us. Richards is meeting us at our next stop. He said they have a few guys already with Luca." Gunner's mouth was like the desert. They hit a dirt road and took off, finally losing their tail. He wedged his hand between the seats, rummaging in the back. He grabbed one of CJ's feet and shook it. "Cinder, you hurt?" No answer, no movement. He shook her foot again, then shouted through clenched teeth. An eerie calm surrounded the cab. His pulse throttled at his neck. He waited to try to regain control of his system.

"Dammit." He unlatched his seat belt and bolted between the seats, kicking his way until he faceplanted on the bench seat. He rummaged through the cover, pulling it away, noticing his fingers were tacky and covered in specks of crimson. "She's bleeding." He whipped away the blanket. Her hair covered the space in a tangled mess. Her face was lodged under the driver's seat. He was calm in almost every scenario, except anything that had to do with CJ. His heart pounded under his sternum like a semi's piston as he checked for a pulse.

"Shhh!" He held his own breath, to focus on hers. Gunner reached under her, trying to get leverage. "CJ, talk to me. Tell me where it hurts." He didn't dare move her in case she had a neck injury. "She's out cold. I can't see where the blood is coming from."

"No stopping. See what she needs in transit. We must get as far away as we can," Hawke yelled over his shoulder.

Ryker tapped Gunner from behind. "Here's a moonbeam. I got eyes here. You make sure she's okay." He tapped him again. "First aid. It'll do, until we stop."

"Roger that," Gunner grumbled. He flipped the switch and turned the flashlight on, propping it in between his neck and shoulder.

She groaned. "My head and..." but nothing legible after.

He got as close as he could to her. "Stay with me, girl." At closer inspection through her blood-soaked hair, he found a cut near her eyebrow. He wadded the covering and placed it under her hair, smoothing what he could from her face. The first aid kit flung against the door, spilling the contents. He ripped open a gauze pad, blotting the wound as best he could in the tight compartment. He slid his hand under her and noticed she had bruising along her cheek and around one of her eyes near the cut.

"Can you move your neck?" Without hesitation, she did. He scooped her up and cradled her close. She mumbled something, so he moved closer, in time to hear his name. "Stay with me. What hurts?" He wedged himself as low as he could, but there wasn't much room. "Angel, you're okay. It's me."

He moved her closer so he could bear most of the weight. He spotted the water bottle on the floorboard next to a mangled, bloody, police baton. He inched the bottle closer with his foot. Soaking some gauze, he wiped away some of the blood from her face with slow methodical swipes as he whispered her name. The crease between her brows flared as she stirred.

"Easy. Don't move, I got you." He could feel his jaw tick. "You're gonna have a lump, and from the looks of it, you are going to have a black eye. The cut above your eyebrow bled a lot, but won't need stitches." He wasn't sure she heard anything he was saying but talking to her helped him.

"G, is she okay?" Hawke yelled over his shoulder.

"Hard to say, but I think so. She was wedged way under the seat and knocked her head good under there or against the door. I've never seen this happen but the baton needs repair too. We'll have to check on her after we make a pit stop."

"It's gonna wait for a while. We need to create a lot more distance right now."

"Figured that's what you were going to say. When we do, we need to dismantle the tracker." Gunner huffed as he swiveled his gaze around. "Ryker, how are we looking?"

"Quiet, my man, but I'm keeping my eyes sharp. Quiet is a no go and I get the itch."

"I hear ya. If you see something, I got your six."

"Take care of Sleeping Beauty. I'll holler if I need you."

Gunner ran his fingers over CJ's hair and spun his fore-finger around her golden amber strands, which were slicked with sweat and dotted with a little blood. Her body trembled and her jaw quivered. He wrapped the cover over her and nestled her closer, then lowered his face to hers to make sure she was still breathing. Maybe, a little dramatic, but with the way he was feeling, it reassured him more than he cared to admit. He exhaled and squeezed his eyes tight.

"No one messes with my girl and gets away with it. Angel, get some rest."

SEVEN

Only one person called her Angel. Gunner, a pet name he'd concocted when they were undercover as a couple in a small rinky-dink town in Nebraska. He used it from time to time, especially when she was at her worst, meaning scared to death. Hearing the name roll off his tongue gave her fortitude in the bleakest of times. She wrapped her arms around him and dozed off into a deep slumber. Somehow, her face and forehead didn't hurt as much and the throbbing in her head ceased a little.

She jolted awake with the nagging feeling she may have spilled the proverbial beans by telling him exactly how she felt. Talking in her sleep got her in trouble a lot, though he'd never said a word. Somehow, she could tell, he just knew. Had she said the L word? Being awake was easy. She spent so many years lying about this and that for the sake of her safety; while sleeping she was on shaky ground. CJ inhaled with a sharp gasp, followed by a murmur.

Her head ached. *Where am I?* Oh yeah, in transit, again. Behind her eyeball throbbed, and the movement wasn't helping. Static and buzzing almost deafened her completely. She fought for clarity but could feel her eye swelling. Wave after wave assaulted her and her pulse quickened.

CJ heard Gunner's voice through the haze, and by the way her body reacted, he was close. She panicked, remembering the gunshots, and twisted to get away, but she was not about to get anywhere. Thick arms cocooned her, and all her senses woke up like they had downed a double espresso. She struggled to fill her lungs. The more she fought, the harder it became. Her face hurt. She winced in pain and felt tears run down her cheeks. Did they finally find her? She whimpered but her throat was parched. Swallowing hard, she tried again. "Gunner!" Her head pounded, and she clawed at the air. "I can't find you. Help me. Please help me." She dragged in a breath, feeling warmth, security.

"Angel, I'm here. It's me. You're safe."

She stopped fighting when she heard his familiar voice.

Everything she held in escaped with an uncontrolled sob. The years, months, days leading to this day flashed in front of her eyes. Everything she bottled up ejected in mere seconds. The more she cried, the worse she hurt. The worse she hurt, the more she cried. The only thing soothing was CJ knew where she was and whose arms were safely around her. She breathed him in and exhaled as her body relaxed.

CJ felt a nudge. "Hey there. How's the head?"

"Ouch." She crinkled her eyes. "I've had better days. Thinking makes it throb."

"Don't think." He shook a bottle of pills, and she winced, holding her temples.

"Shhh..."

"Sorry. My bad. You need to take something and try to get ahead of the pain. I just wanted to make sure you were going to wake up first."

"I passed out?" She turned green and closed her eyes, focusing on her breathing. "I'm bleeding? My head slammed against something and then I got clocked."

"You were."

"Great." She chuckled and held onto her ribs. "What's up with this?" She pointed to her side.

"Don't know exactly, but you were bounced around a lot. You might have taken the brunt over the rest of us. At first, I thought you had been shot, but no bullets got anywhere near you."

"Thank goodness."

"I couldn't agree more. We'll stop up the road, get ice and something to eat, but we need to get you cleaned up and see if you have any other injuries. It's hard to assess the situation. You look straight out of a horror flick, so we can't have you go inside. We can park on the side and sneak you in the restroom."

"I look bad, huh?" CJ tried to sit up and cover her face. "This blows."

"Rocky Balboa may have one on you, but not by much. Doesn't scare me, but watch it. Ryker might hurl; he's a big wimp."

"I heard that," Ryker yelled from the rear of the Humvee.

CJ held off a snicker. "Stop. Don't make me laugh."

He prodded her hand. "Take these. The sooner you do, the better you'll feel." He opened the water bottle and handed her a power bar.

CJ and Gunner's fingers grazed, and she quickly turned to cover her face, knowing full on she was something straight out of a Texas Chainsaw Massacre movie.

"I think not." He shifted, grasping her chin. He gently directed CJ to meet his gaze. "I still see you, not squeamish in the slightest."

She forced a smile. "You're a terrible liar."

"I'd never lie to you, CJ."

"Okay, maybe not, but you've detoured the truth a time or two."

"For your own protection. Like now."

She swatted him on his forearm. "Brat."

"Heads up, we're stopping here."

CJ eyed the old gas station. She twisted around, looking to her left, then ahead. "Are you sure it's safe?"

"Only one way to find out. You have nothing to worry about. As you well know with us by your side."

"Have you seen what I look like? I've learned to expect the unexpected over the years. I swear I have the worst luck. My biggest accomplishment to date is having all of you at my side."

"I disagree. Luck, good or bad, has nothing to do with it. You've been an impact long before we came on the scene. You escaped Ryder and the triple Ds and had already given your statement to the police and the D.A. How can you think we're your biggest asset? It's been you all along."

She shrugged. "It would have been awfully lonely existence without you here."

"I'd have to agree. We've grown accustomed to having you by our sides too, ya know. After all, you were our first big case. We have you to thank for making our business a success. The rest of our cases will fail in comparison."

"Flattery will get you everywhere." She pinched Gunner's cheek. "There is a heart under all that muscle. Who would have thought?"

He rolled his eyes. "Watch her. I'll check the inside and get a key for the men's." He leaped out the door. Hawke reversed the SUV into the closest space near the restroom.

CJ shivered and laced her fingers together. She leaned

forward and asked Hawke, "How much longer do we have to drive?"

He turned and got an eyeful. "Hell, G wasn't kidding about the Balboa comment."

CJ looked into the rearview mirror. "Good Lord! I'm a freak."

"Welcome to the club. We're all freaks. Don't you worry about it. Let's say once your extra extra strength Tylenol kicks in and you take a little nappy, all will be right in the world. Ryker, go get some ice for the prize-fighter."

"Back to where are we going. Are you trying to avoid me, Hawke? I mean you can't exactly avoid me with all of this." She pointed for emphasis at her face. "I'm a hot mess. Guess things will never change. You're always tight-lipped when I ask you where we're going. You are impenetrable."

"Maybe one day you hope I'll cave and tell you." He turned and looked her straight in the eyes. "I don't tell you for your own protection."

"I get it, but one day maybe you'll soften up a bit. I hope I'm there to see it."

"Don't hold your breath."

"We'll see."

Ryker returned with a couple of plastic cups of ice. Hawke pointed as Gunner rounded the corner. "Eye on the prize. Ryker, block the door after Gunner and CJ go in. I have eyes up front."

Ryker opened the door for CJ and gasped after he got a good look. "Geez, that's gonna leave a mark. G is going to have his work cut out for him." He muttered under his breath, "Clean up on CJ's face."

"Aren't we the comedian?" CJ smacked him.

Ryker shooed her into the restroom and handed Gunner the medical supplies. "Good luck." He winced.

"Would you rather?" Gunner cocked a brow, towering over Ryker.

He waved his hands and stepped away. "Nope, it's all you."

"Enough of the comic relief." Gunner had Ryker by a few inches in height, but his fierce look had most people shaking in their skivvies. These guys were so tight, like brothers. No matter how much they respected each other's former military rank, they still gave each other crap.

EIGHT

Gunner held the door open for CJ, but the flickering fluorescent light stung her eyes and she got dizzy.

"Whoa, Angel." He directed her to the commode. "Sit for a minute. I need to clean up, this place is disgusting." He grabbed the Lysol and sprayed the room. "I'll see if you have any more injuries."

"I think I'm going to be sick." She covered her mouth. "I am."

Gunner erased the distance and swung into action. He propped her up, lifted the lid, and eased her in front of the crapper. She dry-heaved as he held her hair back.

"I'm sorry."

"Why would you be sorry?" He ran a soothing hand across her shoulder. "This isn't exactly the first time you've blown chunks."

"Touché." She wiped her mouth with her sleeve and grabbed the water bottle she'd brought in, taking a swig and swishing the liquid around before spitting it into the sink. "First all the jarring around like I was in a jumpy house, then getting wedged under the seat while a two hundred plus pound man did squats on my face." She covered her face and laughed. "That did not come out as intended."

A familiar scarlet heat warmed her cheeks and he tried to make sense of what she meant before he went somewhere totally inappropriate. "I'm to blame with the baton. It was supposed to protect you, not injure you."

She rubbed her head. "I'm a klutz. I'm an accident waiting to happen. If something's in the vicinity, it will find me. Let's top off the day with me barfing the light fantastic. It's not exactly a recipe for a woman to feel purty." She stretched the last word out with a drawl.

"It's all overrated, anyway. Women gussy up more than they need to. I think you're fine the way you are."

"Exactly. Fine is what I aspire to be." She mouthed the word *fine* with her usual sass. "Never mind." She closed the lid and took a seat, rubbing her temples.

"Keep your eyes closed and leave the rest to me."

"I don't think I can move anyway, so no argument."

Gunner yanked several handfuls of paper towels and wet them in the sink. "Let's see what we're dealing with here. This may hurt." He washed his hands and opened the first aid kit. "You ready?"

She nodded up and down. "No time like the present."

She inhaled deeply as he gently wiped away some of the dried blood. "Ah ha. It's a doozy, but the good news is you don't need any stitches." He wiped her face more, cleaning up as good as he could. "Once we get to our stop, you can shower and get the rest of the blood from your hair." He held one of her tendrils and rolled it between his thumb and forefinger. "You're going to have a black eye. It's already looking like an award-winning one."

Her eyes popped open. "Yeah, unfortunately I caught a glimpse."

He nodded. "What hurts the worst right now?" He studied her, hoping she wasn't in as much pain as she looked.

"Equally my head, the parts of my face hanging in there, and my side."

"Let me see what you're talking about with your side."

She lifted her shirt slowly as he crouched in front of her. Gunner hesitated and inched away before pressing a light touch along her ribs. She jerked and watched him.

"I don't think anything's broken, but it's pretty bruised up." He felt her eyes upon him. He lifted his gaze, but the contact never wavered. "I guess you took the brunt of the force on the floorboard. We weren't on the road for most of it. I've been off-roading, and this was off the Richter scale."

"A smidge rough. The flying object took revenge on this girl, did some damage, and decided it wasn't done playing. That's about all I recollect."

"You blacked out." He tipped his head. "It could have been so much worse if any of the bullets had hit you. For that I'm thankful." The thought still shook him. He ran lazy circles over her tender flesh. *What's happening here?*

"Me too. Thank you for doctoring me up." She stood and ran a hand over her jeans. "Do you think I could have a minute alone in here to use the facility? Then you can."

He gathered the first aid kit and threw the blood-soaked towels into the trash can. "Sure. I'll be right outside if you need me. Knock when you're ready." Gunner closed the door and leaned against it, taking a deep breath. His nerves were shot, but he was relieved there weren't more injuries. CJ would feel better sooner versus later.

Ryker looked over his shoulder. "G, I'll go get some grub and energy drinks. Hawke said I'm driving, so I need some wakey-wakey. As soon as CJ's tucked in, I gotta whizz. My teeth are floating."

"TMI, Ry. Why do I need to know this?" Gunner shook his head. "Better make it fast before you soak your tighty whities."

"Funny." Ryker leaned against the building and cracked his knuckles. "Bud, you okay?"

"Yeah." He rubbed his eyes and yawned. "Solid."

"Cool." Ryker gave him a fake jab.

Hawke lowered the passenger window. "Boss called. They're wondering why we're still here." He waved his hand in the air in haste. "Found the tracker too. Hurry up. We need to be further along to meet Luca. Jeffrey just called; he'll meet us tomorrow."

Ryker raced around the corner and Gunner checked around before guiding CJ into the back seat. They took off, Ryker at the helm with his two cans of eye-popping juice, Hawke in the passenger seat ready for a snooze. With Ry driving on the stuff, they'd be there in no time.

CJ had the dozies most of the trip. Gunner loved watching her sleep. It had been his favorite pastime over the years. Something peaceful about it, since it was one of the few times he'd seen her not filled with worry. A gentle spirit in her slumber with no cares about the brutal world she had lived.

He loved the way she survived. Every day she'd take the day on, even if she was afraid. She walked over hot coals day in and day out, but smiled her way through it, covering most of her pain. She didn't pity herself. Yes, she had pain, the deep kind that undid a person, but she took full responsibility for her part.

But when she smiled and looked at him like she did, he knew he'd sacrifice everything as she did, just for her. He'd do it all for another glimpse of a heart without pain. Her heart. His own.

The sun rose over the horizon -- a new day, washing away the days behind them.

Gunner swiveled to catch a glimpse of the rear. No one was looking for a tail, so he kept his eyes sharp. He stretched his legs out a little more to get a better view, leaning against one of the doors. CJ was draped over him and hadn't moved for hours.

He was grateful the pain meds had done the trick, but the dosage was on the low end. Her sleep probably had more to do with the past few weeks and the trial. He ran a hand over her hair through the night, more to help her relax. *Or is it me?* She stirred.

Gunner could sense Hawke's stare. "What's up with nastygram?"

Hawke shook his head and focused on the road ahead. They hadn't seen anyone on the road for hours, but they were closing in on their safe house. A team was already on the premises, keeping a watchful eye.

"It's a go. The premises have been cleared," Ryker said in a matter of fact tone.

Gunner nudged CJ awake, and she groaned.

"We're here."

"What?" she crinkled her eyes and rubbed her nose. "We're here?"

"Yes. How do you feel?"

She stretched her arms over her head. "A lot better than I did earlier."

"Good." He smiled.

"What?" Her eyes bugged out and her mouth hung ajar.

He smoothed a hand over her hair. "Beetlejuice has nothing on you."

"I'm sure I look atrocious."

"Not really, but I'd hate to see the other guy you've been sparring with. About the black eye. Yes, it's a keeper."

"Of course, it is, I do nothing halfway." CJ got a glimpse of her face and crazy hair in the rearview mirror.

"Oh, Lawdy Lawdy. I need a makeover, stat!" she laughed.

"I'm not sure there's enough paint to cover your eye, though. As soon as we get settled you can take a long shower. Or whatever you need to. The teams already got everything set up. But we all must make up some time we lost first."

The small house sat on a couple of acres. If you weren't looking for the structure, you wouldn't see it hidden behind the unruly bushes and overgrown weeds. "We're only here until tomorrow, then we land in your new world with a shiny new cover. We'll get our orders before. Some of us will go with you and the rest of us will either get our R&R or hop on to a new case."

"Will you be there? Or are you going home?"

"I don't know. I probably won't go home, not much there anymore." Gunner thought about the last time he had gone home. He'd to move his mother to a memory facility and sell their family home. With Hunter missing for years and his dad never around, preoccupied with his military career, it didn't make sense to hang on to the place.

Dear old dad had never been there. Mom had taken on both roles. Home was right where he was. *This is home enough. If I could only find my brother.*

"All of us are meeting with the boss of Noble Network."

He scoffed at the thought of home. There wasn't one. Some guys had their places, others didn't. Most like him just continued with work.

"You need a vacation."

"Vacations are overrated. I don't relax much—not in my DNA. I'm spun too tight."

"You should, or you'll have a coronary."

"Honey, the military and this job are enough to give you a

heart attack. I think if it wasn't in my life, I'd probably die over a pina colada."

"There could be worse things."

"Right, but I'm not into the froufrou drinks. Give me a dram of bourbon or a brew and I'm dandy."

"I could use something to take the edge off."

He waved her forward, grabbed her hand, and exited the SUV. "Come on. Breakfast first, then we can see what they have for later. It's going to be a busy day."

CHAPTER

NINE

The place was a mere shack. The interior was a surprise, better than the ruins of the exterior. *Seriously.* CJ was glad this would not be her next residence. There were three rooms, one bedroom with a queen bed and a bathroom, and two rinky-dink smaller bedrooms, one with two bunk beds.

CJ's first thought was how the heck were any of her bodyguards ever able to sleep on them without their feet and legs hanging off them? They weren't very high. It would only take a step and they'd be there. She'd hate to be on the bottom bed when one of them was above for fear it would topple on some unsuspecting sleeper.

The other was about the same, with four small basic beds scattered along the walls like a dorm. Nothing like all of them up close and personal. A hall bathroom and main living space. The ceilings were so low everyone was ducking their heads. She felt claustrophobic immediately.

After the grand tour, which took three minutes with everyone bumping into one another, Ryker showed CJ her space and the clean clothes laid on the bed. Her cue to disappear while they had a meeting of the minds. Thank goodness she was ready for a shower.

CJ had closed the door most of the way, watching the cluster of men around the kitchen table, when Gunner's gaze shifted in her direction and softened. You could cut the tension from there all the way into her little piece of the shack.

They had covered the windows with plywood, so CJ switched on the nearest light and walked to the bathroom, turning on her shower. Putting her head under the warm spray, it shocked her to see how red the water was as it swirled around the drain. She didn't grasp how long she stayed in there, hoping water could cleanse it all away. Was her nightmare ever going to end?

CJ turned the water off with a whistle, thump, thump, growl of the pipes. The last growl was so loud she half expected the pipes to hurl through the shower. She wrapped a towel around herself gingerly. She ached, an ache so deep as she willed herself forward. Wiping the condensation off the mirror, she caught sight of herself and gasped. Wincing, she rolled her shoulders, focusing on the bride of Frankenstein reflection. Her eye was more swollen and hot to the touch. The colors were deeper than before, with redder discolorations, and deep purples were forming where the blood had pooled. The sharper stabbing pains had reduced to tingly and numb.

"Who are you?" She fought for every ounce of willpower. CJ struggled to swallow the fear consuming her life. No matter how hard she tried, the distaste was firmly imbedded.

She looked away, tired of the face she barely recognized anymore. She slipped into baggy jeans, a white tank top, and a bubblegum pink sweatshirt. Wrapping her hair in a towel, she gave the mirror another glance.

"Lawdy lawdy. Aren't you a badass, Cinder?" She shook off

dread as it tried to seep in and leaned on the sink, thinking any moment her knees would buckle, knowing with every fiber of her being, she was opposite. She slipped under the covers, trembling to shake off the eerie coldness. Silently weeping, as she had for years. No one was about to see her cry; no one would see her vulnerable.

"I'm so lonely."

"Angel, you're not alone."

She whipped around in the dark room. She could make out a silhouette of Gunner in the corner, his elbows firmly planted upon his knees.

She wiped a wayward tear with the back of her hand. "I comprehend I'm not alone, but I'm so lonely." She covered her face and bawled. The floor creaked in her ears and CJ lifted the hands from her face. Gunner had crossed the room in three quick strides.

"Please don't. I can't stand to see you cry."

She could sense an unease about him with his jerky movements.

"I don't cry." She jutted her chin forward.

A hiss escaped his lips. "Okay, but your eyes are leaking. It's not the first time." His eyes gave her a knowing look she had grown accustomed to.

Her gaze darted away. "Wow, I thought I'd had you fooled all this time."

"Nah, never. Remember, I barely sleep, and it's my job to check on you."

She shifted to sit up and lean against the headboard. "Not hiding it well?" she said while moving her head from side to side.

He copied her. "Maybe a little at first, but we're trained to use our senses, and most of the places we've been need insulation. Big time."

"Oh. Please don't tell the others."

"Wish it was that simple, but you're not fooling any of us. You shouldn't be ashamed."

She could feel her face distort. "They know too?" *Ugh.*

"I'm afraid so." The bed creaked as he sat beside her.

"I wish I was stronger, not as emotional. It's becoming harder and harder these days."

"I don't. You're so strong. It's okay to cry. This trial had to be tough. It's your last one, and seeing your family for the first time is extremely emotional. There's a finality and closure to it. I did what I could over the years, arranging the phantom texts on a burner phone. I know you wanted to talk to them, its way too risky. But each time you'd shed more and more layers of yourself. I take personal responsibility for making things worse for you." He bowed his head and picked at the dry skin of his cuticles. "I'm sorry."

She moved closer. "I don't think you did. So do not go there. Those texts, though cryptic and anonymous, gave me the strength to move forward. They gave me sanity." She placed a hand on his cheek. "You gave me hope in a hopeless situation. I will be forever grateful."

Gunner inched closer. "Somehow, I feel I've done more harm than good. It tears at my gut to see you like this."

She wanted to wrap him in her arms and kiss him silly. "I will never forget your act of kindness." The walls between them receded every time they had a moment where they bared a little bit of their souls to one another like this. "You are my sanity."

"Ha! Lucky you."

The door swung open, and they both turned, separating themselves from their prior position.

"Heads up. There's movement on the frontage road. We

need words, G." Hawke thumbed the air toward the direction of the open area of the house.

"Can I join you?" CJ asked.

"Not yet. Maybe later. I need to talk to Gunner about a few things." He handed her a plastic bag of ice. "For the swelling."

"Thanks." CJ recognized Hawke's demeanor – he got his nose out of joint when doors were closed. She and Gunner were alone for too long.

Gunner got up and turned. "I bought you a notebook if you want to write." He laid it on the bed beside her.

CJ ran a hand over the simple spiral notebook. "Thank you."

"WHAT THE HELL do you think you are doing, dude?"

"What?" Gunner held his stance wide, planting his shit-kickers solid, anchoring his legs, his arms firm over his chest.

"Seriously? Don't play dumb. You understand exactly what I'm talking about. We've had this conversation before. If the boss catches wind of this, she'll send you overseas, far away from CJ and your little crush. Get your act together."

"I'm handling it. Do you think I'm slacking? Am I not doing my job?"

"No, that's not what I'm saying. You're getting too close. We all are."

"It's been ten years! Longer than we ever thought this job would last. Are you a heartless piece of shit? We're all she has."

"It's hard not to get invested. I get it. I hear what you're saying. I admit CJ's grown on all of us." Hawke got in his face. "You going soft on us? You know if you do, she could end up dead."

Gunner flipped him around, clenching his molars. He

pushed Hawke against the wall. "Bro, say it. Say I'm soft. Say it, and I'll show you how deadly I am."

"I've seen your deadly up close and personal." Hawke put his hands up. "Chill. You go soft and let your guard down, we could all be in danger."

"Haven't I always had your six? In the service, on the job, on a mission? Tell me I haven't done my job and I'll back off." His voice grew louder. "Say it!" He could feel his insides bubbling up. "There's a new threat, one we didn't expect. I will not go soft. Not ever with my responsibility to CJ."

"Don't press your luck, Gunner. We all have a lot at stake here."

"If I don't do my job, I'll walk my ass away." He loosened his grip.

Hawke pulled at his shirt. "I'm not saying I don't trust you with all our lives. She depends on it." He hitched his thumb in CJ's direction. "I'm getting in your craw. Make sure your head is in the game before you slip."

Gunner turned and stomped out the door. "Gonna go cool off, for all our sakes. It will not be pretty if I lose it."

"You do that. I'll see you in a few so we can discuss our next move."

Gunner kicked wind with his size 12 boots, chucking rocks in every direction. "I. Am. Not. Going. Soft," he breathed through gritted teeth. Clawing at his scalp, he loosened his hair from its elastic band. Gunner raked through it again, pulling his long ass strands back tight in the tie, repeating the words again, "I. Am. Not. Going. Soft."

He knew full well if he took a long look at the situation, things had changed exponentially. His thoughts were diverted as he spied headlights in his peripheral up the gravel road. He punched the mic of his earpiece. "Heads up. And someone better have eyeballs on CJ. Vehicle at 12:00. Do you think it's

Jeffrey?" He dropped and rolled head over feet, sailing over the porch and tucking himself behind a tall bush, waiting for his next move.

"She's right here. Could be Richards." Hawke responded. "We got your six."

"Balls to the walls. Eyes on moonbeams. I think it's Jeffrey, but I don't recognize the vehicle. Try calling him. I'm standing until I hear from you."

"Confirmed. It's him."

Gunner got up from behind the bush, wiping the debris off his knees. "Asshat," he mumbled. The vehicle came to a stop and Gunner met Jeffrey. "You came damn close to sporting a metal jacket, ya shit." He gave him a firm shake, then a hug. "We weren't expecting you until later."

"I busted tail to get here. This is important. I had to speed things along and get to you before it was too late. Luca's in my dust. He'll be here in 10—I told him to park behind."

"Too late? What's up? Or should I ask? I've seen the look before. After the last twenty-four hours we've had, I expect you are layering more piss to this show."

"Unfortunately." Jeffrey's demeanor was more stoic than usual; Gunner suspected this was not good news.

Gunner waved him forward and patted him on the back. "Come on in. The gangs all here." Hawke and Ryker stood at the door. "We have a secured meeting with the boss lady and the General."

"Good, I'm not late. I have intel I shared with them." Jeffrey stated. "Your plans have changed." He ran a hand over his mustache. "We need a new location. The other one could be compromised."

"Figures." Everyone headed to the common area.

～

"I'll be there in a minute." Gunner hitched his thumb toward where CJ was.

"Back in a flash." He knocked at the door before entering.

CJ was curled up on the bed, writing in her journal, but set it aside. Her bags were lined up next to her. "Hey there. What's all the ruckus?"

He walked over and sat at the edge of the bed. All of CJ's attention was on him, as it always was. How she licked and bit at her top lip was never suggestive, but one of focus, like the entire world didn't matter when they were together. Her eyes fluttered as concern painted her expression.

"What's going on?"

"Jeffrey's here. We're having a meeting with the boss, something about our orders."

She stumbled over her words. "I—I don't understand." Her brows knitted together, and she took a huge breath. She pressed her temples. "I'm over the repeat already."

"One day soon." He patted her knee. "I'm sure it's just a detour. Nothing to be concerned about."

She ran her fingers over the seam of the bedspread. "Will you be able to tell me?"

"I'll certainly try, if I can."

"I'm counting on it. If it concerns me, I have a right to know," she said, barely audible.

Gunner stretched his neck from side to side, each crack and pop relieving the tension. "Absolutely. I've been transparent with you." He lifted her chin. "You trust me?"

She nodded. "With my life," she snickered.

CHAPTER

TEN

The handlers, including Jeffrey, Luca, and a couple of others, gathered around the table in the kitchen. The phone rang, Ryker pressed the speaker button. "Luca, you did good giving the tail a joyride. I'm impressed." Gunner gave him a high-five.

"Everyone here," the General's voice boomed, followed by their boss, her voice always smoothing over the General's prickly edges.

"Hey boys, how's it going?"

Everyone spoke over one another to get an answer, except for Gunner. The pulse in his neck raced, his gut dipped and rolled. His vibes were always on point; he knew something big was about to present itself.

"We've had a change of plans in the upper echelon; there's some kind of leak in Colorado. Someone broke into the judge's chambers and took files. There's also been a threat to the District Attorney. Some files had information about the witness protection agency, so this is our show going forward. We have all of you and our resources. When you signed up for the Noble Network Security, we were considered a liaison for the government. The stakes are higher and we can't risk going by the book anymore. We decide from here on."

Gunner watched Hawke, knowing full well they were going rogue, but needed to hear the words. "So we're clear...what does this exactly mean?"

"Noble Network has contacts and support from military and some jurisdictions, but basically, we don't exist."

The room was eerily quiet, though it overflowed with half a dozen guys.

"Richards is here as a point person; a lot of our communication has been compromised, so we will find our own way to get our messages through. He's brought all-new devices. We're scrubbing and pitching what you have. This will ultimately mean the cases we're working on will continue, but the teams will rotate. We can't risk our destination being compromised, so we're scrapping it. Jeffrey has the new data." Nothing but silence on the other end of the phone. "Are we up to speed so far?"

"So far. Don't you work for the military still, Jeffrey?" Hawke piped in.

"Retired before the trial. I had an offer I couldn't refuse."

"Good to know. You're a full-fledged one of us now. You may regret it, though."

"Nah, this is what I've been waiting for. Just had to set things right with the military."

"Damn straight," the General grumbled.

Gunner pinched the bridge of his nose, shaking his head. He'd never said it out loud, but the general and he were not on the best of terms these days. Anytime the guy spoke, he fought off an instant migraine. Most of it had to do with his brother, Hunter, being MIA and the general calling off his attempts to find him. Some boo hooey about interfering with what the military was trying to accomplish.

"You and Gunner had my six in the service and helped me with my sis when Devland wouldn't leave her be. I must do my due diligence for the cause." Jeffrey Richards knuckle-bumped Gunner and Hawke.

"Are you still gonna keep the mustache? I swear you look like an 80's porn star." Gunner smacked his pal on the shoulder.

"You wish." Jeffrey ran his fingers over his mustache. "Back to business before I lose my job. I want to see this thing to the end. Listen up, the boss will take it from here." Jeffrey passed around individual plastic bags.

Gunner leaned in, giving his full attention to the lady who had guided him most of his life, and who had gained his respect. "Each of you will get your new phones and an envelope on where you'll be needed. Most of you will stay on for a while, but at any given notice, you'll be reassigned. Right now, we can't risk a new team for Miss Johnson and Gunner. You're heading to another place to assume a new identity until some of this thing blows over. Hawke, Luca, and Ryker will too. The rest of the team will be elsewhere or in the peripheral. There's a big internal investigation into the witness protection program, the government, and any association with either moving forward. We can't risk CJ's life, or any other person associated with the program."

"Do the guys who showed up at point A have anything to do with all of this?"

"Miss Johnson appears to be at the center of it. How else would they have known where you'd be if it wasn't for the latest information at the courthouse?"

"Geez, these guys need therapy. Let it go. There have been

some ticked off people after her since we came on the scene," Hawke said.

The General piped up. "Thompson infiltrated the motor-cycle club, and how we found out.

"You mean Tiny?" Gunner said.

The general paused for a minute and stumbled over his words. "Yes, Gunner. Other members of your team have been dispersed across the country and are reporting directly to us. Your boss and I are doing what we can, since you have your hands full. Some kind of shit is stirring and people are crawling from under a few rocks. Keep a close eye on CJ. Some threats we assumed were not in the picture anymore decided they wanted to mess with us." The tactical energy of the team changed in the silence. "You were commissioned because of your stealth training in the military. You are the best of the best. We are no longer just hired bodyguards or security. Our clients are in the best of hands."

Gunner looked around the room. *Did the general actually compliment us?* Gunner shook his head. *Whatever.*

"Richards will fill you in and pass on the orders. Your move starts pronto, so follow the orders to the T. Get prepared. You have your work cut out for you."

"Godspeed, gentlemen. I have the utmost faith in you. Hopefully soon this will all be in the past. The General and I will check in from time to time, but Richards will be your point man. Hawke, you and Gunner are aware of your duty. Ryker and Luca, listen to them. That's an order."

"Thank you, ma'am. You can count on us."

"Always have. Your wards need you even more. We are doing our best with the time we're given. Take care of your-selves, please. As you were." The communication ended, and in a split second, a scurry of activity.

The hairs on the back of his neck were standing up.

"What's this?" Gunner looked around the room. "Who else is crawling from the sewers? Isn't everyone accounted for?"

"Guess we'll find out. Beat feet, eyes sharp."

∾

CJ LISTENED CAREFULLY at the door but couldn't hear much. The glass she'd grabbed and pressed against the door was worthless. She should have known it only worked in movies, but they talked in code most of the time anyway. Maybe she should have pulled out her shoe phone too, made an emergency call like they did in one of the old movies she and Gunner had watched.

She chuckled to herself and cracked the door a little. By the look on a few of the guys' faces, something was changing. She was itching to see. CJ inched the door open a little wider, but still couldn't hear anything. She opened the door fully, it squeaked so loud every guy turned to look at her. She could feel the heat spread across her face like a hundred fire ants.

She recognized Jeffrey Richards right away. The newcomer had been sitting with everyone from the trial in Solemn Creed and now he was huddled with her handlers. Her keen sense she acquired over the years gave her knowing gut; this band of brothers, went way back in the military. He was handing pamphlets to Hawke, Gunner, Luca, and Ryker. The other two guards present she'd only seen a time or two, they were usually in the background and never got close enough to be introduced. She felt exposed with all of them gawking at her.

The reality her life was anymore. Nothing like her and a room full of beefy man sandwiches giving her the stare down. Her gaze softened as she locked eyes with Gunner, and CJ's body buzzed. Somehow, she found undeniable comfort. His cadence and internal vibe was always *'in the know,'* and she found strength with him nearby. Her shield. Her protector. His friendship was her most prized possession. CJ hated most of the attention, but it appeared her life was an open book. She'd had to turn a blind eye to it over the years, but with Gunner, it wasn't so daunting. Cracking his suit of armor had been a gradual process over the past decade, and she was intrigued to see what lay beneath his steely cloak.

Gunner slid from his chair and treaded closer. "Can I get you something?"

She moved her head from side to side and mouthed the word *No*. "On second thought…" She stepped around him and into the gathering, tucking her hand deep into her pockets. Watchful eyes assessed her, and Jeffrey flipped a map over, anchoring his elbows over it.

CJ squinted her eyes and tapped a finger over her lips. She shifted one foot to the other. "What's that?" CJ leaned over, trying to get a better look.

Jeffrey pursed his lips and furrowed a brow. "What?"

She pointed. "That? The thing you are using as a placemat."

Luca chuckled. "You should give up, Richards, CJ's beat down bigger men than you."

"Never. She doesn't have a chance," he shot back in a matter-of-fact tone. His eyes squeezed into tiny slits, never breaking contact.

Gunner stepped forward and rested his palms on the table. "Don't be so sure. All of us had a similar attitude in the beginning. I'd strongly advise forfeiting while you still have a choice." Gunner gave her a wink.

Hawke interjected, "True story." He gulped the last of his water and pitched the plastic bottle in the nearby garbage.

"This doesn't concern you," Jeffrey retaliated with a cocky attitude.

CJ anchored a fist on her hip and tapped her foot. Waggling

her finger at him, she said, "You don't say?" *Tough guy will crumble soon enough.*

He kicked back his head. "Yes, I said it," he said, emphasizing each word.

"Let me ask you something, Mr. Sassy Man. This placemat of yours appears to be geographical in nature, right?"

He nodded and drummed his fingers over the map.

CJ eyed her bodyguards. All of them had some form of a shit-eating grin. This guy was a piece of cake compared to her protectors, and proudly her experience over the years had strengthened with each attempt. She chuckled and blew at her nails.

"I have another question, if I may? Does this so-called map have anything to do with me? Or, furthermore, is any location you are marking with your fancy smancy crayon describe or show where I will travel or end up?"

Jeffrey swiveled around the room at the snickering faces. "Possibly."

She walked behind him and whispered in his ear. "Then it has everything to do with me, my life, and my safety. I have every right to understand what it is, where it is, and whatever it is. Last I checked, we are all here because of *moi*, something I am not proud of."

"You think so." He held her gaze before looking away without another word.

Got him. "Yepper, Mr. Know-it-all. Your employer said when you were hired you work for me too. You are hired, hired..." she said with emphasis and air quotes. "To protect me."

Jeffrey let out a hiss. "You weren't shitting me, you guys told me she was a pistol." Jeffrey caved and laughed, throwing the map up in the air. "Seriously, she has a point. How can I argue?"

The crew busted a gut laughing. "Told you so, Richards. You wimp."

CJ walked over to the refrigerator and grabbed her favorite white can of energy heaven. "Just kidding. I could care less what's on the map. I only read them if I have to."

"Get up, Ryker. CJ, sit." Jeffrey pointed.

She didn't move.

"You are about to get your first 101 in map reading. You need to be knowledgeable as much as we do. We have routes to travel by, escape, to get lost in. Sit," Jeffrey grumbled.

"She's messing with you, Richards. She's an ace at maps. She's gotten us out of a mess or two over the years when we're so sleep deprived, we couldn't see straight," Gunner echoed.

CJ tried her best to look serious but failed miserably. The entire situation bubbled inside of her. *Another one bites the dust.* She held in a laugh, covering her mouth.

"Geez, that's just wrong on all levels. You fit in well with this motley crew. You're evil. Sit or stand, makes no difference to me, but you should."

Gunner rounded the table and pulled a seat from the table for CJ. "Watch what you say to the lady, Richards. We go back to basics. Don't make me hold you down and shave your manstache. Just for kicks."

Jeffrey teetered his hand, shaking it around. "Trembling, Ward. But I do apologize to CJ. Just seeing how far she's willing to take it, you guys were right. She's a damn warrior through and through. I've scoured over CJ's files, studied photos from the get-go. You seriously ran bloodied, and barefooted to get away from your captors. Saw the mess from one of the break-ins in Wyoming where you split a burglar's head open with a chunk of firewood. Not to mention the guy who permanently speaks soprano after a kick in the balls." Jeffrey winced, crossing his legs. "You have my respect in droves for what you did to take down Barry Ryder and the motorcycle club, getting their drugs off the street." He nodded and gauged the room. "Newsflash: if you didn't comprehend it already, you guys are wrapped around her baby finger."

"Ha! It's the least I can do compared to what everyone in this room has done for me. We're a team. I can't help being the only female here, so I need to work my charms whenever I can. It helps pass the time. So do the self-defense classes we practice when we're bored silly. I guess they have come in handy a time or two." She gave a wry smile.

"Just wait. You won't even know what hit you until it's all said and done," Ryker rumbled. "She will break you quicker than basics, without lifting said *pinky finger*. It's been a slow, treacherous decade, and to think you caved already."

CJ could tell this group of men, including Jeffrey, was a band of brothers. A lot of love and respect amongst them. "Before we get into all the particulars, how did you all meet?"

"Military basic training. After Hawke and Gunner ended their time in the service, they helped me and my sister with the menacing Devland."

"James Devland?" CJ shivered, running her hands up and down her arms.

"Went to school together. Unfortunately, my sister was childhood sweethearts with him. He was a jerk, but not so bad, until he hurt my sister. We had a restraining order against him, but he stalked her. I'd be called away on a mission, so Hawke and Gunner protected Ellie as much as they could."

"How awful. He's an evil man." CJ turned to Gunner. "Did you help Ellie around the same time you were hired to protect me?"

"No. Before you, by what?" He looked to Hawke.

"Maybe two years or so. Then we secured a few more jobs," Hawke answered.

"My sister, Ellie cracked him over the head with a cast iron skillet almost as big as she was after he broke into the house. CJ you've come along and put him in jail. You have my respect. That man and Barry Ryder have hurt way too many of my loved ones. It stops now. Ellie's got a great husband. Connor Winslow would do anything for her."

Feelings swirled about the day of the accident which killed Connor's parents and her part in it. She swallowed hard. "I understand from the District Attorney he's wreaked havoc on your entire family and mine. Small world, isn't it?" Anger swelled in her gut; she flung the feeling away. *Just keep talking. You have no room for hate. Let it go.* "We're from the same hometown of Solemn Creed, Colorado, so you can't be all bad." She winked and extended her hand. "Nice to meet you officially. Mr. Richards."

Jeffrey stood and returned the shake. "Jeffrey, please." He scooted his chair forward and rubbed his hands together. "Let's get to business. We have little time before we hit the road."

CJ looked over at Gunner and smiled. His epic stare could undo her even in a room full of people. He had the ability to pull her from any funk she was in. He was her bodyguard. She could feel the heat rise under her flesh and pulled at her collar, realizing it was suddenly almost stifling. If she had to speak, she would fight for anything audible and make a sappy fool of herself. She tucked a loose hair behind her ear and eyeballed anything other than the man who filled her every waking fantasies.

CHAPTER

ELEVEN

Gunner threw himself into a cold shower and changed his clothes for the next haul of their trip. Strapping his blade to his ankle, he loaded his pistol, putting it in his shoulder holster, then checked the mechanism on the semi-automatic weapon. He tucked his hair under a ballcap and loaded the SUV. Tromping through the house, he gathered CJ's stuff while Ryker and Luca wiped all the surfaces, burning any debris they found in the trash can.

Gunner stood in the doorway with his arms on the wall. "You ready?" Nervous energy floated around his system. He was at his best on missions. Laser focused on the task.

"No time like the present." CJ stuffed her journal in her bag. She tied the blood-stained clothes into a plastic bag and handed it to him. "Burn em'. Gotta travel light."

"Dispose of these please." Gunner threw a bag to someone. "It's going to be a long haul. We're changing vehicles a few times, so hopefully we'll get something super-sized. Not stopping except for gas or switching rides. You sit with Ryker, we're

91

driving straight through to the south, and we'll take turns driving in shifts. You get some rest."

"Fat chance. Why did I drink two energy drinks? I'm slap happy."

"Good. You can entertain us. Just don't sing."

She tried to swat him, but he was too fast. He winked and closed the door, running around to the driver's seat.

Gunner looked in the rearview mirror to the backseat. Sometimes CJ would be a million miles away, looking off into the distance. He wondered what she was thinking about. Other times she'd be talking one of the guy's ears off, being an oxygen thief, but the worst was when she fell asleep on Ryker's shoulder. Ry seemed unfazed, but Gunner was coming unglued. He could feel the heat bubble under the surface and caught himself as the vehicle would veer. All he could think about was... *mine*. She was his, or he'd die trying. *My shoulder she's supposed to be leaning on, the person she tells jokes to. Confides in.*

He gripped the steering wheel and punched the gas.

"Hey Ward, pull off. I'll drive for a while. Trust me. I think I should drive. You're spun a little tight." Hawke preached.

"Aren't we all? I'll switch after we change rides. We're not far, and I'm not tired."

"You should be. You're the only one with zero winks. Seriously, let me know when you've had enough, and I don't mean driving."

"Shut up." Gunner growled and snapped his teeth together.

Hawke swiveled in his seat. "We've buddied it up far too long for me not to call it like I see it. You got the itch bad. If it wasn't for all of us sticking like glue, you'd be off this case."

"Don't threaten me. The rules have changed. We can do whatever we need to survive right now."

Hawke leaned closer and whispered under his breath. "She's not the person you need to survive. I can tell it's already killing you."

Gunner hit the wheel and took a huge intake. "Don't push it, Hawke."

"As always, my friend, I'm just watching your six. That's how I roll. You're just too close to see. You got it bad for her."

"Whatever. I don't fall. Are we having this conversation? Really?"

"No falling, bud. You crash." Hawke raised his shoulder. "Big time and you know it, fool. You're walking a tight line between sanity and insanity. You need to get laid; we need to find a strip club and stat."

Gunner swerved the vehicle over to the side of the road and slammed on the brakes. "Okay, you got your way. You can drive, get out from under my skin. Strip club, come on?"

"I'm familiar with all your triggers, dude." Hawke's laugh echoed in the space.

Gunner curled his lip. "Wiseass! Payback." He exited the driver's seat and switched places with Ryker.

"Front seat." He cocked a side grin, trying not to be too enthusiastic about sitting by CJ. Her hair was every which way. He loved her hair. Clenching his fists, he fought the urge to run his fingers through it so he could see her expressive eyes. He yearned to watch her; she was a very complex character. One slight in stature, but with a giant personality, an ethical dynamo.

Her eyes widened. "Do I have something on my face?"

"Nah." He looked away.

"It's my rat's nest, isn't it?"

"You're perfect", he mumbled. Gunner noticed Ryker look at a text message once he buckled up.

"Got word. Jeffrey's in the command center ten miles

ahead. We switch vehicles again and get our new paperwork and identities. We're on our own until we hear something," Ryker said.

"Is it weird to say, even though this is not always comfortable on the road, I somehow feel safer driving than in one place?" CJ bit at her top lip.

"I get it. Every time we go somewhere and you insert people, things can get dicey. You always have pot stirrers in your business."

CJ laughed and leaned over the front seat. "Remember the one time we were in Idaho and all of you were my husbands? The looks we would get. Polygamy at its finest. Whoever brainstormed the idea, it's a major fail. We were supposed to blend in, not be center stage for all the gawkers. A harem of showstopping men and me. I think I was the envy of every woman around. The communal living was not exactly for me, not to mention being in the middle of nowhere."

Gunner leaned against the door and crossed his arms over his chest. "I admit not having a television or any of the modern conveniences was a bit out there, but it did the trick."

"Cooking on a wood stove was whacked." Ryker griped. "And a bitch of a winter. I froze my nuts off."

"TMI." CJ plugged her ears. "I slayed playing cards, but I need a rematch at Booger Bridge."

"You absolutely did. Maybe if things settle a bit, you will get your rematch."

CJ leaned back and sighed. "Who am I kidding? Will things ever be simple?"

"CJ, you've earned a normal life. I, for one, am rooting for you." Gunner winked.

"Ditto," Ryker said, looking over his shoulder.

"Me too, but come on. Normal is for sissies. Aren't we all bozos on the bus?"

Gunner nudged the headrest on the driver's seat with his foot. "Hawke. Speak for yourself, you clown. I guess the first step is admitting it."

"Up there." Hawke pointed. This is our stop." They turned into an old bait shop and parked beside a rickety Winnebago.

CJ gasped. "Is that our transportation? If it is, outstanding. My parents would take us on vacations when we were young in something similar. It wasn't much fun for us kids, nothing but a sea of Winnies for miles. My pops used to have a sign with wording *if the Winnie's rocking, don't bother knocking*. He had a great sense of humor."

"You get yours from him and I assume where are your old slang words come from?"

"I guess so. It's like keeping him close."

"It's endearing. I can understand why you'd want to do it, but girl, you have a healthy imagination with your vocabulary. Some are just unusual, but somehow they make a weird sort of sense."

"I'll take it as a compliment." She smiled, thinking of her father. "What about you, Gunner? Did you ever go on camping trips or to Winnebago rallies?"

"Can't say I've done the Winnebago thing. My dad was always gone, and we never stuck anywhere too long, so it was an adventure every time he got deployed or new orders."

"Military man?" She perked up.

"The entire family is. For generations. My calling or duty, even though I didn't want it. Growing up, it was strict. They groomed me from the get go."

"I never knew that. You don't talk much about your family."

"Don't want to bore you." He shrugged his shoulders. "I like the more relaxed version these days. I made my own way in special forces. Guess I had a knack after all. I'd never have met my mates here." He messed up Ryker's hair.

"And we all lived happily ever after." Hawke put the vehicle in park and cut the engine.

"I knew you were in the service, but unaware your family was too." She moved closer. "Tell me more. Inquiring minds want to know."

"Another time. We should see what orders Jeffrey has for us."

CHAPTER

TWELVE

Gunner tucked the file under his arm and opened the door for CJ. He swiveled the passenger seat around to face her.

"This looks like a broken-down clunker from the outside, but it's sweet inside. You can sleep on the bunk and run a rocking command center by day. I'm impressed."

CJ took a seat at the table. Sorting through the papers, everything she read was surreal. Could she handle the next cover? Was the universe testing her? *Breathe. Just breathe.* A pulse thudded in her neck. She looked at Gunner and pressed a palm to her neck. He was transfixed on the papers in his grip.

"Gunner, did you see this?" Her shoulders dropped, and she sighed.

"Is this some kind of a joke?" His brows shot up. Gunner edged forward in the passenger seat and gawked at Jeffrey.

She redirected her gaze to Jeffrey, then ping-ponged her sights around the room to gauge the mood. Everyone was antsy.

"That's fire!" Ryker said with a chuckle.

"I'm afraid not." Jeffrey rocked from heel to toe. He directed his eye sockets to Ryker, to Hawke, then to Gunner. "This is from the Boss personally; she chose everything, to the last detail." Jeffrey shoved his hands deep in his pockets. "She said, her way or the highway. If you don't like it, tough." Jeffrey raised his hands in defense. "I'm just the middleman. Don't kill the messenger."

"Go big or go home." Gunner's deep voice boomed in her ears as he read from the paper. "Newly married Angel Ash and Ward Gunn are renting a home and planning a family." A groan accompanied the roll of his eyes.

CJ assessed the overall vibe in the room and kept quiet. If they were uneasy, she should be. So far, she didn't get why they had their skivvies in a twist. *Or is it being married to me?*

"I don't like this one bit. We've never had the entire team present." Hawke stared Gunner down, then locked eyes on her. His brows slashed over his dark eyes. If she didn't know him so well, she would have bolted. Instead, CJ darted her gaze away as soon as she noticed his concern-filled eyes.

"She's toying with us. For sure. Ward Gunn. Married? Is the General behind all this mayhem?" Gunner looked around at his buddies. "It sounds like his mantra." His lips were in a flat line.

CJ noticed a tick in his jaw, and a familiar flash in his eyes. He was always better at handling his emotions than she was. She rubbed her neck, where her pulse beat in hard spasms. *What is going on? You can't toy with people this way.* She had to keep the faith and this was the right thing to do, it was her they were protecting and she trusted the process. *But why does this leg of the road feel so different?*

"Get this. We're splitting up for several weeks. You two are solo, but we won't be far." Hawke's brows knitted together. The crease in his forehead deepened. "What were they thinking?" He eyed Gunner in some unspoken language.

There is something a little weird with my cover name and Gunner's. "Groovy. Angel Ash is from Alabama; I'll practice a proper southern drawl stat. I love Alabama. I'm a hairstylist and you're a… blank, but someone wrote detective over it."

Hawke and Ryker didn't make eye contact.

"CJ, you already have a good mix of dialect, you had a lot of practice over the years. Good thing it's a detective and not a dentist, because there is no way I'm not packing my piece." The corners of his lips quirked into a light smile.

CJ laughed, more from nerves. His timing was good, cutting the stifling tension.

Jeffrey threw the keys to Hawke and Ryker. "Your ride is in the back lot I sent Luca ahead to check the area. Here's all the papers you'll need. Hit the road." He waved away the two.

"Ward, see ya when I see ya," Hawke said as he headed for the door, only to turn and point his finger at his friend. "Be careful, both of you. Watch over each other. I've got the willies about this. You'd better not screw this up."

Gunner saluted him. "See ya if I need ya."

"Bye, Hawke. Take care of yourself. Tell everyone to be safe out there. I'll watch your boy."

He winked and waved off the comment. "I'm counting on it. Summon your inner badass, CJ." He took off, shutting the door behind him. She watched him jog across the drive and disappear behind the bait shop.

Ryker opened the door again. "Hey kids, don't do anything I wouldn't do."

"Get out of here, Ry."

CJ unlaced her fingers; she hadn't realized she had them in an iron grip. She waved them around, hoping the circulation would return. "Anyone else a little stressed, or is it just me?" She blew out a long breath.

"No worries, Angel." He flashed a huge grin and curled his hand around her wrist. A jolt soared through her system.

Jeffrey clapped his hands once. "Mr. and Mrs. Gunn. You're coming with me. Strap in. This beauty is a little rough around the edges. The shocks have seen better days." He turned on the ignition and pumped the gas. The smell of exhaust permeated the air.

CJ coughed and waved the papers fast and furious. "Maybe it's time for a tune up."

"Ah, it's all for show. All I have to do is flip a switch and this thing can fly."

"Let the games begin." Gunner roughed up CJ's hair. "You ready, Angel?"

She raised her shoulders. Memories of years ago flooded her mind. The kiss began this infatuation with her protector. He was the only thing she drew strength from outside of her own will to right her wrongs. He didn't judge her. This was hard enough. *Why do I have feelings for him?*

It wasn't like he'd ever have feelings for her anyway, other than duty. Looking at him, he was not happy about this at all. She was just his ward. Her knees jack hammered with nerves. How would she assume this role with him, especially with no distractions, as they played house alone? Emotions ricocheted throughout her system. CJ was a straight up mess.

THIS WAS A TEST. One he didn't like. They were playing him, setting him up for failure. *You don't mess with people's emotions.*

"I need to make a call. I won't be long." Gunner stomped his way out the door. Hitting the call button and waiting for an answer, he paced back and forth.

"Tell me it's not you. Tell me the General is up to his old

tactics." Only her silence on the other end of the call. "Hello." Followed by a familiar up-to-no-good snicker. "It is you. You're behind this," he said to the voice on the other end of the line.

"Are you alone?"

"Seriously? Of course I am. I wouldn't risk anyone hearing us." He shook his head and sighed louder than he intended to.

"Me behind what?"

"You know exactly what I'm talking about."

"Me? Why?"

"Because they said it was the boss lady's personal request. That would be you." Gunner strained to hear with the loud Winnebago engine behind him, so he walked further. "You're so busted. You are testing me."

"Oh, come on. Testing you? Been there, done that. This is not a test. I'm not playing. This is serious. Your lives are at risk, same as always. Some rules have changed a little, but we still have a job to do. I'm invested as much as anyone else is. We must move forward. The poor girl depends on you, on us, and without Noble Network, she has no one to protect her now with the leak in witness protection. She's even more compromised."

"I know this. Why do you think I'm here?"

"You're here for more reasons than you realize. I thought I'd just give you a little nudge. It's been a long haul. Plus, if there is a leak anywhere, including the team, you are not it. You've kept our little secret since it's conception."

"Does the General know about this?"

"Oh, heavens no. Why do you always call him that? So formal."

"He likes it by the book, but you don't. I'm not sure where this is going."

"Someone, meaning you, has been all business for an eternity. I thought this would be a perfect opportunity to give you a little staycation of sorts. You'll die young if you are all work and no play. Don't think I haven't seen the extra shifts you sign up for."

"I don't get what you mean. I'm a workaholic because it's in the DNA."

"I conquer, but you do not want to end up going in the same direction emotionless, or you will die young. I can't take another loss." She paused and Gunner plugged his other ear to hear better. "All of this has hardened you."

"The military hardened me and..." he paused, raking a hand through his hair. "You know the why. If I go soft, it will be catastrophic. But at whose cost?" He kicked the gravel under his boot, picked up a rock and threw it. "If I side-step, it could hurt CJ. And you are the only one who knows I call her Angel. Seriously. You're relentless."

"I've seen it with my own eyes, the effect she has on you. Smoothing a wrinkle or two isn't all bad. There won't be much to memorize when you get there. This has been a long time coming for both of you, so just jump in with both feet, with reckless abandonment. If you don't, you'll regret it. The teams are in place. You keep close, play your part, and make it believable so there are no red flags. We are dropping you into a safe area. It's been scouted, another team is already there, and you will see Hawke and Ryker in a few weeks."

"Yeah, yeah. It's not a fair scenario for her. You know what happened before." The Winnebago's horn blared. "Jeffrey's getting impatient. Gotta go."

"Gunner. Do me a favor, please. Let your guard down a smidge. It won't kill you."

"This is mutiny. Why did I ever sign a contract?" He laughed. "My guard is intact, lowering it is what I'm afraid of." He hung up and jogged to the Winnebago.

~

CJ PUSHED AWAY the curtain and peered out the side window at Gunner. He didn't look pleased. Who was he talking to? She pulled her hair up and rested her head against the wall.

She jolted when Gunner swung the door wide and leaped up the stairs, ducking through the doorway. The Winnebago rocked and teetered. He gave her a half smile and a quick nod. "You ready?"

She bowed her head and wrapped her arms around her midsection. Yeah, he wasn't good at faking it. He was not happy about the next step they were about to embark on. CJ wasn't so sure herself. She caught another look as she tucked a wayward hair into the nest on her head. She watched him buckle up in the front seat. He swiveled his chair around and his gaze softened. "I'm ready. This could be fun." His broad laugh reached his eyes, spreading small lines outward.

"I am too, Ward, but we shall see." Jeffrey hit the gas again and put the engine in drive. She held on for the bumpy ride ahead. If it's anything like the last one, she'd better latch the seat belt and fast, or layer herself in bubble wrap. Once they ended up at their destination, it would be an entirely different story all together.

Flipping through the folder, CJ stroked her neck, reading the part she'd play and their backstory. *How am I ever going to talk about hair and sound believable? I've gone undercover as a therapist...I'm sure I can adapt to hair-apy. Good thing no clients were ever involved. Fake it till you make it.* She rummaged through the box and found a theory book of cosmetology, flipping through it to get the jargon down.

What am I thinking? This is easy, the other will be a stretch. How does one get close and not get burned? She set the book aside and pulled her knees close.

"CJ, could you come here, please," Jeffrey asked over the roar of the engine.

She dodged and weaved flying objects in the RV that hadn't been secured. "I may risk life and limb with everything flying from the cubbies." She covered her head and darted forward, feeling like an impaired drunkard, never once going in a straight line. CJ trudged forward and landed with a thump between the driver and passenger seats.

Jeffrey shouted over his shoulder. "Listen up. We're almost at your drop off point. Your car is there. The rest of your credit cards and identification are in a small pouch." He thumbed to the rear of the RV, where CJ had been moments before.

"There are a couple of backpacks, and everything's loaded in there. I'll stop for gas, and you go inside. There's a rear exit and your vehicle is waiting."

He handed Gunner a set of keys. "Here you go. Keys are for the car and the residence. There's only one set, so you two are glued together. At all times." Jeffrey furrowed his brows.

His look was almost chilling, snapping CJ's attention onto the seriousness she dreaded, but always surrounded her existence.

"Luca has a backup set." He waggled a finger at them. "Like glue, you are never to be apart. Ever. Got it." He nodded. "This is where we say our goodbyes. If you get in trouble, G, you know how to reach me, but here's a phone with a few minutes." He handed it to CJ. "But only in an emergency. Everything you will need is at your destination."

Jeffrey handed them a map and pointed to the circled area. "CJ, you're in the know now on map reading. It's a co-pilot's job." He took the wheel hard, swerving off the road and into a busy gas station and eatery. "Grab some grub. I heard the burritos are the bomb." He threw a few fingers in the air and whipped them around. "Don't get all mushy. I hate goodbyes. I prefer see ya later. I might show up when you least expect me."

CJ stood up and leaned over, kissing Jeffrey on the cheek. "I can't begin to thank you." CJ forced the moisture away, thinking of her family. "If you have a chance ..." She looked to Gunner and to Jeffrey. "Tell my family I love them, and I'm going to be okay."

"You are, and I will. Enough, or I'll be an emotional mess." He pounded on his chest. "This kind of stuff always gets me in the ticker." He winked. "You two get going and be safe."

They threw everything they needed from the box on the table into their packs and stood at the door. Gunner shook Jeffrey's hand. "See you, partner." He hopped out, looked both ways, and grabbed CJ's hand.

She mouthed the words, "Thank you."

Jeffrey gave her a thumbs up.

THIRTEEN

Gunner stood by the front glass door and saw the exit. He took a cursory glance to the left and right of the convenience store, then behind. He swung the door open for CJ and she followed closely, cowering against his chest.

"I'm not sure how far we're going, so load up on your munchies." He walked behind her, grabbing a few things and a couple of energy drinks. Investigated the motherload she had in her arms, he laughed. "You realize there's probably food somewhere else, too, right?"

CJ's eyes gleamed with excitement. "You've seen it in epic proportions before. I'm a nervous eater."

They loaded the pile on the counter and Gunner side-stepped, directing CJ to follow his cue out of view from the security camera, throwing the cash on the counter. "Keep the change."

He wrapped an arm around her. "Stick close. Time to bust tail." He gauged the surroundings, throwing eye-darts in every direction, tracking every move the other patrons made.

They grabbed their bags and retreated through the rear exit, both stopped mid-step. "You've got to be kidding me."

CJ's eye popped and she scurried forward and pointed. "Wow. Look"

He followed her to the back of the vehicle. *Just Married* was plastered on the rear window in blaring neon orange paint on a flashy electric blue sports car with tinted windows. "What the hell. I swear we're not blending in."

"It's totally cute." CJ slapped her hands to her cheeks.

Gunner furrowed his brow. "Cute. Just what I had hoped to be. Cute."

He opened the trunk to find two medium- sized duffel bags. "I guess we will have a change of clothes."

CJ put the bag of food on the floorboard of the passenger seat as Gunner unzipped his pack. He rummaged through the contents and took out the map. Something dropped on the ground, so he picked up the small box and opened it.

"What is it?" CJ asked.

"Ring."

"A ring?" She tilted her head and squinted her eyes.

"Yes. I guess we better make it official." He wiped his forehead and paused.

She stepped forward, extending her left hand. "It's pretty. I've never had anything so fancy."

Gunner rolled the ring around in his hand, but he fought for the words. CJ yanked the rings from his hand and said, "Yes, but I won't be your old ball and chain." She put it on her left ring finger and held it up. "Geez, what a dazzler. It is so sparkly." Her hand shook.

"I didn't even get on a knee." He bit the inside of his cheek. "Now you're quoting old movies. No one says that anymore. Or is this something your dad said, too?"

"Maybe a little bit of both," she said with a smirk. "Next

time we do this, you can get on a knee." She fluttered her lashes and lifted the ring up again, then drew it into her chest. "So sparkly."

He cleared his throat, and said under his breath, "Just like you." Her gaze searched his.

"Come on, we better get moving." He squeezed into the driver's seat, hitting every lever to push the seat as far as it could go. "I hope we don't have a long drive. This isn't exactly a good fit."

CJ chuckled and skipped to the passenger side.

"Come on, you ball and chain." He failed miserably at raising his voice to an almost shout while keeping a straight face.

Her eyes widened to the size of the retro sunglasses on her head. "Good one, you do have a sense of humor." She squealed, plopping herself in and buckled up.

He handed her the map. "The route should be marked." He tapped it for emphasis. "Get us to our destination, co-pilot."

"Say no more. Looks like we don't have a half a day's travel. Good thing. I'm in dire need of a comfy bed and a hot soak."

Two plus hours of blaring congratulatory horns for the newly married couple. Gunner turned up the music to drown it out, but he couldn't keep his eyes off the ring CJ was wearing. Neither could she. The way it glinted against the sun dazzled her. She looked elated. He relished it, even though unconventional and a sham. She seemed pleased to fall into the fairytale. No way he'd squash what little of life's pleasures to she had to relish in. Fake or not.

"We need to exit here." She pointed to the right and sat up a little taller, edging close to the windshield. "Geez, I've never seen so many cornfields on our trip, and look, palm trees. Guess we're heading to warmer climate."

"We just crossed the state line, so we're in the panhandle.

The sunshine state and retirees. Makes sense. Loads of vaca-tioners and transplants. We might blend in after all."

CJ rubbed her hands together. "We've been a lot of places together, haven't we?" She handed him a piece of licorice. "I bought your favorite."

"I see. Thank you." He chomped on the red vine. "We have." His gaze was introspective and soft. "How are you feeling about everything?"

"I'm nervous about all the changes. Sometimes, I look back and wonder if this was worth it. Testifying." She looked deep into his eyes. "I think what my life would have been like if I'd stayed in the motorcycle club." She shivered.

Gunner ran a hand over her arm. "You might have been dead if you were still with them. Or in prison, or maybe even been a substance misuser. I hate to even think like this, but you might not have had a choice."

She pressed her palm to her lips.

"I realize this isn't the life you imagined or the one you deserved, but you should be proud of what you single-hand-edly accomplished." He tipped his head. "Not just anyone can say they were responsible for locking away a drug ring."

"I am proud. Thank you. But it's cost me everything." She raised her shoulders and let out an exhale as they dropped. "Sometimes I don't see the entire picture. But if I had never done any of those things, it would not have brought me here. I would never have met you, Hawke, Luca, or Ryker. I have a wildly different slice of happy."

"You've brought..." He contemplated. "Bounds of adven-ture too."

She laughed. "I have indeed. Whether I wanted it or not, it came a-knocking." She put another piece of licorice in her mouth. "Thanks for always being there, and for saving my life more times than I can count." She pointed to the sign and peered at the map one more time. "I think we're here."

"You need to stop with the thank yous. We all know how grateful you are." He used the blinker and pulled in front entrance. "This is looking good so far. It's a gated community—even better. There should be a code somewhere."

CJ rifled through the pouch in her backpack. "Here it is." She held up a paper with the code and did a Blake Shelton finger point.

Gunner shook his head and punched in the four-digit code. The arm of the gate lifted, next the second set of two opened slowly. After several twists and turns, they arrived at their destination.

"This is it. Cheese and Rice! Who's paying for this?"

"I have a feeling we've all paid in some way or another for this." He whistled. "Staycation is right," he said to himself.

CJ yanked on Gunner's arm and pulled him forward. "Don't forget the key." They caught two neighbors walking by slowly with their dog. CJ and Gunner made it to the front door, and he peeked over his shoulder. "Yep, still there gawking." He unlocked the door and cracked it partially open. "You ready?"

"I'm ready to see the rest of this mother lode."

"Not yet."

"Come on?" she said in a whine. Her bottom lip protruded.

He hauled her up, took her in his arms, and kicked the front door open. CJ squealed in surprise.

"I needed to carry you over the threshold." He spun her around and she laughed.

"I think I am going to love this." She spread her arms wide.

Gunner smiled, showing his pearly whites. "I am too." He caught an eyeful of the ladies still standing on the sidewalk, so he dipped CJ and kissed her. Most was for show, but the other part was simply he had wanted to do exactly this for years.

"Wow! I mean wow." Her knees wobbled and her insides were nearly exploding. She exhaled and caught sight of their audience, so she strolled to the door and waved at them.

"You're an ace on how to put on a convincing act. If there is an encore, I'll give you an ovation." She waved at her face to cool it a little.

The space was perfect, with high ceilings and the view from the rear of the house showcased a full bank of glass French doors.

Gunner walked to the exit and opened the doors. "Guess what there is?" He turned and smiled. "We have a pool."

CJ moved closer and her mouth gaped open. "You're kidding me. Not only a pool, but a hot tub, a screened lanai with privacy shades, and a fire pit. I think I never want to leave."

"It beats every one of the other safe houses by a landslide." He waved her to follow. "Let's check the rest of the house. Three bedrooms, the primary, guest, one with a hideaway bed and an office." He walked into the sizable living area. "The larger bedroom will be yours."

"The spare bedroom is fine for me." She tapped her chin. "This is a lot more space than we've ever had in the past. It's larger than we need. But if the troops come, there will be room for them too."

Gunner surveyed the house, inspecting the doors and windows, and noticed a fully operational security system he would check later. He walked by the refrigerator and opened it. "Fully stocked. We have everything we need."

"And a wine bar. This is almost too good to be true."

"Don't say that. It might be, and I'm superstitious." He pulled at his chain where his dog tags hung. "I'll park the car in the garage and bring the stuff in, but first I'll look around the perimeter."

"Can I come with you?" She swung her arms.

"No need. You get settled and relax."

Once Gunner had exited the house, CJ walked around, her rubber soles squeaking over the travertine floor. She whistled and the sounds bounced off the high ceiling and walls. This was a sizable structure, but no home. Not the home she grew up in. She noticed a plush earth tone sectional and frilly pillows in the formal living room. Rich walnut wood and etched glass adorned the furniture. A sheer valance draped in the center of a large picture window with heavy lined taupe drapes and robust rods were more for decoration. There were way too many doohickeys on every surface, but a sterility to it, and reality's ugly head was making its presence known. She went to the primary bath and ran her hand along the smooth, lustrous countertop. She pressed her hand to her face, hoping the coolness would transfer to her hot skin.

She glanced at the largest jacuzzi tub she'd ever seen, with pretty little soaps and lotions lined up. Picking one up, she inhaled its deep notes of lavender and a zest of lemon, calming and reviving her senses. "Ahhhh..."

CJ peeked into the closet and found a plush, canary colored robe. She pulled it from the hook and squeezed it tight. Her gaze caught on a couple of dresses neatly hung on the furthest rack. One was in a white plastic bag and the other looked to be formal attire. She couldn't remember the last time she'd worn a dress, except for the time she had one that looked like a potato sack, reminiscent of the little house on the prairie, and today. She'd felt as frumpy as the role she'd portrayed.

She longed for her family. Would this continue to be her life? She had been certain a light glimmered at the end of the tunnel after the last court date, but evil still lurked. Something new nagged at her gut. A new place, uncertainty, always looking over her shoulder like she had for the past decade.

CJ went to the tub, flicked the plug closed, and turned the water on. A chill spread over her. She glanced at the window, then walked to it and tugged on the lock to make sure it was secure. Subtle light filtered in, but no one could see through the frosted glass.

Her nerves were shot.

Slipping off her clothes, she eased into the warmth of the water, swooshing it around with her hand. A knot formed deep in her throat and all she could do was sob. She longed for home, and Solemn Creed was so close she could almost grasp it. Something deep in her core told her it was time. She might always be in danger, but momentarily she'd rather sacrifice herself to live with her loved ones, even if it could only be for a short while.

"I'm so tired. I want to go home."

CJ pressed her palms to her eyes and wailed.

CHAPTER

FOURTEEN

Gunner sat on the floor in front of the primary bedroom, resting his head against the wall. His gut twisted. The acoustics of the house were amplified and he could hear CJ weeping. It tore at his soul. She'd been in there for over an hour.

He pinched the bridge of his nose and squeezed his eyes tight. If only he could help. He'd risk it all to give her the happiness he had seen on her face staring at her loved ones in the courtroom, again in the private quarters for their first and last meeting in a decade. He was overcome, seeing so much love, even as her sorrow flooded every cell throughout his body.

Gunner lived and breathed loss, the pain when his brother had disappeared. He recognized the hope, like CJ did, maybe one day it would be different. Hope was all he hung on to, hoping one day he'd see his brother again. Alive. He only wished she'd talk to him more. Maybe it would help him. He heard a noise closer to the door and tapped lightly.

"Angel, everything okay in there?"

She peeked her head out the door and jumped, seeing Gunner sprawled in front of the door.

"Sorry, I didn't mean to scare you. I only wanted to make sure you hadn't drowned." He lifted himself from the floor with a groan. "The floor may look nice, but it sucks on comfort," he said in a failed attempt at humor. He raked his hands through his hair and stepped aside, pointing at the 70-inch television in the massive living quarters. "Are you up for one of our old movie marathons? I'll help you pick up more vocabulary, if you like?" He stammered and shifted from side to side. "I can make something, and I thought we could both use a movie night." He gauged her reaction as she looked around. "Doors are locked. Perimeter is safe. I checked them twice." He raised a brow. "You can relax tonight." He lifted her chin. "Or ... maybe we could just talk."

She shrugged her shoulders. "A movie sounds good."

He raised his hands and stepped aside. "Then it's our first cinema night in the new home, Angel."

She turned and sent him a glare. "Do you mean I get to pick the movie?"

"Oh. Nah, hell, I didn't say that." He said, knowing too well this was not about to teeter in his favor.

She took off in her fluffy socked feet, darting in the direction of the living room. "First one to get the remote control chooses."

She ran this way and that around the couch, looking for the remote. "Where is it?" she said with a puzzled expression.

He cleared his throat and said, "Searching for this?" as he waved the device in the air.

CJ anchored a fist on her hip and crinkled her eyes. "Not fair. You had it all along."

"You understand the drill. I check everything, and I mean *everything*. I'll make a deal with you. If you make your special popcorn with all the butter, ranch, and parmesan, I'll let you choose the movie." He crossed his arms over his chest and bit the inside of his cheek. "But…I prefer not watching something sad, that makes you cry." Gunner stepped closer and inspected her. "You've cried enough lately, and I will not compromise." He glanced deep into her red swollen eyes. "You can barely see your black eye. Healed fast. I think both of us could use a laugh or two." He gave a quick nod.

She followed his cue and gave a cursory nod in return. "I'm in full agreement. And nothing scary either. I know it's our favorite pastime, but please not tonight." She gave a half smile and walked one direction, then executed an about face. "I'm lost, apparently. Where's the kitchen again?"

He hitched a thumb in the right direction. "I'll be in to help, but first I'll get the TV set up on the movie list and close the curtains." Gunner scanned the room, repositioned a few pillows, and put a blanket on the chaise of the sectional. He spotted a fireplace, but the heat index was a stifling eighty degrees and he was sweating bullets. He spotted the ceiling fan and flipped several switches until one hit the mark and the long wooden blades whirred to life. He wanted her to be as comfortable as possible.

He leaned against the doorway to the kitchen and watched CJ rifle through the refrigerator and sort through the cupboards for dishes and bowls. He loved watching her do just about anything; it was his favorite pastime. She was so hyper-focused on the simplest tasks and took everything with great exuberance. He edged closer. "How can I help?"

"You can't. I got this."

"No way. I don't want to be a partner who doesn't do his share. We do this together."

She did that thing, biting her upper lip, while she was processing his words. It drove him wild. Her cheeks reddened.

How did CJ not recognize she was the most beautiful woman he had ever known? Inside and out.

"You're razzing me, and it's hard to take you seriously with a smirk on your face."

"Why?" He leaned forward and rested an elbow on the center island. "What smirk?" His second favorite pastime was teasing her. She was the only one in his life who got his humor, but rarely did anyone penetrate his walls. She had, but it had taken years. She simply got him.

She pointed. "That one. Don't mess with me. Be serious."

"I take my job very seriously and we must be convincing, so practice makes perfect. weren't you the one who told me to lighten up?"

"I did, a trillion times?" She chuckled.

"Personally, I don't have a clue on the how to's and what a partnership is, but I want to do my best."

CJ got all flustered and darted about. "I don't either. Guess we are on the learning curve together." She tucked a hair behind her ear. "I take this seriously too. Communication is the secret sauce, so if I need to do something for you, you must talk to me, or this charade will never work."

Gunner hesitated and ran a finger along the edge of the center island. "Hmmm..." His gaze met hers. "I'll do my best."

She tilted her head and tapped her jaw. "Most women see right through things like relationships of a lot of couples. Have you ever seen a couple and think it will never work from the get-go? And it doesn't. It's like a sixth sense. But you have an advantage; it's imperative for your job, I've seen it. You follow your gut."

He nodded. He appreciated the fact she watched him as much as he did her. His lips curved in a smile.

"We have homework to do and there's no time like the present." Her fingers went up in quotations. "*Ward*. Do I have to call you Ward? I'm getting a rerun of a Leave It to Beaver moment that can't be undone." She laughed and held her head. "Can't I just call you G, or G man? I don't care. Anything but Ward."

"You don't like my last name?"

"I do, but not as your first. Don't worry, I'll come up with something to call you, snookums."

"Oh no, you don't, honey bear." Gunner's loud bellow bounced around the room. "Geez. Snookums. Really?" He questioned, rolling his eyes.

CJ retrieved the melted butter from the microwave, put the bag of popcorn in its place and doctored the butter mixture with her secret ingredients to pour over the popcorn. "Get me a tray, would you please?" She pointed to the counter. "Thank you, Love Bunny." He whipped around and she winked. "You are so easy to rile up. This is a side of you I've never seen."

He shook his finger at her. "Watch it. I'm out of my element. This is the first time the team hasn't all been in one place together. I don't have a wingman and we're on a limb here, not knowing what's next." He wiped his brow. "I'm vulnerable in my new role. It's a little more personal than we're used to because we—we—its..." Gunner wiped his nose fast and furious.

CJ stepped closer and touched his arm. "Personal. It's more personal."

"Very."

"I understand you've heard this before, but I want to say this, in the utmost rare form of this personal thing called my life, and this recent journey we are about to embark on." She stepped so she was directly in front of him. "Look at me. I'm alive because of you."

"You have mad skills yourself." He stared deep into her eyes. All he wanted to do was kiss her. He could never repay her for what she'd given him over the years. Anything he did failed to compare.

The microwave beeped, drawing their attention elsewhere.

Gunner plopped a few bags of the goodies they had accumulated onto the tray while CJ prepared the popcorn and their drinks. "Well then, it's settled. What's your poison? There's beer and wine in the fridge. I haven't checked elsewhere, yet."

"I'll have a brewski after I help you."

"Oh okay. You are serious about all this."

"Never been more serious." He winked and watched her skin pink up.

GUNNER SAT the tray on the table and handed CJ the remote. "I may regret this, but it's all yours."

"If this experiment is going to work, I must find a chick flick. I'll teach you stuff most guys will never understand about women, so you will not lose your man card. This is strictly research. Maybe we need to YouTube the book '*How to speak your partners love language*'. Or we could watch a romcom." She extended her hand. "Do we have a deal? I vote to watch a romantical comedy."

"Come on, my skin is already crawling. If anyone catches wind of this, I will never live it down."

"You owe me. I've watched so many...how can I say this politely...dick-flicks with testosterone-fueled explosions, fast cars, and boobs over the years. One chick flick won't kill you." She tapped her foot and gave him a wry smile.

"I'd gladly do my penance to see you laugh." He gave a quick nod followed by a wide smile.

"How sweet." CJ put her hand up, palm forward, as an oath. "Peaches, I swear I will not speak of this to another soul. Your reputation will stay intact. Jeepers." She shook her head.

"You look miserable. Maybe you better have a drink to ease your discomfort."

"I better not. I need to learn this. Though it might take the edge off, Sugar Boo."

She laughed at the nickname. "Come on, you party pooper. It's not like a drink or two will affect you, ya big man sandwich."

Gunner paced back and forth, stretching his neck from side to side. He did a double take. "Man sandwich? You are a unique individual, CJ."

"Inside joke." She covered her mouth. "When was the last time you relaxed yourself?"

He gave it some thought and scratched his chin. "Not sure. It's been years, I know with certainty."

FIFTEEN

What was this sudden change with Gunner? There were nuances she had never seen before. He was usually stoic with a quiet fierceness about him. For the first four years, she'd barely gotten a grunt, let alone a word from him. And she'd tried her darndest to get a reaction, but nothing.

She'd made it her personal mission to break his silence. Pride soared through her realizing her attempts worked. Every year since, layers were shed. Gunner was always the one to notice things weren't right and was overly cautious. But he built and lived behind his own walls. His shadows weren't as dark; in his eyes a whisper of light. The stern look was malleable, with hints of expression she learned to look for. His voice was less cold and softer in nature, but only when he talked to her. Of all her protectors, he was the one who was there ninety-five percent of her time in the witness protection program. She often wondered if he had any kind of life outside of his career path. How could he? Gunner was always there.

They had barely escaped the assassination attempt at the

courthouse and ended up in the mountains, running from Barry Ryder's posse with the fireman in tow, nearly getting set ablaze, and hiding in a cave, until help arrived. Afterwards, as if a dimmer switch had been turned up a notch, an invisible thread tied them together. The connection was merely a feeling deep in the recesses of her core. A connection between her and Gunner, and not because she was a job.

He was the one who gave her strength, the person she drew power from during the trials. Gunner was what she looked for in a sea of judging strangers who deemed her as guilty as the people she was testifying against. If it hadn't been for Gunner, the years in the program would be ten times more unbearable. If she could keep safe a little longer, and no one would look for her. Maybe, just maybe she would be able to go home. Would Gunner consider leaving with her?

A girl could hope.

He ran a hand over her shoulder and squeezed her arm gently. "What's on your mind?" he said, his voice sweet and smooth like syrup.

She wanted nothing more than to be held snug in his arms and be assured everything would be okay. Her pipe dream. Today they were going to watch a romantic comedy and forget the world outside. Silence enveloped them for what seemed entirely too long.

"We don't have to do anything if you're not feeling it, CJ..." His words trailed off.

CJ cleared her throat, bringing her to the present, and straightened up. Stumbling for words, she blurted something unbelievably sassy. "You are not getting out of watching this movie." She pushed a hair away from her face. "I found the perfect one, an oldie but a goodie. We will both enjoy this. It's comical. Who wouldn't love Mathew McConaughey and Kate Hudson?"

"Okay..." He drew out the word.

"I've seen it, but it's super funny. Might be a perfect flick for our situation."

He raised a brow and situated himself on the end of the couch, bringing his massive legs up on the table. CJ lifted her wine and handed Gunner his beer.

"Cheers to new adventures, G- man."

Gunner raised a brow. "So, it's G-man?" he hissed. "Not feeling it."

"I haven't decided."

"Can't wait." He took a long swig of his amber beer, slouching as much as he could on the couch. "Good times."

CJ rubbed her hands together and settled herself on the chaise lounge at the other end, folding her legs beneath her.

As the movie was under way, they both moved a little closer to the tray on the table to enjoy the popcorn and snacks. CJ caught Gunner chuckling a couple of times. Watching him was so much better than seeing the movie for the third time.

"Good times, my love," she said under her breath.

GUNNER HATED TO ADMIT IT, but the movie was funny. Old horror flicks and action movies were more in his wheelhouse, predictable, but watching something different to make her smile resonated in his core. Making her happy just felt right. Kicking back next to CJ without a care in the world eased some of his tight, twisted muscles. But the closer she got, the harder it was to concentrate. He could smell lavender and citrus when she leaned over and their hands touched, grabbing the popcorn. Something deep in his belly stirred. How would he ever forget her when the time came to move on? He knew the time would eventually come. The phone buzzed in his pocket, and he dug for it checking the screen.

"I need to take this. It's Hawke."

CJ clicked the remote, pausing the movie.

Gunner listened to the familiar voice at the end of the line. "Hey man. Everything good?"

"Yep. Ah—um, just chilling."

"We got eyes on you. Luca said he saw you earlier checking the perimeter, but noticed the drapes are drawn and nothing's going on. Sleeping on the job? Just kidding, you're not, you rarely sleep. We're tapped into the exterior security system, but blind inside. I wanted to check in and see if you need anything. Nothing going on here and I'm bouncing off the walls. Staying in character, you might need to lay low for a few days since you're newlyweds. It'll look better for your cover later. I'm told part of your cover is showing up tomorrow and should be delivered at 1000."

"Gotcha, but what else do we need?"

"Need to know basis, so guess you'll get the memo tomorrow. Showtime, Bro."

"Whatever." Gunner ended the call. "Guess our orders are we're making ourselves invisible to the neighbors. After the movie we should go over a few details, but we have plenty of time to study our backstory."

CJ rolled the engagement ring around her finger. "I suppose we should."

"Let's finish this movie. I'm dying to see the end." He winked and leapt over the couch.

CJ WATCHED Gunner pace the expansive room in long strides. The softness of his face earlier had changed to business as usual during the call. His brows furrowed, slashed over his intense stare, his lips pursed together. She curled herself into a ball and covered herself with the throw blanket. Somehow, the movie wasn't as much fun if she couldn't watch Gunner enjoy it. Hawke and their mission were a huge buzzkill.

She could feel her stomach roll and wave, as it usually did when there were so many unknowns. The only sparkle to this entire thing had been the last few hours she'd spent with Gunner, giving her hope maybe...maybe one day she could have a life with a partner and forget this entire decade.

"Any tips from the movie I should apply?" Gunner's deep voice snapped her thoughts to the moment.

CJ moved her head from side to side. "Let's say I won't do what she did in the movie to try to lose you, and you treat me with the respect you always have, and we will roll with the punches and ad-lib the rest."

"Sounds fair enough." Gunner jumped up from the couch. "I'll get the folder so we can test each other on our backgrounds, when we met and so on."

She twirled her finger around a section of her hair. "Sure."

Gunner opened the file and handed CJ some papers. He faced her and crossed one ankle over the other on the cushion of the couch.

"We've been together for five years and met in Vegas at a strip club. You were one of the strippers. Get out!" She laughed.

"Say what? I thought I was a detective. Whoever came up with this stuff is a real comedian. Hey, what's so funny?"

"Did you see your persona?" she covered her mouth. "The Warrior King." She bit at her forefinger to hold off a rip-roaring laugh.

He grimaced and his brows knitted together. "I'm going to kill them."

"I don't think I've ever seen you dance once. "

He growled. "I don't"

"You better learn. Warrior King? Take your hair down for me."

"Why?" he huffed.

"Because I'm your wife and I'm asking nicely."

He scrubbed his face hard, next grabbed the tie from his ink black hair. It tumbled past his shoulders.

CJ gasped. He was undoubtably on the sexy meter at 20000. Her goosebumps had goosebumps. She licked her lip, envisioning him in a warrior king ensemble, doing a glorious Magic Mike performance. She could feel her nipples pebble under her cotton tee. Her vision blurred and when the haze cleared, she could see Gunner close by.

He snapped his fingers. "Get a grip woman. You zoned out, but we have business to do and you're all flushed. Do I need to take you to the doctor or something?"

She waved a hand at her face. "Nope. For a minute, I swear my wildest fantasies came to fruition. How lucky am I to be with such a stud muffin?"

He crinkled his eyes. "Stop it." He attempted to pull his hair up.

"Don't. Leave it. I like it." She said barely able to make the words audible. "Please. It suits you."

"I haven't exactly been able to get normal cuts the past few years. Can we stop talking about my hair and get back to this?" He lifted the papers from the folder.

"Okay, I'll be serious." She eyed his hair and how he screamed *sexy*. He peered up over his papers and stared at her. No words were said; none were needed. His look almost undid her as her heart throttled beneath her chest. She fought air into her lungs.

"I need to get a drink of water" she mumbled and took off to the kitchen. She filled a glass and downed the water, then decided to put her face in the freezer. She stood there, trying to get the feeling of the last few minutes out of her system. As soon as she closed the door to the freezer, she jumped. Gunner was standing behind the door, his arms crossed across his massive chest.

"You scared the living daylights out of me."

"You don't look scared, CJ. I've seen you scared."

She flung her hand up in the air and walked away. "Whatever. You don't know me."

He grabbed her wrist. "I think I know you pretty well."

She closed her eyes, and opened them, but didn't turn her gaze to see him. She couldn't. She felt so exposed. Her feelings were all over, and if he'd never felt the same way, she'd rather imagine it before ever knowing the truth. Some risks were better off buried.

She inhaled through her nose and exhaled slowly. "You probably do, more than I care to admit. I'm sure we will both learn a lot about each other after this cover." The stakes for both were about to climb to another level.

He grabbed her hand and directed her to the couch. "Let's get to work. It's getting late and we need to be up early tomorrow."

He had a way of centering her and calming her most frazzled nerves. If she didn't look at him all googly-eyed, she'd make it to tomorrow unscathed.

SIXTEEN

The sunlight streamed into the window of the kitchen. Gunner had been up for hours. He'd scouted the perimeter of the house, studied the map, and consumed a pot of coffee before he knocked on CJ's door. Cracking the door open, he saw her sitting upright, her legs crossed under her, writing in her journal. Her hair was going every which way, a look he had grown accustomed to. She was deep in thought, so he slowly closed the door and knocked. "Time to get up, sleepy head."

"Come on in. I'm up."

He opened the door. "I didn't want to disturb you, but I'm making us breakfast and it should be ready soon. Here's the last cup before I make a new pot."

She inhaled the caffeinated brew and groaned. "You get an A+ on the hubby scale already today." She smiled. "It won't take me long to shower. We have a big day, honey bunches of oats."

"My cue to leave." He shook his head. "See you in a few.

There are clothes in the dresser. I hope what they picked for you is better than my attire." He winced. "It should be near eighty today and balmy." He closed the door and went into the kitchen, starting a new pot of coffee and throwing several strips of bacon into the pan. He even found a couple of frozen waffles. While the food cooked, Gunner studied the aerial view of the five hundred home gated community; he memorized every crossroad and the quickest route to the back gate.

"Something smells delish."

He lifted his gaze, awestruck at CJ in an orange and cream off-the-shoulder blouse with a pair of cutoff shorts. Her long lean legs were rarely kissed by the sun, but her beaded sandals and matching belt set the outfit off. She rendered him speechless. None of the clothes could ever do her justice. She made everything look beautiful.

He cleared his throat and said, "you can't go wrong with the bacon, ever That's about all I can handle. And coffee. The rest you will have to teach me. I found frozen waffles and syrup."

"Score." She walked over to the pot of coffee and refilled her cup, giving it another splash of cream. She tiptoed to the table and looked over Gunner's shoulder. "What's that?" She pointed to the map. Her proximity made him freeze. He could smell the clean scent of her hair and the citrus scent she wore. He breathed her in to recharge his wandering thoughts.

He leaned away and craned his neck to give her another look. "It's the map of this community. We both need to get familiar with it. When we go out, we will take a more detailed look, but I'm preaching to the choir. You're familiar with the low-down."

"I've been taught well. I'm a little nervous about going in public—I've grown fond of the alone time the last few days."

She took a seat across from him. "I normally wouldn't say this, but the last few days have been..." She picked at her nail. "Different, but refreshing too."

"I agree. It's been different, and what gives me pause." He blew out a breath. "We are in uncharted territory right now, since we are the sole responsibility of the Noble Network. We can handle anything that comes in our way, but this is unprecedented. We have a looser structure." Gunner leaned forward and touched CJ's hand. "I don't ever, for one second, want you to think we won't protect you as we always have. Our job is to disappear until they figure where the leak is."

"Maybe being parted from the rigid confines of the government program isn't all bad? To be honest, I feel more liberated." Her face warmed and she smiled. "I've never felt unsafe in your presence."

What she said resonated, and she appeared to look right through him. Her lashes fluttered, showing her beautiful eyes. Gunner found solace in her words. *I believe what she is saying, and pride fills my chest.* "We've had a solid run, maybe a few side steps, but you're here and safe." He gave his head a quick nod and released her hand.

"I am and look at me." She wiggled her fingers. "Pretend married." She laughed and strutted across the room to push the waffles into the toaster. "Aren't you going to sweat to death in your jeans and combat boots?"

"Yeah, I'm a little overdressed, I guess. I'm not thrilled about it."

"You are going to stick out like a sore thumb wearing that. We're supposed to fit in. I'll find you something." She took off at a sprint to the spare bedroom,

"Oh no you don't!" He took off after her and caught up in a few strides.

CJ ʜᴇʟᴅ up a shirt from the closet. "What about this?"

"I will not wear a Hawaiian shirt ever." He cocked a brow and shoved his hands in his front pockets.

"I've shown you several things and apparently you don't like anything. Let's make a compromise. The only things I've ever seen you in is black, black, black, camo, and black." She grabbed a pair of grey camo cargo shorts and a black tank top. "Scrap the boots for a pair of flip flops and you are good to go."

"What's wrong with my shit kickers?"

"Come on. Didn't you say we needed to be ready by 10:00?"

"Uh huh." He grimaced, looking at his watch.

"Stop arguing and hurry up. I'll step out, so get your clothes on."

CJ waited for Gunner to finish dressing, assuming he was dreading the attire.

"Whoa. I mean Wow. You look so different." Her tongue was thick in her throat and her heart did a little pitter-patter. CJ inspected Gunner, from his pulled back hair to his Ray-bans, to the massive shoulders free of sleeves, exposing his tattoo as dark as his ink black hair. His dog tags hung free from his neck, his shirt hugged his flat abs, and her gaze roamed south to his narrow waist and loose slung camo shorts. She exhaled and grabbed at her throat where she felt the thumping through her veins.

"Do I pass?" He scooped a ball cap onto his head and flipped it around.

"You will do." She gave a tsking sound. "You will do, Mr. Right in all the wrong ways," she said, almost breathless. She grabbed sunglasses and a Havana-brimmed hat.

The doorbell sounded; Gunner peered through the

window. He put a forefinger to his lips, waving CJ into her bedroom. She ran off, eager to comply.

Gunner opened the door, recognizing the delivery person. Luca didn't look half bad, even sporting a fake ZZ Top beard and Lennon shades. He had a clipboard and asked him to sign something.

"What's this all about?"

"Follow me," Luca said. "I need a hand with your delivery." He directed him to the large white van parked on the street.

"What is it?"

"You'll see." He chuckled.

"I don't like the sound of it."

"You'll get along stellar."

Luca opened the van door to reveal an enormous cage.

"Oh no you don't!" Gunner stepped away and held up his hands.

"She's trained for numerous tasks. Axel got her as a pup with two others service dogs and worked with her. She's particularly trained to protect CJ. Wait and see—she'll be an asset to the Noble Network team."

"I don't need any help like this. What the hell am I supposed to do with this thing?"

"You're taking her. Orders." Luca handed the leash to Gunner. "Hurry up. It's time for you to walk your dog. I need to get back asap. If you have grievance, talk to the boss lady. You're experienced, but you need a brief handling her, so listen up."

"I've worked with combat canines before. Kane and Able were my battle buddies."

"All the basic commands suffice: sit, stay, heel, drop it, watch me, yadda-yadda. She has military training with verbal, hand, laser pointer, and her sniffer is on point. The dog knows a ton of commands, but she's extra special. You'll see. She's advanced and will attack an enemy." Luca raised a brow and gave a chuckle. "She's unique to the Noble Network family and so are the other two dogs we've trained. She's been scent trained, so she already recognizes you and CJ." Luca nodded and pointed. "Look at her. I think she's in love."

"Right." Gunner grimaced.

"You better get familiar, and in a hurry, but you shouldn't have anything to worry about." He handed Gunner the book of instructions and commands. "I'd suggest you don't go anywhere until you and CJ get cozy and comfortable with Karma."

"Karma? Figures. Pretty much sums it up." Gunner lifted his cap and wiped his forehead. "Come on, man. Don't leave this thing with me."

"No choice. It's an order. As I said, the dog's been trained to protect CJ. She's scent trained, so she's already hyper-aware, but keep her away from anyone outside of the team. She's a beast."

The dog whimpered and whined, pawing at the cage. "You sure she's not just hungry?"

Luca unloaded the rest of the stuff. "I'll help you bring it to the garage. I'm sure you noticed the sizable, fenced backyard. She can sniff out a threat like no one's business."

"Thanks, but no thanks." Gunner paced the garage with his new four-legged friend and closed the garage door. He knocked on the entrance of the house and yelled for CJ. "Hey, honey, I have a surprise for you. Can you come here?" Gunner stood waiting for her and absentmindedly tugged at the leash. "What are you looking at? One wrong move when it comes to CJ and it won't be pretty. Just saying." The dog tilted her head one direction, then another, her tail whipping back and forth at hyper-speed.

CJ poked her head into the garage and caught sight of the

German Shepard. She squealed and jumped over the two steps. Gunner put himself between CJ and the dog, not knowing what to expect. CJ dodged and weaved around him, attempting to get to the dog. "What are you doing?"

"CJ, they dropped this thing off and Luca said she's cool, but I'm cautious. She might attack." Gunner caught sight of the dog laying on the floor with her belly exposed, paws in the air. Her tongue was dangling from her mouth.

"Ferocious," she said with a chuckle.

"I understand she can be a guard dog to protect you, even kill if needed. Luca said she has a gamut of abilities, including detecting firearms, drugs, explosives, and full protection with an added twist. Guess we will see what the twist is."

"What's the problem?" CJ got to the floor and inched her way closer. The dog whimpered. "She's friendly."

"I'm not taking any chances. Not when it comes to you." He gave her a deadpan look. The dog jumped to her feet and sat up begging in front of Gunner. "Don't give me that. I'm not falling for it." She pawed and begged for his attention.

"I think she knows you don't trust her."

He raised his brows high. "What? No, you don't. Not the two of you against me. I've protected you for way too long to succumb to this pressure."

"Come on, please...your team would not risk you or me with this fluff nugget. You trust them, don't you?"

"I do, but I know them better than this fleabag. Seriously, what's next?"

CJ went to the dog before he could even flinch and covered the dog's ears. "You're going to hurt her feelings." She took the leash and walked away. "She's nice. See?"

Gunner followed them into the house and watched the dog, ready to pounce any moment. Willing to put himself in harm's way, if needed, to protect the women he lo...

Gunner hesitated. He'd never thought it until this moment. He'd realized early on he had feelings for CJ, but love? *Do I love CJ?* He swallowed hard, but the thought made it impossible. *Love?*

CJ guided the pooch around the house and he closely tracked their every move. "Maybe we should go for a walk? Maybe she has to go potty?"

He rolled his eyes. "Let's do this. But stay clear of everyone until we're for sure."

"What's her name?"

"Karma.""

Gunner sorted through the bag that had come with the dog, including her papers. He noticed a vest with the words *companion service dog*. "What's this?" He opened the documents and read along, then scratched his head. "The dog is your dog, which means she will be always with you, because your cover is you have seizures. Wow, this is no joke."

"But I don't have seizures."

"I know you don't, but it's a great cover. If by chance I'm not with you, this dog will always be," Gunner said.

"Isn't that dangerous? CJ asked.

"It could be to the wrong people getting anywhere near you. We might be able to be seen, but I personally don't plan on going to any neighborhood parties. Our cover is to be newlyweds."

"Right. We will be all in love, canoodling behind closed doors." She giggled. "I like karma as a name."

"Hmmm...karma does have a ring to it."

"Leave it to a bunch of former military guys to call a killer dog Karma. Karma, let's go for a family walk." She pulled on her leash and waved Gunner forward.

He followed close, set the security system, then locked the

door behind them. He extended an arm to CJ. "Better make this look believable."

"Thank you, kind sir. Which way should we take our first official stroll?"

He pointed to the right. "Try this way first." He whistled. "Karma." Every few steps Gunner scanned between the houses, looking over his shoulder every few feet. He held CJ tighter the further they got from the residence. "Maybe we should turn back."

"Nonsense. We've only been outside a minute and it's a beautiful day. We could use a little exercise. Hawke told you we needed to be seen roaming the neighborhood, and we haven't even made it around the block."

On cue, Gunner's phone buzzed. "Speak of the devil, it's Hawke. He's messaging me."

Try to act like you're enjoying a stroll with the woman you love and stop acting like you're paranoid. You need to trust the process. We've always had your six. Relax, dude. You have your job, we have ours.

Hard to change my stripes, Bro.

"What did he want?"

"They have eyes on us, so he told me to play my part better and chill." Gunner spotted someone power walking in their direction. "Heads up." The dog tugged at the leash, growling. CJ waved at the passerby. Gunner gave a quick nod of the head.

"Wasn't so bad."

"Right, but wait until someone wants to converse with us, that's when it matters."

"Neither of us are social butterflies, so I don't wish that part on anyone." CJ leaned in closer to Gunner, holding onto his upper arm. "I'm not ready to open up too much of my world yet. I'm perfectly fine with you."

Something stirred in him as he wrapped his arm around her, squeezing her tight. "Good thing, because you're stuck with me for the time being, Angel." He looked upward and inhaled deep, breathing in the feeling. A sensation of calm encapsulated him. She was a healing drug.

CHAPTER

SEVENTEEN

"I think that's enough of a walk for me. Maybe the *little* needs a drink or something to eat." She leaned to pet the pup. "Are you hungry?" she said in a squeaky high-pitched tone.

"Okay, mama bear, let's go home. Karma, come." He resisted the smile forming on his face, then let it rip. Hawke had made it clear; he should play the part. A part of him didn't care if they knew it was an act or not.

CJ flung her hat on the nearby credenza and discarded her sunglasses. "Love, let's get you something to eat and a bowl of water."

"I'm coming, Angel."

She pivoted and said, "I was talking to the dog, but you can come, too. Maybe I can rustle us up some food." No sooner had she said the words the doorbell chimed. The dog took off to the door with her in tow. She held on to the handle and stood there, shaking.

Gunner ran a soothing hand over her shoulder. "It's okay." He opened the interior door after the persistent sound of the

138

ringing, leaving the screen door closed. Two ladies stood on the front step, one with silver white hair with a big black streak, maybe in her late sixties. The other he thought was a decade younger with sparse, brassy hair. The older one opened the screen door, trying to push herself into the house.

Oh hell no. Think twice lady, before you regret it.

Gunner stepped in front of her and played push me-pull me with the door, but the lady persisted.

Let go or else.

He chomped down on his molars. Karma wiggled her way forward, growling and baring her teeth. The women stepped aside, their mouths hanging open. One slipped off the stoop and into a bush. The insistent one pulling at the door had a perm-a-frown. "I didn't know you had a dog. I hate dogs."

Here we go, stacking up points. Reason #2 why I don't like you. "A shame, I'll keep that in mind. Where do you live?"

The older women pointed across the street at the corner house.

"We'll keep the dog away, but she's family, so don't expect us to come visit either. You are on our property." Gunner caught the dog by the collar.

CJ chuckled and leaned in to get a better look at Thing 1 and Thing 2, but the dog intercepted her, guarding her from the intruders.

I guess the dog and I are on the same team, after all. He reached to pet the Shepard on the head. "Good girl," he whispered under his breath.

"We just wanted to see what you've done to the place. We knew the previous owners."

"I'm sorry, ladies, but my wife is under the weather today. Her service dog is very protective when she is not 100 percent. Maybe another time."

"Oh, married? We didn't think you were," the younger one

said as she leaned in for more information, brushing the dirt from her clothes.

"Married."

"When and where?"

"Why so important?" He paused and took a deep breath, plastering a smile on his mug. "We've been married a week; the nuptials were in Vegas. Technically speaking we're still on our honeymoon."

"I assumed you were living in sin. Too bad you're married. You're a mighty strapping fella," the younger lady said as she fluttered her clumpy false lashes.

He shook his head. "I'd love to chat a little longer, but I need to attend to the little woman." Gunner abruptly closed the door, giving the dog a pat on the head. "Good girl." He craned his neck mid-step. "You too." He lumbered with intent to the study, hoping to catch the women on the external camera. The high-tech system would pick up their conversation.

HER THOUGHTS WERE in a deep spiral, but she went through the motions of feeding the dog and getting her some water. She inched herself to the floor and sat by the dog as she ate. CJ tried to settle her nerves by running her fingers over the dog's coarse black and tan coat.

Was this always going to be the case? Being scared for the rest of her life? Would any amount of protection ever make her feel safe again? If it hadn't by now, it never would. At this rate, even seeing her family would be literally impossible. Why did she ever make the stupid decision to like a guy on a motorcycle? The one mistake had led her here. No matter how hard she tried, there was no escaping it, and something as simple as a welcome committee coming to say hi had her shaking in her shoes. Could she ever live without her protectors or live without an alias? Deep in her being, the answer would always be no, unless she was brave enough to run from it all and go home.

~

GUNNER TURNED the volume up on the exterior security camera. The two ladies were still standing on the premises, staring up at the house. His gut told him they were nothing but a couple of nosy neighbors, stirring the pot, but still he listened.

"Something's strange about this couple. I think I will look them up and get information on them. You can google anything."

Gunner picked up the phone and called Hawke. "Heads up. Two women came over here and one of them is overly paranoid. My guess is it's her thing. I heard them on the outside system. I have zero clue why they're suspicious, other than I didn't let her gain access inside when she tried to force her way in. She lives on the corner of Almandy, a green house. She said she's looking up our digs in the public forum."

"We've tagged all the IP addresses from around here and what she searches redirect to us. If she's looking for the owners of your house, it will come up copacetic. We're all over this."

"I didn't get too far on the details of my last name, since I never use it. What will show up?"

"We improvised. It's under Ward R. Deluca."

"Seriously? Does that mean Luca, Ryker, and I are related?" He laughed out loud. "You guys need to use a little more creativity."

"Smith, Jones, and another hundred we've already used up.

There were slim pickings and we had to do it on the fly. What did we have, a minute?"

"I'm just giving you crap. I don't care. Just want to make sure we're covered and keeping you in the know. But I do have an issue with the nuthead who thought up my backstory. A male stripper? Warrior King? Payback is going to be sweet."

"The boss lady said she ran the mission, but we could improvise on a few details, so we ran with it. There may or may not been alcohol involved. Think we all could use a laugh. It's been an intense ride. How are you doing?"

"It's different for sure, but she's a better roomie than any of you any day. It's refreshing to live without a bunch of cavemen for a change. Oh, and thanks for the hairball. CJ loves the thing. Me, not so sure yet, but as far as our two visitors, Karma earned her keep. She's serious biz for giving extra protection to CJ. Having her be a service dog works."

"If you do any domestic things, I strongly advise muzzling her. She means business." Hawke gave a whistle through the line. "Inform CJ we're not far away if she needs us. In the meantime, settle in, and we'll touch base on our end. Let the games begin. On a different note, we heard there's a bike rally for a few weeks, so we're infiltrating it. Ryker and Luca are meeting up with some of the guys. I'm sure if there's any uptick from across the country and the Denver Devils Delinquents motorcycle club, someone will know about it. There's still a few unaccounted for. We have a few sources planted around from the Midwest to south. Don't fret, though. We have the teams tripled and you'll have eyes everywhere."

"Interesting. Can't wait to hear what you learn. Thanks, Hawke, you know I owe you. What can I do?"

"Be safe, my man. What goes around comes around. Stay put and chillax. It's finally your turn, rest. You could use a little staycation; you've been pushing hard for too long. Take care of our girl. Later, Dude."

"Later." Gunner hit the end button and sat back, clasping his hands behind his head. "Hopefully no news is good news," he said to no one.

He kicked off the flip flops and tiptoed into the kitchen, which was eerily quiet. He spied CJ on the floor, her hand over her face, her hair tumbling wildly. She didn't hear him come in which meant her thoughts were far from here. The dog was laying in front of her, but sat up, sensing his presence.

"Good girl," he whispered. He grabbed a chair and saddled it. "Talk to me."

CJ raised her gaze. "I didn't realize you were here." She pulled her hair up, stretching the elastic band from her wrist and swirling her hair in some casual bun of sorts as she gave him a lazy smile.

"Angel, please talk to me."

She raised her shoulders, then lowered them with a sigh. "You can't miss it I have good days and bad. Earlier was the good part. I had fun. After...When the women were at the door, everything raced back. It becomes so tiring. I miss my independence, not that I've had much. I did early on and look what I did with it." She tried to paint on a smile. "I'm over-blaming myself most of the time, but it rears its ugly head more than I care to admit lately. I think seeing my family for the first time at the trial brought up so many emotions."

He sat there, taking it all in. Gunner needed to be there for her if he could he'd absorb it all. "Thank you for sharing this with me. I wish I could take it all away from you. Maybe both of us should use this time to have a little fun." He peered out the patio door. "And maybe we should christen the pool. It would be a waste if we didn't take advantage of it. No one can see us with the huge cage and the six-foot high fencing. The dog could run in the yard. There's a firepit. Maybe we could make a list and go to the store."

Her eyes brightened with the possibilities. "Really? We could?" She clapped her hands. "I'll find a piece of paper and a pen." She darted around the room with renewed excitement, then erased the distance and leaned over his shoulder, kissing him on the cheek. "Thank you so much. You always know the exact right thing to say to get me out of my funk." She kissed him again.

He turned his chair, watching her scurry about and jotting something on the paper. CJ was so strong. He thought of the women in his life. His mother had battled her diminishing memory, and his Tia, who had taken over as any mother would. She'd protected them from the heartache as he and his brother Hunter were fighting their own war for their country. Tia had fought for answers after Hunter went missing and had begun the Noble Network in their honor. *Where is my brother? Why can't they find him? He's alive. I feel it.* Gunner snapped out of his thoughts when a cabinet slammed shut.

He cleared his throat and rolled his shoulders. "Did you see Karma with Cruella de Vil and Gladys Kravitz?" He thumbed toward the front door. "I thought the hairball was going to pummel through the door and tackle them. I don't think they'll return anytime soon."

"Mrs. Gladys. Kravitz." A high-pitched laugh burst out, followed by a snort. "Good one! *Bewitched* nosy neighbor." She laughed and slapped her knee. "Told you there's nothing better than old reruns from back in the day. My grandparents got my mom hooked on them. We would watch everything when I was little." She smiled wide. "Our new neighbors are rude humans. They wanted in the house bad. If they're not nice, they're not welcome."

"Our visitors were salty. I admit your prehistoric obsession has grown on me over the years." Gunner studied her. She was intoxicating. "Karma gained my respect protecting you. I saw the look she gave the ladies, baring her teeth. I was almost shaking in my skivvies myself. She was out for blood."

"I feel better with the two of you here." CJ ran her hand along the dog's full coat and lifted her gaze, almost peering straight down her cherub little nose. "And I heard the *little woman* comment you made earlier. Puh-lease." She stretched the word with attitude.

He grimaced and slapped his forehead. "I may have adlibbed. One thing, you're not a little defenseless woman. I mean maybe in stature, but you are a strong, confident woman, and never have been a meek little woman ever."

She lifted her chin. "Thank you. Somedays, I'm not sure I measure up."

"You do for me."

"What I mean is—you always find the right thing to say. Watch out. My head may balloon up from all the compliments. Thank you."

"There's enough room around here for over-inflation. This place is better than all our digs combined and then some. You'd never let that kind of stuff go to your head anyway. It's not who you are."

"One could hope, but thank you just the same." She tapped the pen on her chin. "Marshmallows, chocolate, and graham crackers. We could do s'mores in the firepit sometime if we have wood. I better go check."

"Sure, or a hot tub pool night if you're up for it?"

"Sounds dreamy."

Gunner watched her intently. Her excitement seeped in. Everything about her had coiled around him from the start, even though he had been a headcase when he had first taken the job. His aunt pleaded for him to take the sole job of protecting a young woman trying to right the wrongs of her past. She must have seen it long before he did, but as Gunner glanced into her eyes then and today, he saw himself.

Our souls are forever intertwined.

In the beginning, he was nothing more than a wounded soul who could see CJ's effect. Days became months, which led to years, but the more time he was with her, the more he craved her presence. He was on a path of healing; she cloaked him in powers she possessed unbeknownst to her. Gunner had seen his own reflection when he looked into her eyes and dug himself out of the crater he'd merely existed in.

Her will and exuberance to make the most of a terrible situation was admirable. CJ quenched and satiated the demons that fought to take him away after he watched his mother dwindle slowly, until she could no longer remember him. Long after the years he spent trying to find Hunter when he'd disappeared into thin air. A spiritual rendering and cleansing of every action in the service. Every enemy he'd extinguished, every gut-wrenching travesty he'd witnessed, over the years never forgotten, but had given him a paradigm shift. CJ had seen death and heartache, but she would not let it penetrate who she was at the core. She'd made a stand for justice, and though the cost insurmountable, she did it anyway. He learned and thrived from her presence, and she was resilient. He respected her spirit.

"I think you're pretty special," he said under his breath. His blood raced in his veins, along with the pummeling under his solar plexus, and somehow he felt so vulnerable as she whipped to attention and stared at him. Her gaze literally penetrated him, not as her guard, but as Gunner Ward. *Did I just say that aloud?*

EIGHTEEN

CJ watched Gunner intently; the longing she saw in his eyes struck her. No mistaking it: something epic was happening between them. "What did you say?"

"Ah, nothing." He turned away. "It's nothing." He rubbed the tense muscles along his neck and dipped his chin.

"You can run, but you cannot hide. Look at me and tell me what you said." She put a hand on her hip.

"Can't remember." His voice lowered.

"Funny, you remember everything." She gave a half smile. "That's okay if you can't recall. I heard exactly what you said. You said, I was pretty special." She could feel her cheek get warm and a shiver struck, giving her pleasure. Time to dismantle the façade. *Here I go.* "I happen to think you are pretty special too." She leaned in and gave him a kiss on the cheek, but didn't pull away. He turned. She could feel the warmth of his breath prickling her skin. "Are you going to kiss me?" she said, barely able to catch her own breath. Her fingers ached to touch, to caress.

He leaned in and rested his head against hers. He blinked and looked deep into her eyes. "I'm afraid if I do, I'll never be able to stop."

She inhaled, hoping the exhale would give her an extra dose of courage. *Here it goes. All in.* Still not moving, she threw the inhibitions she'd bottled up for so long out in the universe. "What's so wrong with that?" She ran a finger along his goatee and his razor stubble, her hand shaking for control. She closed her eyes, pulled her shoulders back, hoping her inner warrior got the memo. He pressed his lips along her jawline, and she quivered with the contact she had merely dreamt of. Was this it, finally?

The doorbell rang and the dog pounced forward, almost taking her in tow. The guttural sound coming from the dog gave her goosebumps and prickled her skin. She gasped.

Gunner leaped off his chair and it slid across the floor. His eyebrows knitted tight across his forehead and his eyes were dark as a turbulent storm. He put a finger to his lips. "Stay here. I'll check the camera and see who it is." He glanced through the window. "Don't move." Karma growled again and her nails scraped against the tiles. She looked back, then darted to the front door. Her barking became insistent, and she clawed at the door on her hind legs at the shadowy figure.

Panic jabbed hard at CJ's stomach. Her heartbeat grew louder in her ears, muffling the dog's warning. She tried to move, but she was glued to her spot. The deafening sound was a familiar one and she knew it would pass as soon as she took control of her breathing.

"Breathe in a calming breath. Now breathe out." *Out I said. Dammit.*

She closed her eyes and latched onto the side of the chair for balance, then decided to sit. She jumped when Gunner's phone buzzed on the table. She peered at the call screen:

Hawke. CJ grappled with the phone, almost dropping it to the floor, but secured it tight against her chest. She swallowed the lump lodged in her throat. "Hello." The word trailed off in a puff.

"Where's Gunner?"

"He's looking at the security camera. Someone's outside."

"Don't let him get anywhere near the front door. Sounds like Karma's got it covered. We don't recognize who it is, and we can't identify the license plates. I'll stay on the line while you get him."

CJ rocketed from her chair with wobbly legs and took off to the office. She whispered *Ward* and tugged at his shirt. "Gunner, it's Hawke on the line. He said don't answer the door." He pulled her close and ducked into the office. Gunner reached for the phone in her jittery hands, but stopped and planted a kiss on her lips. Sitting CJ on his lap in the office chair, he cradled her. "Hawke, what is it? Uh huh, got it."

She breathed in the scent of his Bravo Sierra shea butter and coconut body soap, remembering he liked it more for the name alone. But the combination of him wearing it had become her favorite. Adding in the rich leather notes of his boots, his hair tie and the old tattered bracelet she'd made him years ago, he'd become a perfect soldier in her fantasies. His calming touch soothed her.

She wanted to tuck herself in and escape, but how long would they have? She felt his thick thighs underneath her, his muscular arm around her waistline as he ran lazy circles over her sensitive flesh. Sitting there made her feel safe. The adrenaline faded away as his scent wrapped around her like a warm blanket.

Like home, familiar. The only home she'd known over the past ten years. Gunner was her home, him. This time there was something more to it and her core clenched. Her eyes drifted to his lips and CJ couldn't help the growing desire to know how he felt against her own.

His hands were molten hot as he rubbed her fear, but it sparked more inside her. Unable to fight the burning desire, she slid her finger to his neck. Gunner shivered when she softly slid her fingers through his long hair and over his shoulders.

He focused on the monitor. "Hawke. Whoever it was just left. Everything here is locked tight. Good. You should follow them. Keep me posted."

"Nah. We go it covered. Radio out," Hawke said and hung up.

Gunner held the phone to his ear, but stayed as still as he was prior. "Angel, they're gone. No need to worry." Slowly he rocked her as she nestled closer.

"Okay. Do you think it was the people following us?"

"Probably not, but Hawke's on it."

She didn't want to know if whoever was chasing her had found her already. "What a relief," she said, but her thoughts drifted. *How could they and so soon?*

Gunner drew her hair away and kissed the sensitive part of her neck. CJ wanted time to stand still at this moment. She didn't want to move for fear Gunner wouldn't do the thing he was doing to her. She'd waited years for his touch, one moment showing her he felt the exact way she did, not all the reasons they shouldn't. She sensed he was knocking around the idea why they shouldn't be teetering in this direction by how his muscles tensed. Emotions welled up and she tracked his demeanor.

He sighed, moving his sharp gaze to blink at the ceiling fan for a few silent moments as he played with the silky tendril of her hair. "We shouldn't. Hawke might call."

"If I know Hawke, he's got it handled." Her eyes strayed to his face, and she kissed his chin. "Shouldn't what?"

"This." He studied her with piercing scrutiny.

"Why? We're two consenting adults."

"You are my ward. I have a job to do. I need to protect you." He struggled to spit out the words.

"I am a lot more than an assignment and you know it. You have and will protect me just the same."

"It can change everything. I'm not sure if I can take the risk."

"Can I ask you something? I want you to be more honest than you have ever been."

"Depends, but I'll try."

"If things were different and I wasn't your ward, if you didn't have a job to do. If you'd met me, would you be interested?"

"Lightning fast, but this isn't the way it is. We're not in those situations. It's too risky."

"Risk I understand. That's all it's ever been. My whole life has been full of danger and risks. Everything else is unfamiliar." Her lip quivered and tears formed in her eyes. "Except with you, I've never known what it feels like to have someone care so much he'd protect me with his life, but I can't explain this any other way. With you, with everything I am, it's so much more. I've never felt so beautiful as I do when you look at me. I've witnessed the truest form of love, whether you see it or not. I see myself in your eyes. You give me hope. I feel love."

He tried to speak, but she covered his mouth. "I want to know I matter. I want to be in your arms while you make love to me and forget everything." She planted her feet on the floor and sidestepped. "I believe you want it to." She ran a soft touch over his arm and leaned over the back of his chair, biting at his ear. "Nothing else matters."

He spun around, leaped up, and pressed CJ against the

wall. "I don't think I'll ever be able to stop," he whispered into her neck in a pained tone.

"Then don't."

CJ lost all self-control and let her body lead her, pulling his face to hers. Their lips met and warmth radiated through her body. Their kiss started gently, hesitant, both unsure of what they were about to unlock after so many years. Who was to say who lost the fight first as they both fell deeper into the kiss. She opened her mouth for Gunner, moaning lightly as he slipped his tongue against her own. A soft gentle caress that quickly built into a fervor of need.

Her fingernails dug into his taut shoulder muscles and the vibrations of his moan against her lips sent electricity straight to her core.

CJ pulled at his black leather hair tie. "I've never been more certain about anything in my life." Straight black hair washed over his shoulders like spilled ink. She fisted her hands, eagerly waiting to comb through his hair. "What about you?"

"I want you so much it hurts. Always has." His movements were erratic, shaking with an internal fury. "Help me, please, Angel." His deep baritone voice rasped with need.

It had been so long since he had been with a woman; he hadn't wanted another since he first had the kiss with CJ. No one else could ever quench his thirst. Nothing could have taken him away from her side over the past decade, except when he'd been away from her for two weeks. He had to take care of his affairs. His family had needed him. Being away from CJ was unbearable, and he'd had to move fast from brink's edge to get back to her. It was as if he couldn't inhale deep enough. His cadence was side-stepping and no undoing his course.

Gunner shivered when CJ softly slid her fingers through his long hair. Heart thudding in his chest, a spark of desire came alive in his eyes. He wouldn't make the first move, not after witnessing her fear.

He was breaking his own code: *do not get attached.* But the path had been forever blurred with CJ, slamming him upside the head, burrowing into his heart.

Today was the tipping point. His need to be with her trumped everything else. He could get fired, a risk worth taking because not having her in his life was not an option. He'd give it all up for her. She was more than a necessity; she was everything that mattered in his universe, and he couldn't fight the longing.

Here she was in front of him giving herself to him. How could she want this? Why would she? He was broken.

"I'm not who you think I am, CJ. I don't deserve you." He buried his head into her hair.

"Let me be the judge, love bunny." She had a way of lightening any situation. Damn, he was drawn to her. If only he could say the words he swallowed every day. The universe was finally giving him a shot at finding love.

Gunner tenderly tipped her face and looked into her glacier blue eyes. They glistened with tears, and he felt his heart clench. "Angel, you're safe," he assured her as he swiped a lone tear from her cheek.

Gunner lost all ability to think of anything other than making CJ his. No going back after this, so when she said, "Take me, Gunner," he didn't hesitate. Lifting her up, he asked, "Are you sure?"

"Yes," she answered breathily. No longer, or any doubt he was the one she wanted in every way. She let out a gasp as he easily lifted her, his hands pressing against the sensitive skin of her bottom. Gunner stumbled slightly as he carried her to the bedroom. She was special and he would take his time with her. He felt his angel deserved to be cherished, not taken on a desk, even if *where* was the last thing on his mind.

Once in the bedroom, he carefully sat her on the edge of the bed. He stepped aside to take her in. The flush on her cheeks and her red, swollen lips almost matched the red in her hair. Her eyes stared at him with hunger, but she'd never match him. He'd given her more.

"Angel," he whispered as he cupped her cheek and peppered her with kisses from her nose all the way to the top of her breasts.

Slipping off her shirt, she reached to unbutton her shorts. Gunner stopped her in his desire to spoil CJ. He brushed her hand away and helped her stand. Kneeling before her, he quickly opened the fastener and took her panties too as he slid them down her legs. He braced her body when she stepped out of them and then stood, towering over her in all her naked glory. He was breathless. She didn't shy away from his gaze, unbuttoning his pants before stripping him in the same way.

SHE COULD FEEL his manhood pressing against her and wanted nothing more than to remove the barriers of clothes between them. Her hips moved of their own accord as CJ's breath hitched and her back arched.

"Gunner."

Her voice pleaded with him for more. More than ready for this, she tugged at his shirt. He pulled it off, revealing the full length of his tribal tattoos on his left arm. Licking her lips, she wanted to trace the dark lines wrapping around his bulging biceps. Everything about him was perfection, and she couldn't wait any longer. Ten years had been enough time. There would be no coming back from this. Her hesitation only lasted for a second before she pressed up against the hard planes of his chest. CJ shuddered, hot desire running through her veins. She needed Gunner to take her, so she guided them against the bed.

FREE OF THE barriers between them, Gunner's cock hardened into an almost painful erection, and he didn't know how much longer he could control himself. While he cradled her head in one hand and kissed her, the other skimmed her soft skin. He trailed his fingers to her center, cupping her and feeling her wetness. A sign she was as ready as he was. Reluctantly, he released her lips and allowed her to slide to the center of the bed. His eyes never left her as he walked to the nightstand and grabbed a foil wrapper.

Her devilish grin almost sent him over the edge as he tore open the wrapper and slipped the condom over his cock. Her pert nipples made his mouth water, and he leaned over to take one into his mouth, licking and sucking while it hardened against his tongue. She moaned, arching into him, his lips grazing over her skin to the other breast. CJ was more than ready to feel him inside of her and her hand shot out to grasp his hips. Without exchanging a word, she showed him what she wanted, pulling his hips towards her.

Gunner couldn't hold back any longer. He needed to bury his cock inside her center and bring her to ecstasy. Pleasing CJ was the only thing on his mind. He climbed on the bed and she opened her legs for him. He couldn't help but think how perfectly her body fit underneath him. "You were made for me, Angel."

"I fully believe I am." she agreed, "Kiss me and love to me, Gunner."

His long hair draped over them as their lips met. Their hands roamed each other's bodies, taking in every curve and line, memorizing each other. His tip pressed her entrance, begging for entry. CJ's mouth connected with every inch she could reach, and her hips rose to allow him entry.

Gunner's arms trembled as he let out a groan. "You're killing me, Angel. I need to be inside you."

He withdrew and plunged inside again, loving the way it elicited cute little moans increased his excitement. He ached to let go, but more than that, he wanted to cherish every moment with CJ.

WRAPPING her legs around his waist, she lifted into him, syncing their bodies as his thrusts increased. Everything in her screamed for release, yet she didn't want it to end. Gunner making love to her was everything she never knew she needed, more than she ever thought possible.

Gunner felt her squeezing as he thrust, looking into her eyes, the one word escaped his lips. "Mine."

"Yours," she answered, deep in the throes of passion. She might regret it later, but she felt it deep in her heart.

With the promises spoken, their movements became frenzied. The warm tingles exploded in CJ's center as her release came to the surface. She cried out his name, sending Gunner over the edge with her. With a few last strokes and trembling arms, he carefully laid on top of CJ, enjoying the warmth of still being inside her quivering center.

CHAPTER
NINETEEN

Gunner rested his head on one of his arms. The other was under the woman he had just made love to more than once. He moved slowly, pushing her hair away from her face. Looking at her like this made him almost want to weep. She looked so peaceful, serene. He could count on one hand over the years when she hadn't sleepwalked or talked in her sleep.

He didn't want to wake her, so he eased off the bed, taking his numb arm with him. Grabbing his boxer briefs, he slid them on. He stepped over the dog, who was still at the door. Karma lifted her head as he snapped his fingers for her to follow. Gunner closed the door so CJ could get more sleep while he caught up with the guys. He entered the office and picked up his phone. He eyed his screen and noticed there were several missed calls and text messages. All were from Hawke. He made the call. "Did you miss me?"

"Why didn't you answer? You always have your phone with you."

"I didn't last night since we'd already talked. CJ was pretty upset. What did you find out about the person at the door?"

"I followed the vehicle from the subdivision to a coffee shop, but nothing suspicious. We're still looking into the plates and registration. It's reasonable to think it's someone in the community. No one else could get through the gates."

"Hmmm. Maybe the welcoming committee? I had a couple of those here early yesterday and they were a real treat."

"Luca told me about it. Nosy neighbors are everywhere. Back to you answering your phone. Keep it affixed to your body. I almost came banging at your door, but instead I took a little walky. The lights were on, and I could see the mutt pacing around. Figured everything was cool."

"Everything's cool."

"You sound different. You sure?"

Gunner cleared his throat. "Yep."

"Okay, but answer my calls, bud. To be on the safe side, stay in today. Okay?"

"Gotcha." Gunner's mind wandered, thinking of a lot of things he wanted to do around the house today. None of them had anything to do with going anywhere. He walked into the room he usually slept in and snatched a pair of his old jeans to slip on. The kitchen was his next stop for a cup of joe and give the dog some kibble. He loved quiet mornings before the sun came up. Most of them were to see CJ, and today he was just as eager. For a fleeting moment, he thought he'd feel guilty about them sleeping together, but he didn't. He wouldn't. She was the best thing that had happened to him in ages.

"Good morning, handsome. I missed you."

Gunner whipped around, almost spilling his coffee, his heart knocking behind his sternum. CJ's cinnamon blonde waves tumbled in disarray, and she was wearing his t-shirt. They locked eyes and he strode close to her. She leaned against the doorway and twirled her hair around her finger, which put a little extra pep in his step. He was aching for her already. He towered over her and leaned in; she gazed up, looking hot as hell. Her eyes sparkled.

"I like what you do to my shirt. It's never looked so good." He leaned closer and ran a finger down the bridge of her nose, then her lips. "You're beautiful."

"Thank you, but you don't need to say that because we, you know, did it."

"Did what?" He licked his lips, "You should be used to it. I said it enough last night," he whispered in her ear and continued the descent of his finger, running a soft caress over her chin and along her throat. She squirmed and wrapped her arms around his waist, scoring her nails along his hips. "Are you hungry?"

Her lashes fluttered over her bright eyes. "Are we talking food?"

"Yes, food. My woman needs nourishment."

"You sure?" She giggled as he picked her up and carried her to the table, easing her into a chair. "You Tarzan, me Jane," she said with a laugh.

"We need to stay close, so we'll have plenty of time for play. I think the pool is calling to us." He sauntered across the room on a mission. "First, we eat. I can make a mean egg and I think I saw some pastries in there. Your coffee, Angel." He sat her coffee and cream in front of her along with the pastries. "The eggs are almost done."

GUNNER KICKED his feet up on the table and patted his stomach. "Pretty good, if I do say so myself."

"Yummy. Thanks for pointing me in the direction of the

pastries. Maybe we should go for a walk and a swim. I'm sure Karma needs some exercise."

"Hawke said we should stay here. I'll let him know when we head out. If we don't go too far, he may not object. I'm sure they'll be close by if we do. He said we do need to stay put for another few days before we leave the community." A smile stretched across his face. "A bummer, isn't it."

"A total shame." Her gaze lowered and she tucked a hair behind her ear.

GUNNER AND CJ took a leisurely stroll past the dog park and decided to let Karma run off some of her energy since no one was there. Gunner threw the ball as far as he could, and Karma got it in seconds flat. The dog was a machine. CJ ran around, playing with her, until she heard someone drawing near. "Heads up."

Gunner latched the dog on her leash and CJ grabbed his hand. As they drew closer, he recognized the two men. One was wearing a bright orange Hawaiian shirt, baggy cargo shorts, and sandals with bright white socks. The other was sporting a liberally softer edge than he was used to. At least he'd tried to cover most of his tattoos. CJ released Gunner's hand as she saw her handlers approach.

"Hey, you two." She skipped forward. "Hawke, I've missed you." She gave him a quick hug. "Ryker, I almost didn't recognize you." She looked him up and down, covering her mouth. "Just say no to sandal socks."

Ryker knelt and petted the dog, who recognized him. "I had to improvise."

"I think you nailed it, Ryker," Hawke said with a laugh.

"I knew you'd show up, but neither of you are blending in, if you ask me," Gunner added.

"You think you do?" Hawke replied.

"I think it will be hard for any of you big strapping men to blend in. You guys are a scary bunch. I'm lucky to have you on my side."

"I thought Ryker and Luca were leaving today?"

"Later. They're waiting on rides to show up. Axel is coming in for a few days while they're away. I'm supposed to have a video chat with the boss and Jeffrey later. I'll fill you in when I know something."

The dog's ears perked up and her stance went rigid, leaning against CJ. She exposed her teeth and growled. All eyes were on an approaching couple with two small dogs approaching the park.

"We'd better head out first. Keep your dog leashed; she might consider the littles a snack." Hawke nodded and Ryker shouted, "Nice meeting you. Welcome to Blue Heron Crossing."

"We better bring Karma on the big dog side and keep her gated. Once the couple comes in, we can bolt."

"Shouldn't we go talk to them?" She braced herself, only to bite at her nail nervously.

"We will see how Spaz is first, but I'll muzzle her just in case."

CJ waved at the nice couple as they smiled and brought their little dogs into the small dog side of the park. They looked harmless enough, but CJ couldn't risk it. As if on cue, Gunner put a hand around her waist and guided her to the exit. Outside of the gate he extended his hand, and they walked to their house.

"Will I ever get over being so fearful?"

"Part of me hopes you do. On the other hand, my rational brain had witnessed a lot of reasons you have to be leery. I'm hopeful you always remain careful." He squeezed her tight and kissed the top of her head. "Once you live with fear long enough, it unfortunately becomes part of your DNA. You have nothing to worry about. I'll be by your side to make sure nothing happens to you."

"I can't imagine not having you in my life." She stopped. Gunner looked at her and squeezed her shoulders.

"I can't imagine my life without you in it either."

She gave a half smile. She couldn't fathom what life would be like without him in hers, but all the signs were leading there.

"Come on, Angel. It's getting hot. Time for a dip in the pool."

"I'll make us something cool to drink."

GUNNER FASTENED his hair with the leather tie and threw on a pair of shorts. He tromped off to the kitchen making a couple of cocktails, then placed the frozen concoctions on a tray with chips and salsa.

"I couldn't find a swimsuit, so I had to improvise."

Gunner licked his lips at the sight of CJ in a bright rainbow striped boy short set and tank top. "Not complaining, gorgeous. I didn't have much luck either. We could always swim in our birthday suits?" He raised his eyebrows and his face lit up with a delish grin. Even with the privacy net, the thought of anyone seeing CJ naked stirred his protective instinct into the stratosphere. His jaw clamped down at the thought. *Mine.* No one will see her naked on my watch. "Unless you want to scrap our pool day all together. I could always be swayed." He waggled his eyebrows.

"Oh you. Stop it." She smacked him on the arm lightly. "We both need the hot tub and a swim." She opened the French doors to the lanai and crossed the space to another set of patio doors that led to the screened enclosure extending the full length of the house and around the pool area. "It's been so long since we could relax, and we both need it. I noticed a couple of floaties outside. How will we manage navigating this shack." She kicked her head back in a laugh he had grown so accustomed to over the years.

"I'm claiming the flamingo floatie. You can have one of the others." She crinkled her eyes tight.

"I don't think so. I am not using the unicorn; you couldn't pay me enough. I'd rather rough it and use the green alligator. At least it has more edge and no pink." He rolled his eyes. *I'm going to torture the pranksters who prepped this house.* He sat the tray on iron table and expanded the teal umbrella.

"We're roughing it. What a life!" She lifted her face to the sun and said, "Ahhh...relax—relax—relax... A girl could get used to this."

Gunner handed CJ her drink, then raised his pool-worthy plastic glass. "Cheers."

She popped a chip in her mouth. "We've had some, shall I say, unique living experiences."

"We have indeed. What's been your favorite?"

"I don't even have to think about this. Right here, right now, is my number one."

"Mine too." Both stepped closer and CJ got on her tiptoes. "You are my favorite place."

"You've always been mine." He tapped her nose. "Let's get in the pool. Last one in is a rotten egg."

CHAPTER

TWENTY

Gunner was in and across the pool before she could even process what he'd said. He was so fit, and man, could he swim. After he sprang from the water, his inky hair looked even blacker. All she wanted to do was get closer to him, so she failed at her own plunge. He was there to catch her when she resurfaced, picking her up and spinning her around, only to plop her on the unicorn inflatable. He pulled her around.

"Other than here and the now, what were some of your favorite places?" he asked.

There weren't many. Maybe it would be easier to say what were the worst. "I wasn't fond of the cave or the small cabin in Colorado, the commune in Idaho, the rail car, the double wide in the north, but I was fond of the two-story boathouse in the Keys, the one docked in the boat repo lot, at least until a hurricane came a knocking."

"Yeah, a close call for sure. I recall you didn't like Alaska either."

She shivered. "I'm still getting thawed six years later, but a fun Christmas."

"That's when I first fell hard for you."

"Not until then? I got you beat. The trek in Montana for me You were great on the ranch and the no shirt thing was a plus."

"Ha! I like hard work and it was hot."

"You're not kidding, it was so hot." CJ's cheeks reddened. "But I can't believe you didn't like riding the horses."

"I felt sorry for all of them because we were not petite little flowers. I thought Tiny would crack his horse in half."

"Extremely funny watching all of you. Where is he anyway?"

"Unlike you, you were a natural on a horse. He's been deep in the motorcycle clubs and cross-country rallies. I heard he's not far away, so maybe you'll get to see him."

"That would be nice. I haven't seen him in so long. Can't say I can see him on a motorcycle, though. I loved doing a little horseback riding. I felt more freedom then. It helped having lessons with my sister when I was younger. Dad would be proud it paid off."

Gunner latched onto the floatie and rested his chin on his arms. "Anytime you ever want to talk about your family, I hope you know you can confide in me."

She swallowed hard. "Thank you. Sometimes it's too much. I'm a pretty good sounding board if you ever want to talk about your family. You never do. You know almost everything about me. You do have a family, right?"

He nodded and looked off into the distance. "I do, but maybe another day." He suspected if he started flapping his jaw regarding his mom and brother, he'd never stop. He rarely spoke of them, except to his aunt.

CJ paddled the water to reposition herself for a better look at Gunner. "You can tell me anything. I won't judge."

"I do indeed know this about you, it's not who you are. You will be the first to know when I do." He went under the water and flipped CJ over, only to catch her and kiss her underwater. He said he loved her, but she didn't hear him. She was his safety net, and he knew it.

"I'll freshen up our drinks and bring them to the hot tub. You game?"

"That would be dreamy. My body hurts from last night."

He winked. "I'm sorry. I'd never hurt you intentionally." The blonde strands dispersed through her fiery hair shone like golden threads he'd seen in the Middle East.

"You didn't. It's a good kind of hurt, like a deep tissue massage when your muscles are tight." Her porcelain skin turned a soft shade of pink. "Or something like that." Her voice hitched.

CJ had a shyness behind all the grit and toughness she showed the outside world. He on the other hand, saw what lay beneath in the most fantastic way. She was funny, smart as hell, and her toughness and vulnerability had earned his admiration. She gave all facets of herself to him, and he loved every nuance, because it was the trust she gave but rarely received. Trusting him. Giving her heart and body was the reason he could never have another woman. He'd waited so long for the chance; he would never leave her side. He knew he couldn't live without her.

Gunner watched her through the window as she hopped from the pool and sat at the edge of the hot tub. He didn't deserve to be this happy. A nagging part of himself was waiting for the other shoe to drop. Guys like him didn't get this lucky. Out of instinct, or fear something could happen, he did an inspection of the windows and doors when he went to the pool again. He handed CJ another drink and placed his next to her.

Gunner paced the enclosure, being sure to tug at the exterior screen door.

"Did you see something?" CJ asked.

"No, but one can never be too safe." He shifted and took a good look; her posture was rigid, and he hit the concrete in her direction. "You should never worry when I'm here. Look, we have Karma here on alert." He pointed to the dog taking a siesta. "We're safe and secure." He dangled his size twelves in the water. "Get in. Maybe it's time I help you relax and give you a massage." He climbed in behind her and pulled her close, brushing her hair aside and working her tight traps.

"I have died and gone to heaven."

His stomach dipped and rolled at the thought. "I understand what you mean, but you dying is not an option." His voice sounded so pained he hardly recognized it.

"Hey."

He didn't answer, and his hand stopped.

She placed a hand over his and spun around. "You look ashy. I'm sorry, only a figure of speech."

He turned his gaze away.

She leaned closer and wrapped her arms around his shoulders, running her fingers through his hair.

He pulled her close. "I can't lose you."

She bit at his ear and whispered. "Don't worry. You are stuck with me." Her light glacier blue eyes sparkled. He inhaled deeply and rested his nose to her little cherub nose sprinkled lightly with the teeniest freckles. He wrapped her legs around him and held onto her. "I love you," he said in a breath before claiming her mouth.

HE SAID what she was too darn scared to speak aloud. *I love you, too. I don't deserve you. I'm a coward.* CJ loved him, but who was he in love with? She didn't know who she was anymore. She didn't want this to end, but it would. Everything does.

"Come back to me, Angel. Nothing else matters. Just you and me." His eyes darkened and his breathing was uncontrolled. There was something almost unhinged about their union this time. A frenzy.

CJ trembled as he took off her tank top, her nipples pebbled, goosebumps assaulting tender flesh. She yearned to be closer. Their tongues danced and swirled. Her center ached for him, a closeness she craved with no other, lost in his touch. Gunner caressed her breasts and suckled her neck. Goosebumps covered her skin with anticipation. The stubbly hairs on his goatee tickled her face. He slid her boy shorts down and threw them across the concrete pool surface. CJ clawed at the waistband of his boxer briefs, cupping his bulge. Yanking them away, she freed his engorged manhood. She grabbed the tip and slid her grasp down as he groaned, calling out her name. He raised his gaze to the heavens. She crawled on top of him, positioning herself, and slid on top of his erection, taking him slowly, then to the hilt. Her shrill had his eyes upon her. Beads of sweat littered his forehead and moisture filled his eyes. He grappled, showing a glimpse of vulnerability. Her chest filled with warmth and pride that it was her he showed this side of him.

A deep rumble came from his chest. "You're undoing me, Angel. I need you so bad. I can't get enough. It will never...be enough," Gunner said with breathless abandonment. He thrust harder, and she took him in over and over with every crescendo. Her body quaked. He ran his palms over her backside as they made love. His groans became more panicked, and he bit her neck between his teeth. They were powerful together, over the top powerful, and it frightened her to think she may lose him. Would lose him one day. He inched her to the other side of the hot tub. CJ longed for their connection again when he raised one of her legs for better access, entering her again, easing in and out of her, all the while never letting his lips separate the insurmountable connection. He wrapped his arms around her. She could feel his heart thumping wildly against hers.

"Do you feel that?" she whispered.

He rested his forehead against hers, placing his lips on the soft spot on her neck. His words were barely audible. "Yes."

The layers separating them were discarded and thrown to the wind. So surreal and moving, it almost took the air completely out of her lungs. She struggled for clarity and the sensation rivetted deep in her soul. His guard was down. Obliterated. And he was solely hers. His armor was finally dismantled. His walls crumbled into dust. Gunner gave himself to CJ, and so much more than lovemaking. It was spiritual in nature. He looked at her with so much love it encapsulated every molecule. *I am his, and I know he's mine. We are us. There's no need for words. None would do.* An unspoken language between them. A cosmic unification of two broken souls finding their soft place to land.

TWENTY-ONE

They laid there, fighting to catch their breath and slow their heart rate, feeling satiated and united at a different level than before. They were aligned. CJ and Gunner held each other close as the soothing water swirled around them. "It's been a pretty epic day."

He laughed. "A huge understatement, Angel." He widened his arms. "I mean huge understatement. Whoop!" he hollered, raising a fist up in the air. "You always make me laugh when I get in my head. I don't know how you do it, but your timing has always been impeccable. Thank you." He stood up and ran his hands over her shoulders. "I always hoped it would be this way between us, at least in my dreams I hoped. Watching over you has been a privilege."

"Me too, the privilege part. But not the watch over the part. This is way better. You never appeared to sleep much."

"I've adapted to combat naps since my years in the service. Anyway, watching you was well worth it and did more for me than sleep."

"I seriously don't get how you function. All this life on the run has taught me to sleep when you can. I dreamt of you and wished for us, but I had no clue we would be this absofrickin-lutely ah-maz-ing." She blew out an attempt at a whistle. "I've never been able to whistle, geez."

"So you're not perfect, I guess."

"Far from it."

Gunner's phone buzzed from the nearby table, and he leaped out of the pool in nothing but his birthday suit. He wrapped a towel around his waist.

CJ tried to whistle again but failed miserably. Talk about the perfect specimen. Why did he have to cover up all his magnificence. She anchored her elbows on the side of the jacuzzi and laced her hands under her chin. CJ studied his expression. One of his team, or maybe his boss, was on the other end of the line. A sure tell sign when he went into his serious mode, followed by him clawing through his hair and pacing here and there. He had a good stomp, even barefooted.

CJ climbed out of the whirlpool and scurried to get a towel. Without turning around, Gunner had one in his hand and gave it to her. *I swear he has eyeballs in the back of his head.* She sat at the closest chair and instantly her stomach went in waves. She could feel her pulse build momentum. *Here we go again.*

Gunner ended the call. "We better get dressed. The gang is coming over. We have a meeting." He crouched for better eye contact and rubbed the side of her leg. "Don't worry yourself until we have further information. They're nearby, so we have little time." His eyes widened and a crease formed between his brows.

CJ ran a hand up to her chest. "What?"

"Uh-oh. You have a whisker rash on your face, and I think it's clear I gave you a love bite. More than one."

CJ took off into the house with him at her heels and caught a look at herself in the primary bathroom mirror. "Oh my.

What are we, in middle school? I haven't seen one of these on anyone's neck since I was younger." She caught a glance of Gunner behind her with a furrowed brow. "You might need to take a look-see at your own self. It looks like I mauled you." CJ blurted out a laugh followed by a snort. "Told ya. Don't mess with me when I'm hungry." Her words fell from her mouth in a frenzied mess. She rested her hands on her knees and laughed uncontrollably to cover her nerves. *Did I just say that?*

He stepped closer to the mirror and stretched his neck from side to side. "We're so damn busted, it's not even funny."

She rubbed the raw skin on her face. "We're screwed. I have zero turtlenecks and it's a balmy 85 degrees." CJ dashed this way and that around the bedroom, throwing clothes everywhere. She wiggled into a bathrobe, pressed her hair onto her neck and flung the towel over her hair. She caught another glimpse of herself in the mirror, threw a couple of punches in the air and cracked up laughing. "I look like a prizefighter. This time the bruises aren't on my face."

Gunner reached for her hand. "A gorgeous one. I'm sorry. Did I hurt you?"

"No, not at all. You didn't hear me complaining. My skin will have to be acclimated. Which I plan for another round." She bounced around like a boxer winning a fight. "Come here." She directed him to lean on the counter in front of her. CJ pulled his hair forward. "Good thing your hair is longer. You might camouflage it some." She lowered her gaze. "Pants might help. Use the towel and put it around your neck like mine."

He waggled his brows. "Pants. Do I have to?"

She gave him a playful slap. "Unfortunately."

Gunner took off out the door.

"Don't look guilty either or they will get suspicious."

He laughed. "They're already suspicious by nature. This is

going to be a big fail. The towels?" he yelled as he retreated across the house.

"Think positive. I have a plan." CJ yanked and pulled all the drawers and cabinets until she found some thick face cream, more to remove makeup than moisturize, but her face was red and prickly. She slathered the junk all over her face.

The doorbell gave ping as she darted to the entrance of the bedroom, leaning against the door and trying to act cool, but Gunner's expression had her in a fit. She hadn't heard him laugh so loud and she began laughing, making some of the goo from her face fly.

The outside door creaked. She heard shuffling steps and the brass door handle squealed before the door swung open, only halted by the security chain.

Gunner stopped dead in his tracks and almost hit the floor in a fit of laughter rumbling through the house. "What the...? How are you going to explain that?" He pointed.

"Have you seen my etched-up skin?" She lifted a thumb to her face. "I must do something. I panicked."

He continued his uncontrollable laughing, planting his hands on his knees. "I assure you I won't keep a straight face." He looked up at the ceiling and rolled his shoulders. "I thought I could pull it off. No way now." He wiped his eyes.

"Whatever. I'll convince them." She gave a quick nod and moved some hair sticking to the cream away from her face. "You wait and see."

"Hey! Open the door." A voice echoed through the small opening.

"Okay, but don't take offense if I can't look at you. Seriously, you look like a meme right now." He lumbered to the front door after the bell chimed again.

CJ positioned and repositioned herself, leaning on the door frame, shifting and wrapping her robe lapel snuggly.

He unlatched the chain, swung the door open and three of the bodyguards, Hawke, Ryker, and Luca, barreled through the entrance, their heavy steps echoing on the tiled floor. Each of them entered and glimpsed CJ. Hawke was first—he did a double take, then took the chair furthest away. Unfazed, his dark eyes assessed her. Ryker and Luca, on the other hand, did a cartoon-worthy rendition of eye bulging out of their sockets and the over-the-top jerking motion CJ had seen on a blooper show. The silence erupted into hysterical laughter.

"What the hell happened to you, CJ? You look like you just got hit with a pie in your face." Ryker said as a laugh rumbled from his chest.

"What are you laughing at—my attire, r my face?" CJ bit at her inner cheek, trying not join in. She had to look utterly ridiculous.

"Uh...the frosting on your face, mainly." Ryker jabbed Luca and they cracked up.

"If you must know, I didn't use sunscreen today. I didn't think I'd get much sun under the big bird cage, and my face got the worst burn I've ever had." She pointed her thumbs to her face. "This cream is cooling it off so I don't blister." She flicked some dangling on her chin in their direction. "I'm glad you find me so hilarious. Have a seat."

Hawke looked at her, then to Gunner. "Everything peachy for the married couple?" he said and lifted a brow. "Spa day?"

Gunner grumbled, "Enough." He grabbed a chair from the kitchen, scooting it across the floor. He saddled it, never once making eye contact with her or Hawke. "Yep, hotter than hell and you told us to stay here. Didn't think the Mrs. would be allergic to too much sun." He chuckled under his breath and pulled his hair forward, covering his neck.

The room was long, perfect for gatherings. CJ sat in the furthest seat in the opposite direction of Hawke, making sure the bite side of her neck was not closest to his suspicious gaze. She fiddled with her hair, the fire under the cream stinging, and waved her hand over her face. She blotted the cream and scanned the room before looking up at the slow-paddling ceiling fans. "Is anyone else getting hot in here?" She smiled, and Gunner bowed his head. Then CJ caught Hawke's laser beams staring in her direction again. "Dazzling, huh?" She squirmed in her chair.

He leaned forward and cleared his throat, directing his attention to Gunner and whispering something she couldn't decipher. Gunner's posture immediately went iron straight. He jumped up from the chair and squared his shoulders to go one on one, getting into Hawke's face.

TWENTY-TWO

"You had to do it, didn't you?" Hawke said under his breath.

"Do what? You should mind your business."

"She is our business. Have you forgotten?"

"I've been around her more than anyone. I'll never forget she's in danger."

"You'll risk her life if you go soft."

Gunner pointed a finger at his buddy. "Say it one more time and I'll pop you in the snoot." He ground his molars so tight he thought he'd break a tooth.

Ryker stepped in between the two. "We have a problem here. I'd prefer discussing business instead of you two having a lover's spat."

Gunner paced the room, stopping near CJ. The dog followed and Gunner snapped his fingers, pointing for her to sit. The dog followed the command.

"Look at you two protecting CJ." Luca said. When his eyes roamed over to CJ, he cracked up and slapped his knee. "Sorry, CJ, but you're ghosting something fierce."

"Ha ha, funny guy. Trust me, if you saw my face under all this goo, it would be much worse."

Hawke clapped his hands once. "We have a lot to discuss before Tiny comes around."

Gunner gave Hawke the evil stare down. He was still peeved.

"Tiny?" CJ perked up. "He's coming?"

"Not tonight. Tomorrow," Hawke said.

"We've had Tiny and a couple of guys infiltrate some of the motorcycle clubs across the country. Everything was cold until yesterday. Ryker and Luca hung around for a few hours and it's looking like a hornet's nest. For the past few years, there's been nothing about the triple Ds, but we've locked in on a solo rider who doesn't belong to any club. He recently came from there. He said twelve years ago he was part of a pharmacy burglary near Solemn Creed, Colorado."

Gunner saw CJ shaking in his peripheral vision and inched closer. He could see the sheer terror in her eyes. She covered her face with the towel and yelled. "No!"

Gunner leaned closer and brushed his lips to her ear. "Hold on. We know nothing yet." He watched her movements. She was worried.

CJ inhaled deeply and smoothed her hands over the fabric of her robe. "That's around the same time frame I was involved in the pharmacy burglary." She blotted the towel at her face. "I can't breathe."

Gunner squeezed her shoulder. "Easy, CJ. Breathe in." He emphasized, taking a huge inhale in hopes of guiding her.

She craned her neck, looking straight at him. "There's only one person who was involved and not put away. It's Trent. They called him Taz. And trust me, he's psycho." She clutched her fists to the towel. "All of it is his fault."

"Fuck." Gunner took off to the office, Hawke chomping at

his heels. Gunner had a hand full of files and spread them across the coffee table, knocking an artificial flower vase onto the floor. Hawke had opened the laptop and Ryker was on speed dial with Jeffrey. Gunner handed Luca half of the files and they sorted through the data.

CJ popped out of her chair and Gunner instinctually grabbed her hand as she teetered from side to side. "Angel, breathe. You have nothing to worry about." He said the words for them both.

CJ scurried to the bedroom, and he followed close behind until she froze in front of the bathroom mirror. The sounds were barely audible. "First, I need to get this stuff off my face. It's burning me." Gunner whipped on the cold water and she shoved the towel under the spray. Gunner pulled the towel from her shaking hands and blotted her face until most of the cream was off.

"I think you made it worse."

"Famous last words."

He rinsed the towel again and pressed it over her red face. "Talk to me. Start from your earliest recollection. I've memorized your dossier, but I need recall on this guy."

She nodded her head and took a huge intake of air. "I'll try."

"Take as long as you need," he coached, squeezing her hand.

"When I was younger, I met a guy hanging around the ice cream shop where I worked. He was older and nice, I thought. I was smitten because he rode a motorcycle." She raised her fingers and air quoted. "The bad guy image. What I didn't know was, he was part a motorcycle club. I get most of the clubs are cool, but this one was another story. I was naïve then. Stupid."

"Stop doing that to yourself, please." He cupped her chin.

"The Denver Devils Delinquents have wreaked havoc on everyone for an eternity."

She nodded. "It was his bike I was on when they burglarized the pharmacy and caused the terrible accident. They forced me to go because I saw a couple of things I shouldn't have. I never went into the pharmacy, but I was guilty by association."

"Shhh...it's okay. We understand you were forced against your will. It's been years since I've heard anything of him. We all thought he was dead. Trent "Taz" Kingsman, right?"

"Yes." Her teeth jackhammered up and down. "It will never, ever end. Ever." She stammered. "The worst part is...I remember his voice from the cabin in the mountains. I wasn't certain until now. I thought he was dead. I blocked it out." Her voiced cracked. *It sounded like him. Oh my God. Couldn't be...or could it? It is. He will kill me. He said he would get even.* She wanted to flee. Dizziness sliced through her system. CJ slapped her hand over her mouth, holding back her scream.

"You recognized one of the voices?" He pulled her hand away from her face and stroked it "I promise you: you will have closure. Nothing less. Trust me. Come on. Let's tell the guys."

Gunner guided her to her chair. "Anyone want a bottle of water?" He handed CJ one and passed the rest to the team, then sorted through the files. "Here! Trent Kingsman, nicknamed Tasmanian Devil." He looked at CJ. "This is him, right?"

She nodded.

"Damn, CJ, your face is red as hell. It looks like you got in a cat fight, not a sunburn," Luca jested.

Gunner threw a pillow at Luca and another at Ryker for good measure. "Leave her alone and focus." He put two digits near his eyes and aimed them in their direction.

"That's it, it's him. We heard someone saying he goes by Taz." Luca and Ryker nodded.

Gunner flipped through the file. "Last known sighting was maybe six years ago when a grainy image of him from a convenience store robbery showed up with law enforcement, but the trail went cold." He held up a picture and showed it to everyone, then to CJ.

She looked closely at the photo and grimaced. "Geez, time has not treated him well at all. Gross." She gagged. "I hate to say this, but I wish he was ten feet under. After I first testified, he disappeared. I thought he was running scared, but the D.A. said they picked him up on some drug charge. He was released before they could get the papers to convict him. Then he disappeared. Nothing. He had a healthy habit of booze and cocaine before I escaped." She raked her fingers through her gold and cinnamon waves, and Gunner caught sight of the hickey on her neck.

Gunner watched her intently, his thoughts veering from their conversation and recalling her naked beneath him. He raked his own hands through his hair until Hawke went all eye wonky. He'd seen the hickey. Pressing his hair smooth, he refocused on the case. Gunner rubbed his nose with a fist, fast and furious. "We need to move on this, strike while we have this new info."

"Tiny is slipping away tomorrow; he can fill us in. The rally isn't far, so it's a toss-up. We don't want anyone to get suspicious and follow him here. He said he ran into someone he recognized and had to make himself scarce."

"Tiny?" Ryker let out a gasp. "Fat chance of him blending in. We're screwed."

"Hope not. We need the stats on what he's seen before it's too late."

"We better bolt and go home and see if we can rack out. Best you sleep too. I'll touch base in the a.m. Lock up and get ready. I'm not saying you need to pack your bags, but be ready for anything." Hawke walked to the door. "I'll take the files and the laptop, and I'll pass this new intel to Richards."

CJ walked up to Hawke. "Do you think I can talk to Jeffrey?"

"Why?" Hawke anchored his fists to his waist.

"He told me if I have any questions, I could call him, but I don't have a phone."

"You can use Gunner's phone."

She bit at her nail, then looked over her shoulder. "I'd rather not."

He scratched his head and shifted his holster under his jacket. "I can arrange it, but..." He looked over to Gunner. "I don't think it's a good idea to go behind anyone's back here, especially Gunner's."

She teetered from one foot to another. "Never mind. I simply wanted to get a message to my family. My sister is getting married."

"You're not a prisoner, CJ. I can get you a burner phone. If that's your agenda, I'll tell Jeffrey you want to message him. He can take it from there."

She stepped forward and grabbed his arm, getting on her tippy toes to kiss him on the cheek.

"You better get the thing checked on your neck. I think it's contagious." He gave a stern look that had Gunner's hackles up. "Careful. I don't want either of you to get hurt."

CJ diverted her gaze to Gunner, who was slowly approaching.

"You too, G. Stay alert."

"Got it." Gunner gave him a two-finger salute and shut the door. He ran his hand along her arm. "I'll go check the perimeter and secure the lanai area."

"I'll fix us something to eat. Can we forget everything for the rest of the night?"

"Yeah, sure. Whatever you want."

"You can pick a movie." She fluttered her lashes and gave him a wry smile.

He looked at his watch. "Give me thirty minutes to do security first." He caressed her cheek and she burrowed into his touch.

She nodded. "I'll make some chicken wings, throw in French fries and a salad. I can whip dinner up in thirty."

He nodded as he walked through the French doors to the exterior to the lanai. "Better make it a double batch, or there won't be any for me. I've never seen anyone eat them every night and never tire of buffalo, boneless, or fried."

"There must be some perks for a girl. When all else fails, there's always food." She bit her top lip.

He swung around and squeezed her tight. "We've had a big day. Tonight, we recharge. If you need to talk, I'm here." He kissed her on the head. "I'll be by your side before you miss my ugly mug."

"Ugly is not the word I would ever describe you." She moved to the refrigerator and pulled out the bags. "Hurry, or I'll just wither away." She flashed her pearly whites.

SHE WAS SUCH a complex character who could throw herself out of an awful place for a reprieve. He'd learned so much from her. Tonight, she needed a friend, a confidant. He wanted to be everything to her.

He stalked around the perimeter and flipped open his phone, calling his boss. "Hey, pretty lady."

"I figured I would hear from you." The woman laughed as she answered.

"Tia, I need all the help you can give me."

"You have it. CJ will be okay."

"How do you know what I'm talking about?"

"A woman has an arsenal of talents, and I know you pretty good, sonny boy. I've watched you over the years. You've never been this committed to anything outside of the military. I mean...this case has been your life since I had you take her case. She's familiar in a sense. I knew you would be the perfect person to protect her."

"You realize I'd protect her with my life, Tia. I'm in deep."

"I was afraid that would happen, but you can't do this to yourself. You took on CJ's case after you couldn't find your brother."

"I know he's alive to my core, like I sense CJ when I'm not with her. I can't breathe without her. Another piece of me, gone." Gunner trudged through the darkness, walking the perimeter of the house, pulling, lifting, and tugging on windows and doors.

"Okay, now you're not going to make this old woman cry. Stop, I'm a hopeless romantic."

"Yeah, I'll stop. I don't even know what I'm saying anymore. Maybe Hawke is right. I'm going soft."

"Is it the worst thing to happen?"

"No. Losing her would be."

"There's your answer."

"Tia, as much as I feel Hunter is out there, I hear there's more people who can harm CJ. I will do everything within my power to make sure the rest of them find themselves behind bars. I need a big ask from you."

"Anything. What do you need?"

"More reinforcements. We are fully prepared to do what we

must do, but I need reassurance we are using all our resources. I will not ask the General, not if my life depended on it. He's fallen short in the past, it's his mantra. But maybe you can?"

"Jeffrey is already calling in a few favors. I'll do what I can. It's done as soon as we hang up. Gunner, thank you for asking me for help. I've been waiting. Try to get some sleep. You have a big day ahead of you."

"You too, Tia. I'm sorry I bothered you."

"Never ever a bother. Hey, speaking of the General, he asked about you the other day."

"Now don't go ruining my night."

"He said he was proud of you. He's working on some secret project, so I barely hear from him, but you always come up. He said new intel crossed his desk and he had something to share."

"Good, he told someone how he feels. It's a first. I've never heard any."

"He's a complicated man. Like someone else I know."

"Don't remind me. Love you. I better finish my rounds."

"You be careful. Assure CJ she has nothing to worry about. This too shall pass."

"She doesn't suspect your family, but she said a woman boss rocks."

"She will in time, my love. She's destined to."

"Okay. I'll leave it at that. You've been reading too many romance novels. Not everyone gets a happily ever after. Look at Hunter."

"Don't ever lose hope."

"Hard not to, Tia. Love you."

TWENTY-THREE

CJ threw the chicken nuggets and french fries on a baking sheet, popped it in the oven, and set the timer. Feeling the sting on her raw face, she opened the fridge and felt the cool air float over her skin. She spotted tortillas and decided on quesadillas, the perfect carb-fat combo for her nervous munching escapade. Things were changing again, and who knew what tomorrow would bring? She learned a long time ago life careens in a snap. Tomorrow wasn't guaranteed. After speaking to Hawke, she hoped he'd be able to get a phone to call her sister.

The front door opened, and her hackles went up. She peeked around the corner, holding a towel full of ice on her face. She pointed at Gunner and gave him her best squinty-eyed stare. "You and your stubble. I'm dying here."

He kicked his steps into high gear. "Oh. Love muffin. I'm sorry."

Gunner's predator saunter had her thinking of something else altogether. "You are not."

He shrugged his shoulders. "Maybe for having you in pain, but not for the reason."

CJ put the towel over her lips. "These hurt too."

"These?" He ran a finger over her lips.

She nodded. "Can you kiss a boo-boo?" She stuck her bottom lip out.

"Damn straight, Angel, but isn't this the path that led to your lips and face getting in the crosshairs?"

"Yes, but I still think you are the best cure for what ails me."

"I'm not complaining. Since you are insisting, I aim to please." He hoisted her up, licked her lips with his tongue, then his full lips traveled along her jawline and chin.

She groaned. "Alright, stop or we will never get sustenance. We must eat." She peered over her shoulder. "And, by my sniffer, it's ready."

"What can I do?" Ge anchored his fists on his mighty fine narrow hips.

CJ was temporarily distracted, taking him in. All layers of his complexity drew her.

"Nothing, I got this. You get the movie ready. Remember, it's your choice."

"Anything?"

She shrugged her shoulders and said, "Yes. I'm game for whatever you choose. I'm interested in what you pick."

"Pressure! I can't take it." He pulled his hair from his face and raised a brow.

"Silly." She swatted him with a nearby towel.

CJ strolled into the living space and set the tray of her heavenly go-to comfort food with an enormous bottle of ranch dressing. CJ expected the normal movie her man preferred, not to mention the rest of her bodyguards: guns, blood, and action. Her heart leaped when she saw he had the selection on a comedy. The true measure of a man is to see what his woman needs and to take care of her first. She stood there, speechless, clutching her hand to her chest. Her heart leaped a beat.

"What?" Gunner said with the remote pointed at the television.

CJ chose not to say anything, but her heart swelled at the incredible gesture. This man had the biggest heart. He'd protected it for way too long, and she was awestruck when she got to see a glimpse. What a waste those many years were, but what they were experiencing was worth its weight in diamonds. She might not have appreciated it in the past, nor would he have been ready to show her what was inside his steel fortress. She walked over, sprung up on her tippy-toes, and kissed him on the forehead. "You're a keeper, Gunner Ward."

"I bet you say that to all the guys."

She cocked her head and swayed her hips. "I haven't had many choices in my life. My first boyfriend, you know how it turned out. So, the way I see it, things are looking up." She handed him a paper napkin. "I didn't see any ketchup, but I have it on a list for the store if we don't have to leave tomorrow. I've never run across anyone who can put ketchup on everything he eats."

"I haven't touched the stuff on my fries since you showed me the treasure of ranch dressing. I've been reformed." He tapped her nose.

"I guess I'm rubbing off on you after all."

"In a matter of speaking." He leaned over and snatched a few fries.

CJ tucked herself close to Gunner on the couch. "Thank you for being my person."

"Ditto." He pushed her hair off CJ's shoulders and kissed

her neck. "I need to be someone's person. I used to be my brother's and my mom's."

CJ pulled away and comprehended what Gunner had said. "You mentioned your mother suffered from dementia. You visited her as much as often as possible, but you never said you had a brother."

He stilled for a moment and seemed so very far away. "My mother doesn't recognize me anymore, but it gives me some peace she doesn't grieve for my brother anymore."

"You grieve. I see it." She squeezed his hand. "If it's too difficult to talk about, it's okay. I'll be here if you ever need to discuss it."

He gazed into her eyes and ran one of his fingers along her jawline. "Thank you. I don't talk about my family to anyone who didn't know them personally. It's sacred ground. I guess you bring it out in me."

"Gunner, I feel honored."

He looked away and pressed the palms of his hands over his eyes, then gave an exasperated sigh. "It's such a long story, it could take years." He slumped over.

She moved closer and nestled in. "Can we start with his name?"

He studied her and a smile lifted his lips. "How do you do that?"

She cocked her head to the side, not understanding what he was referring to. Had she pushed too far?

"The way you look at me, for one, makes me want to bare my soul. I've never felt this way before. I'm on shaky ground. I never do this. Ever. With you, I want you to know the real me."

"Don't you think it's time? I'm an open book."

"Ha! Since you put it like that, maybe so." He cracked his neck and let out a deep exhale. "His name is Hunter. Was Hunter."

"Was?" CJ's voice hitched. She sat up straight and covered her mouth.

"He's been missing for six years. Poof! Gone."

CJ ran her hand along his leg. Her heart ached for him. She'd experienced first-hand what it was like to lose the ones you love. "But how?" She tilted her head.

"After our tour was up, Hawke and I were recruited for Noble Network Security. My brother, Ryker, and Luca still had two more years in the military, then they'd join us. He came back for a visit after he served his eight years, but Hunter said he had one more run first. I'm not even sure if it's with the military. He said he couldn't disclose anything." Gunner shook his head and worry lines creased his forehead. "I pleaded for him to forget it, I'd help him, but he was my bull-headed little bro. My biggest regret? I should have pushed harder. He said this one was a game changer. We heard from him a few times, then nothing." He let the words trail off. Gunner had a deep-set frown marring his face.

"How can someone just disappear?" She massaged the tension from his neck.

"I've followed every lead. So has the rest of the team. We get a lead, then it runs cold. I've turned over every rock I can until our General forced us to abort." He pushed his spine upright and gave in to the kneading. "Feels good."

"Your general? The same general you take orders from with the security detail?"

"One and the same. He's not the boss of us anymore, but he does have a say when we stick our noses where we shouldn't. He can be a real ass." Gunner shifted and held CJ's hands. "Thanks for letting me unload." He looked at her hands and took one, running lazy circles across her flesh. He was silent for a while.

CJ leaned in and wrapped her arms around his neck. "It's

okay, I got you." They'd lived side by side for a decade and they had both lived a life of loss for so many years. "If you want to keep talking, I have strong shoulders. If you don't, we discuss it another day." She gave him a quick nod.

"I could think of other things I'd rather be doing. This might be our last night here."

They snuggled on the couch and CJ ran her hands through Gunner's long inky hair, raking her nails along his scalp. His breathing was soft, and she could see the rise and fall of his chest. He dozed off and one of the first times she could see him relax. He needed this. She'd never seen him sleep much over the years. Many times in the past she thought he was sleeping, but somehow, he'd sense her watching him from afar. Once he opened his eyes, his gaze had so much intensity in them she often had to look away.

So much had changed this past year. She craned her neck and witnessed the hard lines of his expression softened in slumber. She brushed her lips against his ear and whispered the words she held so close. "I love you, Gunner Ward. I have loved you for years and I will continue, if I'm allowed."

He moved his arm and grasped her hair, pulling her lips close to his. The look in his eyes told her the same thing she was thinking. Tonight could be their last night together. They greedily took from one another what the other needed.

GUNNER SAT in the chair across from the king-sized bed. CJ was still sound asleep. He had been up since dark-thirty, and the dog was panting nervously. He whispered. "Come on, Karma girl, let's go do your business and look around." The four-legged beast must have caught his vibes—he was unsettled all day.

What will Tiny tell them? His gut said something big was about to go down. He checked his phone and checked it again. No word from Hawke or the rest of the guys, but they were like clockwork. He suspected they were already taking care of business at hand. They had worked together for way too long not to know the others' routine. They'd all had each other's six for as many years as he could count. The only time he trusted leaving CJ was at Hawke's guidance. He entrusted him with CJ while he followed a lead on his brother. The weeks had given him purpose to follow a cool trail of Hunter's possible whereabouts. But being away from CJ was horrid. The only other time he had been off the clock was when he'd put his mother in a care facility.

Gunner's phone buzzed; he answered the call. "Hey, Hawke. Whatcha got?"

"Tiny should be around in a couple of hours. Ryker and Luca will let him in the gates, and I'll come over before. We can go over the plans while I'm there."

"Should I gather our shit?"

"You know the drill. None of us can grasp onto what's going on until we see Tiny. Jeffrey's standing by. Throw some stuff in your car and we'll have the crew tidy up if we bolt."

"See ya when I see ya." Gunner ended the call and listened at the door of the bedroom. He jumped into the shower of the spare room, then threw on a black tee, his well-worn black jeans, and his old shit kickers. Gunner placed a blade in the ankle strap and checked his Glock and sharpshooter. He shoved a few things in his duffle and loaded them in the event they had to haul ass. Life was a fine line between paranoia and being prepared. He was ready for anything.

~

Old scenarios flashed through her mind, spinning, spinning, spinning until she couldn't breathe. Cold sweat soaked her. Panic set in. Memories swirled over and over from the last weeks, strangling her at the hands of the Denver Devils Delinquents. She tried to open her eyes. Only deep-seated darkness.

Barry Ryder had had all the guys in his grip. He and his second in charge were ruthless, and they treated the women like they owned them. Every attempt at escape was thwarted; they were always two steps ahead. They kept a watchful eye on her after the pharmacy heist and the Winslow- Parker accident they'd caused. She knew too much. They had guilted her and tried to gaslight her, saying she was as guilty as they were. She was so naïve, a prisoner long before she realized she'd been captured.

No one was allowed inside or out without Ryder controlling it, except for the drug runners. It had been a revolving door of booze, money, and drugs. Parties every night on some plot of land in the foothills of the Rocky Mountains with nothing more than a few dilapidated buildings and a few dozen tents. CJ hid most of the time because Taz had become a loose cannon. He snorted anything he could up his nose. If he wasn't doing drugs, he would chug a handle of whiskey until he passed out.

But one thing was for certain—he'd never touch her again after what she had seen. The first robbery had killed innocent people. The club had robbed several pharmacies to make their drugs; they were getting into the hard stuff. They'd hired chemists to make a hybrid drug. Their dealers were selling all over the state. She'd heard innocent children were dying. Women were being exploited, several members overdosed or extinguished for crossing Barry and James, but no one outside the club knew their identity. The bigger the operation, the more paranoid and violent they became. She knew who they were, and they'd kill to keep their dirty secret.

What they didn't count on CJ having a plan. CJ had grown up not far from there and remembered a horse ranch a matter of miles from where they were. She'd slipped away in the middle of the night, running with nothing but her bare feet until she came across an unmanned forest station. She called 911 for help. If it hadn't been for everyone knowing the Winslows and her family, she would have never been in the position to go into hiding. Everyone in the state of Colorado had been looking for the motorcycle club and people who caused so much heartache. One of her many regrets was her family couldn't know she was alive or they'd be in danger.

A knot of fear cinched tighter in her gut. CJ tossed and turned as her breathing hissed in panicked bursts, her heart thudded like a kettledrum, and her pulse raced. She clawed at her surroundings, seeing their faces over and over. "Run! He's coming for me; Taz is going to kill me. Run! He's closing in, they'll kill me!" she screamed at the top of her lungs. She ran and ran, getting nowhere. "He's got me!"

CHAPTER

TWENTY-FOUR

Gunner bolted through the closed door and flung himself on top of her.

"Baby. Wake up."

She fought with everything she had. "Help me!" A horrid scream bounced off the walls and tore at his system. He'd heard screams the similar from fellow soldiers in the war's aftermath.

"Angel. You're having a nightmare."

Her eyes flung open and she gasped for air, dragging in anything she could. Her chest constricted. Gunner wrapped her in his arms and held her close. "Shhh...I got you. It's only a bad dream."

She shook uncontrollably. "He's going to kill me."

He pushed her disheveled hair away from her face. There were flames of red in her cheeks. Sweat beaded her upper lip. "He won't get anywhere near you. I'll kill the fucker myself if I must, but no one will harm you, I promise."

She inhaled deeply and clung on to him as he rocked her

slowly. Her eyes fixed on him as her nails bit into his flesh. "Why? I want it to be over." She buried her face into his chest and sobbed.

"It's all going to work out." He said the words but wasn't certain he believed them himself. *It must, or she will snap from the pressure.* No one else could have made it this far. He could see her unraveling little by little. "Hope is a son of a bitch." He kissed the top of her head. Through it all she still had it; she'd powered through all the trials and all the years in the Witness Protection Program. Watching her lose her shine was not an option. She'd fought too hard to teeter into the dark side now. She could dip her dainty ass toe in there, but she was not taking up residency.

"Why don't you take it easy this morning? I need to talk to Hawke about plans before Ryker, Luca, and Tiny show up." He lifted her chin up. "Doesn't a hot soak sound good?"

He moved her chin up and down, coaxing her to agree. He slid away and pulled the covers around her. "Wait here. I'll fill the water for you." He handed her a box of Kleenex.

She wiped her eyes and blew her nose. "Gunner, you don't have to do this."

"Yes. I. Do. Please let me." He swooshed his hand in the water. "It will take a bit to fill." He sat on the edge of the bed. "Come here." She inched over, and he pulled her hair high on her head, then wrapped an elastic band around her mass of curls. He took her hand and guided her into a standing position. Lifting her arms, he eased her little strappy top over her head. She covered herself.

"Never hide from me, Angel. You are perfect, and I accept all of you. Every bit. Don't you ever forget it." He knelt and wrapped his arms around her waist, slowly sliding her panties down her legs. He took her hand and laid it on his shoulder.

"Lean on me." Gunner lifted her foot and kissed the top of it, shucking her panties onto the bed. He smoothed his hands along her legs, then stood. "Come on. It's time to forget it all and relax."

She followed him to the big soaker tub and wrapped her arms around him. "I don't know what I'd ever do without you."

"Relax your mind, Angel." He helped her in and turned off the light. "I'll bring you something to drink."

He watched CJ as she eased into the tub. The waterline was to her neck, and some of her loose tendrils floated on the water as she let out a huge sigh. "There you go." He backed away as she ran a cloth over her face. "Take all the time you need."

"Gunner. Thank you."

He nodded and eased out the door, closing it gently behind him.

Squeezing his eyes tight, he stretched his neck from side to side, then raised his shoulders and rolled them around and around. The dog whined. "She's okay. Let's give her some space."

The dog tilted her head and panted; her long tongue hung over her canines. Gunner tapped his leg. "Come on, girl, I'll get you a treat." He hurried to the kitchen with the dog in tow. He filled a mug with hot water, dunked a couple of mint and chamomile tea bags in, loaded it with honey just CJ like it, and popped two pieces of bread in the toaster. When they were done, he slathered each piece meticulously with butter and sprinkled them with cinnamon and sugar. His attempt would hopefully give her warm and fuzzies from her childhood like she always mentioned.

"Sit, girl." He gave the dog a quick look for good measure. "Stay."

He tapped on the door lightly. "Angel, here's a little something to calm your nerves and settle your stomach."

She pulled the washcloth off her face and smiled.

He sat the napkin-covered plate and mug on the side table near the soaker tub. "Are you ready for a treat?"

Her eyes were wide and her lip trembled. "You made this for me? It's my..." She licked the corner of her mouth and sat up a little taller, but her eyes filled with moisture.

"Favorite from your childhood. I did. I don't have mad culinary skills, but this I managed." Pride filled his chest, knowing he made her feel better. "Now, no crying. This will make the rest of the day better. We all have our days. I've had so many bad things happen this is nothing."

"I've had a bad run, but I'd love to hear more about your brother. Maybe later?" She shivered, but in the depth of her light blue eyes he saw compassion and warmth, which gave him the courage to shed more of his burden.

"You are a dynamo, CJ. I've seen it with my own eyes." Gunner put a finger in the water, testing the temperature and turning the spigot on. "Let's warm this up a little. I'll make myself scarce and let you be. You have all the time you need. I must take care of some business." He winked and leaned over, giving her a kiss on the forehead. Gunner took her robe off the brass hook and laid it next to the tub, then leaned in to kiss her lips. He turned when his hand was on the doorknob. She was smiling. Of all the things he'd done in his life, doing this for her had been his biggest accomplishment. He exhaled and closed the door.

He traveled past the side window and saw Hawke. He and Karma took off to greet him.

"Hawke, can I get you anything? There's a fresh pot of Death Wish coffee." He hitched his thumb in the direction of the kitchen.

"Nah, maybe soon."

"Pull up a chair. Let's hang here for a while. I need some fresh air."

"You okay?" Hawke crinkled his forehead.

"Yeah, I'm good, but CJ had some night terrors about Taz. I heard it from the kitchen. She's almost at the end of her line. I've never seen her this way. This is deep level shit."

"I can imagine it brings up old wounds. All of us are spun tight. Usually, we have a minute to get settled, but first comes the change. We're built for the long haul, trained for maneuvers like this, but she didn't deserve this. She was yanked from one life, then another, and a life in witness protection."

Gunner placed his hand at top of his head and bent his neck the opposite way, tugging on it for a good stretch.

"Looks like it's seeping in on you too." Hawke gave him eye darts.

"What are you trying to get at?" Gunner crossed his arms over his chest.

"Trust me you have it bad for her. Hard not see it over the years. But this, whatever it is...it's risky. Not only for her, but for you. You're circling the drain."

"Don't you think I don't recognize the gravity of all of this? If anything happened to her, I think I'd lose it."

"And why I'm not preaching again. I'm concerned for both of you. I'm invested. I want everyone to win here, but right now, as your battle buddy and best friend, we need to dial it a few notches and focus." Hawke leaned in and whispered, "You and me." He reached forward to shake Gunner's hand. "I got you brother, and I got her. I will be pissed the fuck off if anyone gets hurt and we don't end this triple D shitshow permanently."

"Amen," Gunner said, reaching forward to give his mate a knuckle bump. "I want to pass something by you. I found it this morning when I researched some files." Gunner stood. "I'll go get them."

"I'll take some of the potent stuff now. I need a jolt."

Gunner craned his neck. "Help yourself. You know your way around, but don't make any noise. CJ's recouping and needs quiet. We're not going to have much for the foreseeable future."

Chapter

TWENTY-FIVE

CJ licked her fingers after polishing off the toast. Thoughts of her family stuck with her. Why had she wanted to grow up and flee? How could she ever be with her family if she was always in danger? And her reason why she'd gone into the program. Yet she'd felt no relief when James Devland and Barry Ryder ended up in prison. Taz was free and probably still after her.

She pushed away the things she could not change and focused on her childhood. It had been a good life. Maybe one day she could make more than memories.

She eased out of the tub and wrapped the robe around her. Slipping on a pair of black capri yoga pants and a matching top from the top drawer, CJ tied a lime-colored jacket around her waist and donned her new pair of running shoes. She eyed her go bag near the door, then stuffed a few things in it. She brushed through her hair, setting it in a high topknot, then slipped her journal in her backpack and set it next to the other bag.

She pressed a hand to her skin. The stubble rash on her face had cooled and was barely visible. She got an eye full of the hickey on her neck and decided to cover it. Today she would not get razzed by the brotherhood. Dabbing a little concealer over the purple skin, she noticed a green bandana sticking out of the bag she'd brought in and tied it around her neck. "Perfecto." She returned her makeup to the duffel near the door.

The doorbell rang, then she heard what sounded like a bunch of circus elephants parading around the house. "It's show time." She gazed into the mirror again, pulling her shoulders back and lifting her chin high. "Thatagirl."

CJ cracked the door open and peeked out. Gunner's eye fell upon the crevice in the doorway, as if he had sensed her. He lifted his hand and directed her to approach. She opened the door wider and got an eyeful of three of her long-lost friends. Axel, Jett, and Tiny completed her inner circle. Tiny looked like he was healed and one hundred percent.

"Well, well, well, what do you know? The fam is back together. Come here, you big lugs." She extended her arms wide. "Bring it in. I missed you." Axel and Jett didn't hesitate, but Tiny hesitated, then inched closer. "I didn't realize you two were coming. What brings you here?"

"You, of course." Jett waggled his brows and she noticed Gunner giving him the evil eye.

"Alright, Romeo, don't overwhelm the lady." Gunner gruffed.

"She doesn't mind." Jett replied.

"I don't mind. I love all the attention." She felt her cheeks warm.

"Since when?" Axel piped in.

"Just kidding. I know I couldn't fool you." She winked, gazed at Gunner, who had a territorial vibe going on. She winked at him and walked past the boys, running a hand along Gunner's back.

"Tiny. How are you?" She observed he was all sweaty and uncomfortable, unlike the rest of the crew.

He gave her an awkward half hug. "Good to see you, CJ."

She nodded and said, "Come on, everyone, take a load off. Don't let me stop your business."

Hawke stepped from the kitchen and waved CJ to follow. "I talked to Jeffrey. He said you can reach him on this." He handed her a burner phone. "There's a couple of numbers programmed in there, if you have any kind of emergency." He looked around. "Hide it."

She stuffed it in her shirt.

"This is against my better judgement, and no one has intel to this but the boss, Jeffrey, you, and me. I don't much like keeping secrets from Gunner, but something in my gut says you need this. Having a short conversation with your family now and then won't hurt." He teetered from heel to toe. "Don't make me regret this, and please don't go crazy with this little bit of freedom. Keep the calls short, no information, and use it if you're in danger. Got it?"

"I appreciate it. I don't enjoy hiding anything from any of you, especially Gunner." She looked away. "I promise to treat it with the utmost respect. Thank you."

"You care for him, don't you."

She turned her head from the left to the right. "I don't only care for him. I'm head over heels, I mean madly in love, with the big buffoon, and it ticks me off."

Hawke chuckled. "Ha! Buffoon, I can't disagree." His smile changed to a flat line and his brows knitted together. "Hurt him and I'm done with you. I mean it. He's been through enough."

CJ held her hand to her throat. "I don't intend to. It's my heart I'm afraid he'll hurt."

"He's in the same boat as you. I'll be done with him too, if he plays you." His expression softened. "Good talk, Red. Good talk."

CJ followed Hawke into the living area. The place was busting at the seams with her seven huge bodyguards. She giggled to herself, thinking about one of the funny sayings she had with her sister. A male meat sandwich was an understatement. This was a smorgasbord of awesomeness.

She watched them as they planned and researched. Tiny wasn't himself. He was usually jovial. Something was off, and she couldn't unsee the discomfort. But she wasn't alone. Gunner had a twitch when he suspected something. His attention kept drifting to Hawke and again to Tiny. All the while, a muscle ticked in his jaw and the crease between his eyes deepened.

"Tiny, let's rewind a ways. I want you to pick up where you left off with us, and then Axel, Jett, and Ryker can tell us what they witnessed. The hornets' nest has been stirred up and you identified Taz." Gunner paced the room. "Don't leave anything out. You three shared this information with the boss lady and the General, but we need to hear more. Something's making me twitch."

"I saw that." CJ giggled.

"You did, did you?" His expression changed. "Guess it's official. She's part of the crew," Gunner boomed.

The room echoed with yee haws, whistles, and claps.

Ryker looked at Gunner and CJ. "I guess things have changed around here."

"Funny ha ha." She lowered herself to the floor, feeling her face heat. CJ patted the floor beside her for Karma to approach. "Good girl," she whispered. The dog laid beside CJ as she smoothed her fingers over her thick coat. She could feel the eyes upon her. Maybe if she was quiet long enough, the stares would go away. Gunner tapped his fingers on the wall, followed by a hand rap to snap the attention to the business at hand. How did he always know the right thing to do with her? It seemed instinctual.

$$\sim$$

"Listen up team. The floor's yours Tiny." Gunner splayed his hands wide.

Jett jumped up from the chair. "Before he speaks, I have something to say." Jett's tone bounced off the walls. His demeanor was point blank and matter of fact. "Something's up, that we know. But I feel, and I'm not alone, there's been a shift. It's directed toward Tiny." The focus turned to Tiny, and he wiggled uncomfortably in his seat.

"What's your take on this, Tiny?" Hawke asked.

Tiny leaned around to get a better view of CJ, but Gunner got in his face. "What did you do, Tiny?"

"I screwed up big time. I said the wrong thing to the wrong person, and he has it out for me."

Gunner grabbed Tiny's Harley tee, clenching it in his fist. "What the hell did you say?"

"I didn't mean to, but this guy was shady, and word had it he was in the triple Ds. My gut said he was our missing piece of the puzzle, so I pushed the envelope." Tiny wiped the sweat from his face. "I blurted out I heard a girl wreaked havoc on one of the clubs near the Rockies."

CJ gasped and drew her legs to her chest.

Tiny whipped his gaze to her again. "I'm sorry."

"Don't you dare look at her. You did what?" Gunner ground his molars so tight his teeth hurt.

Tiny put his hands up in defense. "I was shooting the shit after throwing a few back, and this guy came out of nowhere. He said, Cinder Johnson? He said her first and last name. No one knows her identity but those who were involved. We've protected her identity since the beginning, and it wasn't until the last trial anyone knew who she was.

"At first I thought he was one of our guys, until I got a look at him and knew." Tiny blew out a long breath. "The guy had been ridden hard for years, and booze and evil were seeping from his pores. Straight up tainted. But he was familiar.

"I played dumb. I didn't say I knew anything, other than people talk on the road. Ever since that night, I felt his beady little eyes on me. I'm not paranoid. I keep thinking he's following me, but I haven't seen him since." Tiny wiped the sweat from his brow.

"Why are you just telling us this?" Gunner raked his hands through his hair. "You could have been followed and compromise all of us."

"Tiny, why didn't you say something before? All of us rode from there earlier, and we didn't have to come far from the rally." Jett hissed. "You put everyone in jeopardy."

"And Ryker and I were there too," Luca put in.

"I messed up. My ass is chapped," he huffed. "Riding across the country on something smaller than a trike under me. These leathers suck ass." He squirmed. "We haven't heard a peep, and this was my chance to end it." He dropped his head and hunched his shoulders. "I've done the same thing you always ask me to do: I flush out the threats."

"Royally. But you knew we were here and did it anyway?" Gunner grumbled.

"Let's regroup. We're getting nowhere fast." Hawke said, but the chatter elevated.

"Stop it!" CJ screamed. "Please." She was standing in the middle of the room, white knuckling her fists.

"Where did you come from?" Hawke asked.

"I'm from Solemn Creed, Colorado, and right in the middle

of all this god-forsaken turmoil." She stomped her foot hard. She held up a photo of Taz and got up close and personal with Tiny. "Was this the man?"

"Yeah, it's him, but you wouldn't recognize the guy. I didn't at first. He has a bunch of tattoos on his face and neck. Some are satanic. Huge gauges in his ears, a bull piercing through his septum, and missing a few of his chicklets."

Gunner stomped off to the window, his steel-toed shit kickers thudding with purpose, and inched the curtain away from the window as he scanned the street. He spun on his heels, cocked his weapon, and traveled to the rear exit of the house along with two other men. They split up and checked their surroundings, then gathered in the kitchen.

"We'll take shifts. No one leaves tonight. We need to get Jeffrey on the line ASAP and find a new safe house. Two of you need to position yourself at the gates. We fan out at 0600 hours."

CHAPTER

TWENTY-SIX

Adrenaline coursed through CJ's veins. Her mouth was bone dry and her ticker thumped wildly. She knew what she needed to grab while the guys did the job they were great at doing.

She'd learned a thing or two from them. Pack light, never get settled in, keep something on your person to defend yourself, and be ready at a moment's notice. She loaded her fingers with multiple rings and made a fist. She placed a well-worn pair of combat boots near her bed, along with an adjustable waist bag for a few choice weapons. She could take care of herself after all the self-defense the team taught her.

CJ scurried to the kitchen to fill a bag with protein bars, jerky, and snacks, then loaded coolers with ice, water, and electrolyte drinks. She pulled the dog's supplies and loaded half of them in the vehicle with a first aid kit and flashlights, then put the rest in her duffel bag. Her thoughts swirled with the fast-paced thumping in her neck. She had to remain calm and control her breathing.

Breathe.

Multi-tasking was her jam and her part of being on the team. She looked around at all the guys, who were laser focused on their mission. Voices hummed, computers beeped, and phones shrilled. The mood had shifted as quickly as it had before. These were warriors on the battlefield, excelling in their craft. Warriors who had protected her for the long haul. Pride filled her chest as she watched them work together. Maybe luck was on her side this time. She closed her eyes and steepled her hands in a silent prayer.

Hawke whistled. "Listen up, guys. Jeffrey's at the meet site. He has our orders. He's calling once the line is secure." The chairs dragged across the floor as they gathered around in a circle.

CJ watched them carefully as she leaned against the kitchen counter. She focused on her dominant, protective alpha. Gunner's tan skin and the golden warmth of his hazel eyes melded together perfectly. His razor-sharp jawline, thickly corded muscles, and his devilish grin were a great distraction from the bitter tang of regret coating her tongue.

His sharp gaze landed on her. She blinked and looked away. If only they'd met in the outside world before this mayhem. Somehow, deep in every atom, she sensed they were closing in on the end of the line. Gunner lifted himself off the chair every time the phone rang, only to plop down.

She fiddled her fingertips into a loose honeycomb towel with faint rosettes. CJ flung the towel on the granite counter-top, realizing she was destroying the uniquely detailed design. She swung around, squeezing her eyes tight, pushing away thoughts of the inevitable. She plugged her ears, not wanting to hear anymore. Curling her shoulders in, she tiptoed out of the kitchen with her furry four-legged sidekick close behind. CJ closed herself in the bedroom, locking the door behind her.

She awoke cradling Karma. Not knowing how much time had passed, a knock on the door startled her.

"CJ, can I come in for a minute?"

She pushed her hair from her face and scooted off the bed, unlocking the door.

"Are you okay?" His concern was evident on his face.

She opened the door more and sat on the edge of the bed. "I got everything together, I thought I'd relax in a soft bed for a while longer." She pushed a laugh out. "Who knows how long it will be before this happens again."

"Jeffrey said it shouldn't be long." He ran his big, calloused hand over the comforter. "It's my favorite bed," Gunner said with a sparkle in his eyes. Grabbing her hand, he brought it to his mouth, pressing a soft kiss to her knuckles.

Her cheeks flushed warm red. "Mine too." She leaned in and nudged her shoulder against his. "This house is definitely next level." She ran her nail over his bare arm. She had this irresistible pull to him every time he was near. She could let her guard down and hopefully the same for him. "We've had a pretty good run, haven't we?" She barely got the words from her lips. Saying it pierced her soul.

He weaved his fingers through hers. "Why are you saying this in the past tense?" He furrowed his inky brows. "Who says we're done?"

She shrugged her shoulders. "It's a gnawing feeling I have."

"Please don't think such a way." He looked pained, and she wished she hadn't said anything.

"We both knew one day this would end."

He moved closer and towered over her. "I'm not going anywhere, CJ."

She pasted a smile on her face. "I don't want it ever to end, but both of us need to be realistic."

"Neither of us has been anywhere near realistic since we

met, so you can throw this way of thinking far away from here."

She clung to his arm and kissed his bicep. "I'm spun tight here, and with everything happening, I don't want any words unsaid. No regrets."

"Good segue." His eyes caressed her. "I love you, Cinder. If you think you are getting away from me that easily, you are mistaken." He brought their mouths within the same breathing space.

"I love you too. As much as I hate it, we're set up for failure."

"What are you saying?" He jerked and his brows knit together.

"We're not exactly a Hallmark movie. Come on."

He chuckled. "Nope, can't say we are. Far from it." He covered his mouth with his hand. His gaze intensified. "Something unexpected came from all of this for both of us. Right?"

"Beyond my wildest dreams, and scares me senseless. Something could happen to any of us, and it could end." She snapped her fingers. "Like that."

"I understand what you're saying, but I don't want you to worry about the bad stuff. We can revisit this conversation another day. Today we re-shift a little, nothing more." He extended his hand. "Do we have a deal?" He ran slow circles in her palm with the pad of his thumb.

She slid him a cursory glance. "Yes, we have a deal."

He looked at his watch and jumped up. "I'm heading for the gate shift. Someone will be here with you. I'll be back in a few hours."

"Wait!" She popped up and wrapped her arms around his waist. "Can you feel that?" His heart pounded hard as she came to a halt, squeezing him tighter. "I mean really feel the magnitude between us?"

Gunner wrapped his arms around her. "Angel, you have no idea exactly how much I feel what we have," he said, his breath tickling her ear. "After tonight, when I have you all to myself, I'll show you exactly what I mean." The sparkle in his eyes spelled mischief. His lips meshed with hers and he broke away.

~

CJ HAULED the rest of her things to the doorway by the garage. Hawke had come in from his shift and Gunner was on his way. Hawke's radio sounded, Ryker on the other end.

"Has anyone heard from Gunner?"

"No, I just got back to the base."

"I heard gunfire from his headset and then his radio went silent."

"Luca head that way. Hurry." Hawke ordered as he paced the room.

Luca called on the radio next. "He's not here at his post at the back gate, but it's wide open and there's blood and empty shells on the pavement. Calvary's here. Has anyone heard from him? We're following a blood trail. Looks like he's heading your way."

CJ got up close and personal with Hawke while waiting to hear word. She was ripping off her thumbnail.

"Make a sweep and find him!" Hawke yelled.

CJ ran into her room and grabbed her boots, frantically shoving them on. "I'm looking for him," she shouted, snatching the dog leash and something for a weapon.

"You're not going anywhere." Hawke got in her face.

"I am too. He's out there and I must find him," she yelled at the top of her lungs.

"He's probably on his way. Someone needs to be here when

he does." He handed her a pistol and cocked it. "Remember what we showed you?" He pulled her into a safe corner.

She fought him every step, digging in.

"Stop! I need you to listen to me. Focus. This is the safest place for you. I want you to point the gun at anything that moves into the house. We will give you a signal if it's us."

"Hawke stomped off to Gunner's room and returned with a shirt. He handed CJ one of the handheld radios. "Ears open and eyes sharp. You'll be able to hear anything going on." He took the leash from her hand and snapped it on Karma's collar.

"Karma. Go find Gunner." He put the shirt up to her nose. "Go find."

Hawke pulled on her collar, then stomped away. "I won't be long. Point your weapon at all the entrances." He stopped and looked over his shoulder as the dog pulled him in a frenzy. "You got this, kid."

She nodded so fast she could feel her teeth jar. Hawke ducked through the door. CJ whipped one direction, then the next, pointing the gun with an iron grip. She sunk against the wall, listening to the radio for anything other than her racing pulse.

"We heard more shots fired. There's a breach at the front gate. They're ramming the gates."

"I see him," Tiny shouted. "Ryker do you have a shot? Anyone see Taz?"

CJ scrunched up in a ball and listened to the radio.

"I had an eye on him, but he's with half a dozen guys, and a handful took off. Jeffrey called for backup. Balls to the walls... you need to find Gunner and get the fuck out of Dodge. We will hold them off as long as we can."

CJ panicked as the voices buzzed through the radio.

CHAPTER

TWENTY-SEVEN

Gunner used his high-resolution spotting scope and scanned the area. The night was eerily quiet but for the howl of the wind. He locked eyes on movement in his peripheral and swung his scope in the direction. Someone on foot had snuck in the bushes to his right about a half a block away. He shifted to see if he noticed anything.

A tree across the street rustled. He was getting into position, but out of nowhere he heard revving engines from behind. He whipped around at the deafening sounds of gunshots. One bullet whizzed by him and the other sent a shockwave of pain slicing through his shoulder. The slow agony of wincing pain hit him as he dropped off the retaining wall at the gate. He hit the grass with a thud. His shoulder felt numb and wet.

Gunner was fighting to get to his feet when another bullet hit the wall, splattering debris. He sought his earpiece, but it wasn't there. Gunner searched the grass around him—he needed more men. Shots were coming at him in succession from two directions. He was being hunted. He flew head over feet to one of the nearby houses.

A shot rang in his ears, busting a potted plant at a neighboring residence. He slid behind a tree and flung his rifle over his shoulder, pulling his Walther 99 handgun, Gunner released the safety Lights flickered on. He wiped his hand across the blood trailing from his shoulder. A dog barked across the street, getting his attention as he tracked any movement in the darkness.

He tucked tail and ran in, not away. Someone was going to pay. Adrenaline soared through his system, but the pain in his shoulder was no longer a sting. The smell of sulfur and copper filled his nostrils from the bullet wound. He took off and did a homerun slide into a cluster of trees. Shots came at him from behind and he turned, firing off a few rounds. He heard the snap of a tree limb, and someone hit the ground at a run.

"I'm gonna get the bitch once and for all," he heard through the whipping wind. Gunner took off on foot, pelting after the bastard. Was this Taz? He wrestled the man to the ground, pounding on him until an explosion of pain erupted in his side. He'd been hit. He dropped to his knees, barely able to focus. The assailant turned, so Gunner took the money shot. His target flew and hit the ground.

"Son of a...," the guy grunted and got on his knees. He flipped around and pointed his gun. Gunner blasted another round, sending him flying into the air. His assailant landed, splayed in front of him.

"Son of a bitch. Got him."

He heard movement and sent another blast, dropping another perpetrator. Gunner fought to get up, but a volcano of pain was thrashing through his side. The pain was heightening and if he didn't move his ass, CJ would be next. He pulled for every ounce of strength and pushed the pain away. He had one mission, and one only: to protect her. He crawled to the side of a shed and checked where he'd been hit. He'd seen wounds like this. Gunner knew he had little time, either from losing consciousness from shock or blood loss. Worst case scenario, a hemorrhage if one of his organs had been hit.

Gunner pressed his shaky hand on the searing pain. His shirt was soaked and a crimson river of red gushed down his leg. He growled. His left arm hung, useless from the shoulder wound, but he'd survive that one. The other was a crapshoot either way. He'd soon be a goner.

"Dammit."

Waves of dizziness assaulted him. He shook his head. The ringing in his ears was turning into a roaring freight train and he was seeing black specks. The only thing he could hear was his own breathing and the throttling under his sternum. "God, please, don't take me before I get to her. I'm begging you." He limped forward, each step a thunderous shockwave of pain slicing through him as he fought for consciousness. He could hear footsteps pounding toward him and a dog barking. Then everything went blank.

CJ GRIPPED THE WALKIE-TALKIE. She recognized Karma's frantic barking outside. "CJ, we're heading through the garage. Open the door stat. I have Gunner. He's been shot." CJ ran for the entrance. She flung the door open, and Hawke staggering inside, Gunner's body hanging limply over his shoulder.

"He's bad, CJ. Get my med kit."

CJ clawed at Gunner.

"CJ, now! It's in the rear compartment of the SUV." He threw her the keys. "Use the fob to lift the hatch."

She took off at a run, slipping on the blood trail. She fell over her own feet on her way to Hawke's vehicle. The big black plastic box was heavier than she'd expected but with a burst adrenaline-infused energy and earth-shattering fear, she lugged it forward. Once inside, she hoisted it on the counter near where Hawke had Gunner's limp body resting against the center island. She swiped her hand across the top of the island, flinging everything around the room.

"Help me," Hawke yelled. CJ jockeyed Gunners legs as Hawke eased him in a laying position. "I need to assess the damage. He's bleeding out."

She supported Gunner's head as Hawke poked around. Her hands shook as she saw the color leave his face. "Gunner!" she wailed, cupping his face in her hands. "Don't you dare die on me."

Hawke grabbed her arms and shook her. "I need you to focus on my words. Get me towels. A lot of them. Roll one under his head to keep his airway clear." He nodded. "You hear me? I need you to help me or Gunner is a dead man."

Need to help Gunner or he will die. Help Gunner or he will die...

She squeezed her eyes shut for a split-second, then took off to find what Hawke had asked for. She rolled up a towel for his head and didn't waste another second getting everything else. She picked up a bowl from the floor and threw it in the sink, filling it with hot water and soap. Handed the wet cloth to Hawke. He tore at Gunner's shirt, ripping it apart and exposing his bloodied torso.

She looked over her shoulder and gasped. "So much blood." Her stomach rolled and nausea hit her. "He's been shot!" she whimpered.

"Sit here." Hawke pointed to the chair next to him. "Don't pass out on me. I need you to focus. He's lost a lot of blood. We need to stop the bleeding." He pulled her to the chair and pushed her into it. "CJ." He shook her.

"The hell if I am. There's blood coming from here." She pointed to his shoulder.

"I need you to apply pressure to it. We have another bleeder somewhere worse. Apply all the pressure you can."

She knelt on the chair and locked her elbows over the wound, then leaned close to his ear. "Gunner, please don't leave me. I swear, if anything happens to you, I will never forgive myself."

Gunner wrestled to get up, but collapsed.

"Here it is. Shit!"

"What?"

"Do you have any tampons?"

"Tampons?" She jumped, her mouth hanging open at his odd request.

"I need it for bullet hole."

She jumped off the stool and took off into her room, rummaging through her go bag. She returned with a box and ripped it open.

"CJ, get two pairs of gloves. We can't risk infection. Put yours on first, then help me with mine," Hawke said in a calm, direct voice. "Good. We need to turn him over and see if there's an exit wound. I'll show you how." He pointed to where she should stand beside him. "As soon as I lift him, find where the blood is coming from. Once you see it, clean the wound with soap and water, dry it the best you can. I'll need you to insert the tampon."

"A tampon?" Her mouth gaped open even as she did as she was told, locating the exit wound and unwrapping the tampon. "In the wound?"

"Just do it." Hawke look was pained. "Stops him from bleeding and he's lost a lot of blood. What type is yours?"

"Mine?" She shook her head to clear her thoughts, then shoved a tampon in the hole, trying not to think about what she was doing. "The universal one. My dad made sure I knew it. I donated when I was younger."

"Good. Give me your arm."

She rolled up her sleeve and whipped it in his direction. Hawke squirted alcohol on her arm.

"We don't have much time. Anything at this point gives us a chance." He wrapped an elastic band around her arm and slapped it to find a vein.

"Hurry! Do it already! What are you waiting for?" She ripped open another tampon with her teeth and shoved it into the other wound.

"Hold still, will ya? I'm trying to get a line in." Hawke pushed his earpiece. "Gunner's hit. We need medical transport nearby asap, or he's not going to make it."

CJ pointed a finger in his face. "Don't you dare say that again." She spat the words like they were venom and soap the cloth with warm soapy water and another gauze pad. She yanked the package open, cleaned his wound, then covered it. She watched her blood drain from her arm, into the tubing, and shook her head. *This is not happening.* "This can't be happening," she said in an emotion-choked voice, then repeated it in a whisper.

Hawke pressed the button on his earpiece. "Where the hell is backup?" he shouted.

"Ryker's on his way. Should be here any minute," Axel replied.

"Now what?" CJ rocked back and forth.

"CJ, listen to me. As soon as help gets here, you need to get your stuff and Karma. We're leaving. Karma is amazing. If it hadn't been for her, I never would have found him."

"It's done and, in the car, except my go bag." She craned her neck and saw the dog, then the counter where the keys were. She stretched to retrieve them, but Karma pounced forward and retrieved them for her. CJ's legs were locked. She never moved from where her firmly planted feet resided. "Come here, Karma." She tugged at the leash and shoved the keys in her pocket. "Fetch my bag." she pointed. "Go.".

"Don't trip over the tubing."

She rummaged through the case and grabbed a couple of compression wraps, shoving them in her pack. She scanned the room. *Blood, Gunner's blood.* Her muscles jumped under her skin. She wanted to scream.

"You've done good, CJ. I'll get him into the SUV. Keep your arm still and hold the bag. Head through the garage." He hoisted Gunner over his shoulder. "You okay?"

She nodded opening the door and climbed in so Hawke could move Gunner into the back seat. He started the engine as CJ crawled in next to Gunner. "You're not going."

"The hell I am!" She tugged, she pulled with her free arm as Hawke blocked her.

"Sorry, CJ, but I need you to listen to me." He locked his palms on her shoulders. "You have your phone, right?"

She nodded yes as she tried to get inside the vehicle, to no avail.

"You heard the front gate's breached. I need to get Gunner out of here. Jeffrey is waiting for you. Press one and call him. Ryker's coming around from the side of the house. He's going with me."

"I can't leave. If anything happens to Gunner, I won't be able to tell him how much I love him. It's all my fault."

Hawke glanced at her arm. Ryker ran to the SUV, took the blood bag from CJ, and pulled the needle gently from her arm, applying pressure and wrapping it fast. He took off at a run and hurled himself into the rear of the vehicle, hoisting the med kit like it was light as a feather. CJ held her arm and limply gestured. Time stood still, but it had been only a matter of minutes from the time Hawke and Gunner arrived at the house to now. Every agonizing moment had taken years off her life.

"With your blood, we may be able to keep him from going further into shock. There's a military medical helicopter waiting for transport. We need to get you as far away from here as possible before Taz finds you. It's time to go." His voice elevated.

Time. She'd aged a lifetime in mere minutes, but Gunner was running out of time. "I don't care about me."

Hawke ran his hands over CJ's shoulders. "You may not care, but Gunner does. When he wakes up, he will be pissed I didn't take care of you. Please, for me and for him, do what I ask. Jeffrey is waiting. The rest of the team are ready to roll on my command." He wiped a hand across his forehead to rid the sweat.

Her breath busted in and out. "I don't want to leave him. He never left my side." She didn't recognize the shrill in her voice. She wanted to rip her hair out and scream.

"You will see him soon enough if I must carry him there myself. Go say what you need to say. You have only seconds; his life is hanging by a thread," he said fast and furious. His eyes were blinking rapidly.

She whipped the door open and heard Gunner's groans.

"Shhh..." CJ wiped his hair away from his face and kissed his forehead, then whispered in his ear. "Don't you dare leave this earth, or I will cease to exist. I love you, Gunner Ward. And I plan to marry you for real." He tried to push himself up but fell against the seat. She wiped her face and hugged Hawke. "Take care of him. Please. I'm begging you."

CJ tugged at the dog's leash, but her feet wouldn't move and her legs felt like jelly. She jammed her clammy hands under her armpits. This could be the last time she'd ever see Gunner.

Hawke ran around to the driver's side and stood on the runner. "You need to follow me through the gate. Once you exit the gates, go two miles. Press 1 on your phone. Don't stop anywhere until you see Jeffrey. There's a tracker in the car. Jeffrey will take it from there."

CJ stumbled to the car, lifted the seat forward for the dog, then leaped into the driver's seat and reversed into the street, waiting for Hawke to lead. She fought to put her seatbelt on. How would she ever be able to drive? She pressed her hands to her face. *Gunner.* Everything was moving too quickly to process. She hit the brake instead of the gas. The dog whimpered. She blew out a ragged breath. "Focus, CJ. You know what you need to do. Gunner will make it." *He must.*

Hawke sped off in one direction and waved at her to go the opposite way. She could see Ryker doing something to Gunner and almost veered off the road. CJ clutched the steering wheel so tight she thought it would snap off in her hands.

It was all the blood, Gunner's blood, ripping her heart to shreds.

She opened the phone as instructed and pressed the number one. Jeffrey picked up right away.

"I'm a few miles to your south, stay on this road. I'll catch up to you. Remember the command center we drove you in? I'll be there. CJ, you did good. You helped stabilize Gunner so he can make it to the helipad."

TWENTY-EIGHT

CJ pulled the car alongside where Jeffrey had the Winnebago, greeted by someone she didn't recognize. "Keys," the guy said as he waved his finger for her to comply. "You won't be driving. We got this. I'll grab your bag." He pointed to the RV. "Richards is in there."

CJ reached for the door, but saw her hand in the headlights, covered in Gunner's blood. She fell to the ground. Visions of what could be flashed through her mind.

The guy pounded on the door. "Need assistance."

Another guy dressed in camo swung the door open, knelt, and scooped her up. "We've been waiting for you."

CJ couldn't speak. Gunner was dying. *All my fault.* How could she ever forgive herself?

I MUST GET TO HER. No matter how fast he ran, he couldn't reach her. The vision played over and over in his mind's eye. He couldn't move except to pull at straps around his wrists. He rocked his head from side to side. Something was in his throat. Gagging. He didn't recognize the guttural noise coming from him and felt a hand on his chest. *CJ?*

A familiar voice laced with anger assailed him. "It's about damn time, G." Heavy boots tramped across the space. "Sleeping Beauty has woken up."

Gunner fought to open his eyes. Once he did, a hazy wrinkle like everything was under water hampered his vision. He squeezed his eyes shut and open again. Shadows were approaching. A frenzy of activity surrounded him, but he couldn't move. Someone pulled and a tugged at his arm, so he fought it.

"Still giving me the business. I'm trying to untie you. You have a breathing tube in. Patience is not your virtue, but you can't go yanking the thing out yourself, partner."

He tugged at the strap.

"Hear me?"

Gunner winced in pain.

"Don't move, or you'll need another surgery."

Gunner splayed his fingers wide and tapped the bed.

"Good boy."

Despair gnawed at his guts. He had so many questions. Fog flitted through his brain, tapering off as his vision cleared. He scanned the room, fighting the brightness. When he didn't see her, his frantic gaze searched the medical staff. They were poking and prodding. Alarms beeped. His eyes locked on Hawke's like a magnet. He rubbed his eyes with the base of his palm, the one that didn't hurt like a mother...

"O2 is good. He's breathing on his own," he heard one of the staff say.

Get this thing out of me.

"I'll count to three, and I want you to cough."

He lifted his bad wing and signaled 1-2-3 with his digits.

"Be a good patient, G." Hawke gave him a knowing look.

He felt the pulling from deep in his throat and wanted to gag. Gunner focused on his task and coughed. *Get it out.* He cleared his throat, but it was raw. He tried to speak but coughed again. The nurse handed him a sip of water.

"Where is she?" he said in a gravelly whisper. Hawke leaned in and Gunner repeated his question. "Where is she?"

"Good, your brain still works." Worry still etched Hawke's eyes, but a smile tilted his lips. "I'll tell you everything you need to know, but first let the staff check your vitals."

Gunner's side throbbed with an extra pulse. He watched curiously as they lifted the sheet, checking some tube sticking through his side. Fear prickled his scalp and he cringed, remembering he had been shot. He was still alive, but what would the consequences be? He focused on the florescent lights. Gunner closed his eyes and pinched the bridge of his nose, remembering the harrowing experience. "How long?" He struggled to sit up, but pain shot through his side. "Could you please set me up, man?"

"Will you play nice?"

"Do you think I'm in any position to play at anything?"

"I've seen you in action a time or two." Hawke chuckled and grabbed the remote to move the position of the bed.

Gunner winced and cradled his arm to ease the process. "Son of a..."

"It's a doozy, isn't it?" Hawke failed in his attempt to laugh it off. He got in Gunner's face. "Don't you ever do that shit again."

"Hawke, how long have I been here?"

"Too long." Hawke looked at the calendar on his phone. "Almost three weeks."

"What?" Gunner failed miserably at his attempt to get free of this prison.

Hawke pressed him back and got in his face. "G, stop it. Listen to me. You almost met your Maker. You've had three surgeries since you've been here to repair the damage the bullets caused. When we got here, you were barely hanging on. You'd lost a lot of blood. They had to put you in a medically induced coma because you kept ripping yourself up trying to bust out of here. On a positive note, you can eat whatever you want—they had to remove your gallbladder and some of your gut, the bit you can do without. Thankfully you were sedated while they took the hose from your nose. You were damn lucky, bro."

Gunner gulped for air. "You're not telling me something. Where is CJ? Don't tell me I was too late. Did Taz get her?" He cupped his hand over his face. "Please tell me she's okay."

"How much longer do we have to drive before you tell me where we're going?" CJ said as she paced a few steps. "Any more news on Gunner?"

"Not since the last time you asked two seconds ago. You're wearing a path. You should sit." Jeffrey tapped the passenger seat beside him. "I promise you will know as soon as I do. You're not doing anyone any good with all your nervous energy. He's in expert hands." He gave her a sympathetic look, then turned his gaze to the road. "We're stopping at a motel. We should be there in a few minutes," Jeffrey said over his shoulder as he piloted the Winnebago.

"I don't care about me. It's my fault Gunner got shot. They were after me."

"Gunner knew the risk when he was assigned to this case." Jeffrey scrubbed his upper nose hard. "Hell, I'm worried too."

"I'm sorry. I realize you've been friends for a long time. I'm freaking out." She waved her face to detour the tears threating again. She bent and ran a hand over the German Shepard's fur. "I'm forever in your debt, Karma. Thank you."

CJ walked to the rear of the RV and plunked on the couch. She looked at the phone she had in her pocket. Nothing. She sent a quick text—**I need help**—then waited for a reply.

Jeffrey returned with keys and a bag of snacks from the motel lobby. He threw her the key card. "You go in and shower. Room 2." He pointed. "We don't have a lot of time. I'll make a few calls and check on you when we're ready." Jeffrey rocked from heel to toe. "The guys helping me are in your car right behind us. They should be here any minute. You'll go with them to your next safe house in Missouri."

"I hate this. I should be with Gunner, not going further away. I'm over this." CJ shifted her backpack, threw the duffel over her shoulder, and tugged softly at the dog's leash. "Don't expect me to take long. Please. I need answers." CJ opened the motel room door and rifled through the bag for another set of clothes to change into. She was freezing and couldn't get warm. No way she was about to shower. Instead, she whipped her hair up and threw a washcloth in the sink. Her phone buzzed.

Who's this?

Sissy, it's Pissy.

She stared at the screen and waited for a reply.

I thought it was you. Are you okay?

CJ typed as fast as she could. **No. Can you tell Roman and Brady I want to come home? Someone found me here. One of the guards has been shot. I'm not sure he'll make it.**

Where are you?

I can't say. I'm with Jeffrey and they're taking me to another safe house. I can meet R&B somewhere. It's not safe.

Good, you're with Jeffrey. I feel better. What about your bodyguards?

Not for long. They have two new guards I don't know. Please help me, Sis. I want to come home and see you before I leave again. I can't risk anyone else I love being hurt because of me.

Don't you worry about us We have an army to protect you.

I thought I had one here, but anywhere I go, those I love, get hurt. I need to disappear. Everyone would be better off.

Don't you worry. I'll tell the brothers. You can depend on them.

CJ noticed the phone and directory, then she spied a motel pamphlet of area attractions. She rummaged through her bag and pulled on the map. **As far as I can tell, I'm somewhere in Alabama. Next stop, Missouri. Tell them I'll keep in touch.**

Jeffrey tapped at the door. "CJ, we're ready to go."

She swung the door open and handed him the key. "All done. But I need to take Karma to go potty."

He looked at his watch. "I'll update you before we go."

CJ stood, frozen.

"Get going. The dog's bladder takes precedence, then we can talk.

She hauled off at a run in the other direction. "Be right back. Hurry, you beautiful beast."

Jeffrey sat on the step, waiting for her return. She almost tripped as she hauled rear in record time. He handed CJ the new documents for her next destination.

"What are you not telling me?"

"Gunner made it to the base hospital. He's going into surgery."

CJ knew he wasn't telling her everything. "Is he going to

die?" She cupped her hand over her mouth preventing a blood-curdling scream.

"Hawke is with him and he's stable. That's all I know. He said he'd call me when he was out of surgery."

"It's all my fault."

"You keep saying it's your fault, but I've witnessed Gunner in action. It's in his blood to protect and serve. You are not responsible for his decisions."

"Who in the hell else would you blame?" she yelled. "The decisions he made last night were for me and I know it."

"Maybe so, but they were his decisions to make. Any one of your bodyguards would do the exact same thing. The way I see it is you didn't shoot him someone else did."

"He's a different breed all together. He is a better human than I will ever be. I'm responsible. He did what he did because he loves me, and I will live with that for the rest of my days." She wiped her cheeks with the back of her hand. "I need to get as far away from all of you if you want to grow old and gray." She looked at the papers for her new identity. "Why can't I just be Cinder Ashley Johnson from Solemn Creed, Colorado?"

He shrugged, so CJ gave Jeffrey a half hug and pivoted to the waiting car with her new keepers.

Nothing will ever be the same.

TWENTY-NINE

"You can't go anywhere; you still have a drain in your gut. They're doing another scan to make sure you're cleared to move."

"I'm losing my cool here. Can someone please get me in contact with CJ?"

"Jeffrey is calling soon. Maybe he can arrange it, but they're sending her off with Liam and Denver."

"This is the first time they've had a ward." He gritted his teeth. "I'm teetering on the edge, if I don't talk to her soon. I need to know she's doing okay." Frustration wrapped his words.

"Gunner, you know her better than most of us. Don't you think she can handle it? I do. It's them I'm worried about."

"She can. You may have a point. But I'd feel a lot better if you'd go to her next stop. For me."

"It's a big ask, G, but I'm not going anywhere. You are my priority. I need to keep an eye on you or you will go after her yourself. You're not physically prepared or got the mindset."

"I get the physicality part, and it appears I don't have a

choice, but what kind of asinine comment is the mindset thing?"

Hawke walked over to the side of the bed. "You got her on the brain. You're a lovesick schoolboy. My job is to make sure you get strong so you can go get your girl." He shook his head. "I know I've given you a shit ton of grief on going soft, but look where it got you."

"Watch your tone. You would have done the same thing. We prepared ourselves to get the hell out of dodge, but Tiny was who compromised us. I fought hard for years, shoving away everything I felt for her. This is new terrain. I never expected to fall in love."

"Oh, hell no." Hawke shook his hands wildly in the air, then cupped his ears. "Don't say the L word again. I just yacked in my mouth."

"Shut up, fuckface." Gunner held his side and winced in pain. "Don't make me laugh."

"Seriously, I saw it coming for years. Hoped you wouldn't cave, but I'm happy for you. If you haven't figure it out by now, she saved your life in more ways than one."

Gunner's eyes went wide and his head jerked. "She did?"

"CJ was my wingman when I hauled you to the house. She helped stop the bleeding and even gave blood. She didn't even get lightheaded, which was pretty amazing. It took both of us to get you stable. She's something, man. A mighty warrior." Hawke let out a sigh. "She can multi-task like no one's business, and that dog? I would have never found you if it wasn't for Karma. She led me straight to you. I couldn't have done it without her for damn sure." He shook his head. "Not to mention CJ telling you to fight your ass off and whispering sweet nothings in your ear." He thumped his chest. "Hate to admit it. Got me in the ticker."

Gunner threw a plastic pitcher at him, then winced in pain. "Stop."

"You think you have it bad? You're in perfect company with her. She told me more than once to make sure I told you she loved you. I practically had to drag her off you. She didn't want to leave your side. What's with you two? You must be drinking the same jungle juice. Keep me away. And get your shit-eating grin off your mug. You're freaking me out a little."

"Yeah, I'm lucky. You will be someday. You wait."

"Not for me in this lifetime. You are both lucky. Take a knee and rest. In a day or two, maybe we can arrange a reunion. I'll be hanging close, so don't get any harebrained ideas. You and I, we leave together or you don't go at all." He pointed a finger and gave Gunner his best *don't mess with me* look.

~

CJ LEANED FORWARD. "HOW MUCH LONGER?" she asked her new bodyguards.

"About two hours."

"Where are we going?"

"You're better off not knowing for your protection."

She rolled her eyes at his reflection in the rearview mirror. "Whatever, you're no fun. My other handlers always gave me the 411. It's not like anyone ever let me out of their sight." She stretched and sighed, adding another sigh for extra effect. "You know, I'm not a prisoner."

The guard in the passenger seat, Denver, leaned over to the driver. "She's right. What will it hurt? The lady could use a break. We were told by the boss to treat her like one of our own."

Liam gave him a look, then caved. "We're heading to the Springfield-Branson area."

"Thank you. Was that so tough? I've never been there." She snatched the map and a notepad, then circled the map near the Branson/Springfield airport. "I'm working on a project for all the places I've been. I'm nearing forty-seven states. Maybe one day I'll make it to Hawaii." She pulled her backpack onto the floorboard, then shifted to lie behind the passenger seat, curling up beside Karma. "I think I'm going to rest my eyes for a while. Can you let me know when we get close? I've heard Branson is a sight to see." She closed her eyes and slipped her hand into her bag, then sent a text.

ETA 2hours Branson/Springfield Missouri looks like we go by the airport on this route.

Your dream team hopped a flight asap after your message to Kansas. Waiting for instruction.

CJ's heart pounded so loudly she thought she'd go deaf. **Text you when we get closer. Can't miss us blue sports car with Just Married on the rear window.**

What? Never mind, her sister responded.

She wanted to jump in elation, knowing it would only be a matter of time before she saw her family. She opened her eyes as her dog gave her a stare. Karma got her—she knew something was up. No matter. Her big brothers would find her and bring her home. She closed her eyes and sank into the backseat. *Only a matter of time. My life. My rules.*

"You ready, G?"

"You know, another few days and you'd be in tip-top shape, but you are flipping driving me insane."

"We're heading to Missouri to see CJ first. When is Jeffrey supposed to check in?"

"He should have by now; I don't know what's keeping him.

He's been radio silent for the past few weeks, cleaning up things."

"Something isn't sitting right. Why? We have other people to do that. He's been our first line of communication." He counted his fingers. "You said almost two weeks? When did you hear from him last?"

"Richards checked in and said two bodyguards were taking her to Missouri to the new safe house. He had to meet Luca and Ryker regarding the DOA at the scene." Hawke scratched his head. "The boss and the General were here the first week you were in the hospital."

Gunner jerked his head back. "They were?"

"Learned a few things." Hawke crossed his arms over his chest and rocked from heel to toe.

"You don't say. Enlighten me." Gunner peered out the window.

"It wasn't so much of what they said, but how they acted." Hawke walked over to the window beside Gunner. He could feel his hot poker eyes boring fire through straight to his bones.

"What?" He winced. "Why are you rubber necking?" He did not want to have this conversation. "Not a clue what you're talking about."

"Yeah, you do. We've known each other too long."

Gunner stood frozen. "I meant to tell you, but they swore me to secrecy until they figured out the leak."

"I've known for a long time about the Boss being your Tia. Why do you think I'm hanging around? But the General? I know how much you didn't get along with your dad, but knowing he's the General, now I see why. He's cock-blocked all our attempts to find your brother."

"Don't remind me. I'd rather forget. Sorry, man. I hated lying to you."

"Me too. I also hate to admit this, while you were in la la

land, I did some checking around. Even though it's classified, the General is still searching for your brother. He may not want us to look for him, but he's still looking for Hunter. It's his personal mission."

"All of us have been. Luca and Ryker still have a few connections they're calling in some favors. I don't get why the General told me to stop my search. He always gave orders, all my life, for no reason, but this one was the last straw. I loathe the man and his ego."

"Can't blame you. I'm not a fan either. He was one of the biggest reasons I left the service. On a different note, you are a hell of a lot better looking than him and you definitely have more hair." Hawke tapped his phone to his lips. "Come to think of it, I haven't heard from them either."

CJ SAT up and rubbed her eyes. She must have fallen asleep for a few winks. Eyeing the clock on the dash, she realized she had been asleep for an hour and a half. She surveyed her surroundings as the green mile marker showed her approximately where they were. CJ eyed the map and realized there were only four miles from the airport. She frantically grabbed her phone. **Four miles to airport 266 to 144.**

Waiting at convenience store 1st exit past airport look for the big heart. Go to restroom. We're waiting behind there in grey sedan.

CJ stuffed her phone into the backpack and sat up straight. She scanned the area to get her wits about her and saw the heart sign off in the distance. "I don't feel so good. The sandwich I had earlier is at war with my belly." She grabbed her stomach and groaned. "Yep, I think you need to find a bathroom stat, or we are getting to know each other in a way I prefer not to." She leaned forward and pointed. "You better take this exit. I might have food poisoning."

"Can you wait a little while longer?"

She groaned and the dog got up on her haunches. "I swear I'll poo the light fantastic right here." Liam hit the pedal and swerved onto the exit. "Say no more."

She tapped her feet and wiggled around, moaning and oohing and ahhing. She closed her eyes, wincing, or they'd be sure to tell she was adlibbing. "This one right here!"

She took off with her bag and the dog in tow practically before they stopped and ran to the side of the building.

One of the guards stumbled to follow and ran after her. "Wait! I need to check the bathroom first!"

She turned and ran past the bathroom, then behind the building, ducking under a couple of bushes and pulling her four-legged sidekick along. She ran to the waiting grey sedan, thrilled to see her brother's familiar face.

"Haul ass! They're right behind me."

He opened the back door and the dog jumped in, with CJ right behind. She flung herself forward. Karma growled, and CJ heard a vaguely familiar voice.

"Get the hairball off me before someone gets hurt, meaning me!"

"Karma! Off!" CJ leaned forward. "What are you doing here, Mr. Firefighter Man?"

"Guess who your brothers recruited? I'm their backup instead of your sister coming along. She was not happy either."

The car spun around, flinging gravel in its wake.

CJ stared out the rear window. "Poo, that was close. Hurry, the sports car has a lot of gitty-up-and-go."

"They haven't seen me driving."

"And he has this." Brady turned and put red lights on the roof of the car. "Hey sis." He gave her a knuckle bump.

She gave one back, along with the biggest hug to Brady and Roman.

"I see you're still up to no good, causing your big brothers to prematurely age." He ruffed up her hair. "Seriously, Sis, what have you been waiting for? This has been awesome."

She wrapped her arms around their necks. "I love you so much." She fought the tears. "You don't know how many times I've dreamt of the day I'd see you again."

"Glad we could assist, CJ. Where to?"

"Home. I want to go home."

Jax pushed his way around the dog, who was licking him half to death. "We suspected as much. We have help in Solemn Creed readying for your arrival. I know your sister and your parents will be ecstatic to see you."

"Guess Karma likes you. She knows good people. I bet she knows you're family."

"Good thing. I'd hate to be on her bad side."

"We better take a few side roads and fast if we want to lose these guys. I'm assuming they won't give up without a fight."

"I don't know them, but I checked the gas gauge. They won't make it far. The gas was almost on empty."

"You've learned a few tricks over the years, sis. Have we told you how proud we are?"

"I could hear that every minute of every day and never tire of it. Keep talking." CJ rested her chin on her hands.

"Why do you look so sad?"

"I've done so much wrong in my life. I was thinking about one of my bodyguards, one who protected me from the very beginning. He was shot and I have no way of seeing how he is without them sending someone after me."

"Shot?" Jax piped up. "Who?"

"Gunner." CJ lowered her head and rubbed her hands

together. "He must make it through, but I haven't heard if he did."

"That sucks. I'm sorry. I know how close you were to your guards. Especially him."

"We will see what we can do. Maybe Jeffrey knows?"

"No! Not right now. Get me home first, please. This time around, it's on my terms."

CHAPTER

THIRTY

Gunner shifted in his seat and looked at Hawke, who was driving. "What the hell do you mean, she's not in Missouri anymore? We're on our way." Gunner pressed the speaker button so Hawke could hear.

"Why have you not been answering any of my calls?" Hawke yelled into the phone.

"I've been swamped. The entire team has. I have some good news and some bad news."

"I want the news on CJ first."

"You'll have to wait. This takes precedence."

"You're walking a fine line, Jeffrey. I'm a ticking time bomb."

"Relax, my man. Take a deep breath."

"Get with it, Richards. Trust me, it's not pretty here. He's on edge." Hawke shifted his peepers in Gunner's direction and whispered, "Chill. You know him. If she wasn't okay, he'd tell you."

Gunner nodded, taking a huge pull of air into his lungs. He closed his eyes. "Go on."

"G, you got him. The guy at the back gate who shot you was Taz. We found him in the bushes with a couple of your bullets in him, and we arrested the other guys who hit both the gates."

"He's the fucker that shot me? Where is he? I'd like to thank him and the rest of them."

"Taz hung on for a while but didn't make it. He died. I'm sure it will get blazing hot where he's going. The rest of them are behind bars. Another guy is facing attempted murder. We recovered his weapon, and a match to the scene at the gate."

"There were a bunch of them outside the gate, but two were trailing me." Gunner flung a hand in the air and Hawke gave him a high-five. "You're shitting me?"

"Afraid not. We've been working our asses off cleaning this mess up. You weren't in any shape during most of this to hear anything. I wanted to make sure there weren't any loopholes. And why we've been off the radar. Luca also did a little checking on the nosy neighbors who visited you."

"Cruella De Ville or Mrs. Kravitz?" Gunner piped in.

"Mainly the one with the black and white hair who lives in the house on Almandy. She has a nephew with ties to Taz; that's how Tiny was followed. It wasn't to the subdivision, but away, as it turns out."

"Why am I only hearing this now?"

"The Boss Lady told me you needed to focus on recovering. You gave us a scare."

"I hear ya. Great news, but friend or not, I'll give you another scare if you don't tell me where CJ is."

"I guess I've kept you lingering on the line long enough. First, she's safe. I can say from personal experience she's a pistol. She drove me nuts and was relentless, trying to get to you. I assured her you were getting the best care you could."

"Okay..."

"We had a couple of new recruits' step in since everyone else was tied up. They got her to Missouri, but she gave them the slip. It was planned."

"Gave them the slip? Where is she?"

"She's in Solemn Creed, under protection with Cade Winslow, his boss Sutton Bishop, and about a dozen more people in her family."

"You're there?"

"Of course, I am. I couldn't disappoint my buddy, leaving the only thing that took his edge off unprotected."

"You're kidding me. She's there."

"She's a hell of a lot safer there right now than she's been. I suggest you get there and talk some sense into her, because I don't know how much longer I can hold her off."

"We're on our way. Hey, do me a favor. Don't let her know we're coming."

"Gotcha, but you better hurry. If she catches wind of it, she may bolt."

CJ sat in her bedroom on a fluffy side chair near a window with a beautiful view of majestic mountains. Her heart swelled at being where she grew up. Off in the distance grazed a herd of deer near the trees. It was great to be in Solemn Creed and the last few weeks she had shifted from place to place. But the familiar faces of her loved ones gave her peace. Precious time with her parents, her grandfather, her brothers and sister had filled her well.

She lifted her journal, the one Gunner had given her. Jeffrey had told her Gunner was out of the hospital, but she hadn't heard from him. Would he forgive her? He'd almost gotten killed because of her. The ache was so deep she gasped for air.

"I love you, Gunner."

She swiped a tear from her cheek. Sooner or later, her time would end here in Solemn Creed too. Would she have the strength to slip away once again for love? She'd caused a stir, but they needed to get their own lives back, not constantly watch over her. No one would ever be safe in her presence. It had been nice, being Cinder Ashley Johnson again for a while.

She spread the map across the bed. She had almost all the spots marked. "Where to next?" She picked up her phone and pressed the 1 key.

His deep voice resonated through the line. "Hello, CJ. What's up?" Jeffrey said.

She paced across the rich wooden floors. "Have you heard from Gunner? How is he?"

"He's getting better every day."

"Did you give him my message?"

"I did," he said.

"Does he have my number?"

"Yes, I gave it to him."

"Oh, okay." She clutched her chest. She couldn't breathe. He hadn't forgiven her and didn't want to talk. She'd hoped she could at least tell him goodbye. She inhaled deep through her nose and lifted her chin high. "Do you think you can get me another alias? I think it's time to leave."

"Sure."

"I think I want to go to Hawaii."

"Hawaii? That's a tall order. I'll need a few days, and will require a flight."

"Go big right?" She tried to laugh, but her heart ached. "You only live once."

"I'll call you when I get everything arranged."

"Thank you, Jeffrey."

"I RECEIVED another text from Jeffrey. CJ asked for a new identity. He's trying to stall to give us time to get there." He looked at the three dots, waiting for the next text to come through. "She asked about you, again. It's killing me to see her in so much pain."

Gunner tried to dislodge the boulder-size lump in his throat. He turned to Hawke, who was driving. "How much longer before we get there?"

"We'll be there by morning at the latest."

"Go to my place, not the house. I have new tenants. I'll be in the barn waiting," Jeffrey said.

"See you." Gunner ended the call. "Hawke, you need to take a knee. I'm golden, I can drive from here."

"Okay, as long as you're solid."

"I'm antsy as hell. Whose idea was it to drive anyway?"

"Your girl. She was supposed to be in Missouri. Remember?"

GUNNER SHOOK HAWKE AWAKE. "Come on. We're here." Gunner leaped from the vehicle and opened the barn door.

"Hold on. Let me test him or he'll fill you full of lead and you'll never get to profess your love."

Gunner craned his neck. "Already did while you were sawing wood." He laughed and met Jeffrey inside.

"Boy, does this place bring us a few memories." He turned and looked at Hawke.

He hitched a thumb in the huge cluster of trees across the property. "We spent many hours watching for James Devland to make a move on your sister. One small break and she gave him an iron wallop instead."

"She sure did." Jeffrey shook Gunner's hand, then Hawke's. "Looking good, Ward. You gave everyone a scare. Looks like you lost a little weight."

"Don't worry, I'll find it again." He laughed, then his lips went into a flat line. "Thanks for updating me on CJ."

"Look at you. You got it bad."

"That's what I've been saying." Hawke's laugh echoed in the space.

"Come on in. I'll fill you in on everything else and arrange for us to see CJ." He waved them to follow him up the stairs.

"I appreciate it, but I need to do this alone."

Jeffrey raised his hands. "I'll get you there, but you won't get anywhere near her until I make some calls to Cade, his boss, and a team with the DEA. Trust me, they are taking their role very seriously. Then you have Jax, who came to get CJ with her brothers, Connor Winslow, Dan, Evan, and so on. We may need to recruit a few of them, especially her brothers. The account of her getaway was impressive. Maybe CJ needs a job?"

Gunner rubbed his hands together and stomped this way and that. "I'm ready now," he growled.

"Relax for a minute," Hawke said. "Let Jeffrey do what he said." Hawke patted his shoulder. "Come sit for a minute." He pointed to a huge leather couch in newly renovated loft Jeffrey spent time in when he wasn't on the road.

"Yeah, you guys relax." He handed them a couple of waters. "I'll make a few calls, but we need to be discreet." Jeffrey moved into the other room where his office was.

"G, use your head."

"You know I've never put CJ in harm's way. This is different. She was, and I wasn't there. It's eating me alive, knowing I couldn't do more."

"You fucking shot Taz and almost got yourself killed. Give yourself a break. You were fighting for your life. It's impossible to be there for her 24/7. You're at the end of your tether. She was responsible for her actions and she's smart. What kind of life will you have if you do this kind of shit?"

"She could have gotten killed."

Hawke leaned forward. "But she didn't and she's safe. You weren't. You almost died trying to get to her. You knew the risks of running, what, three to four blocks with shrapnel in you, bleeding profusely. You're lucky to be sitting here."

Gunner nodded. "You're right, but all I thought was I needed to get back to her."

"Not cool, bro. Near catastrophic. You always put your safety first. I've known you a long time and hurts like hell. You're my best friend, but you weren't thinking about your own safety. I'm pissed off. You did the same thing with your brother. I get it that's what we do, but..." He paused and rubbed his eyes. "I almost had to bury my best friend."

Hawke's reprimand had an entirely new level of compassion to it. "You're right. This time I didn't either. I'm sorry."

"You're forgiven this time, but don't let it happen again." His stern look softened. "You don't think CJ is a mess over this piece of information? She's blaming herself for you getting shot. More than likely, why she ran off."

"I didn't think of anything but her. I know she's been unraveling. I guess I've overstepped when it came to protecting her at the cost of myself and the safety of the team."

"First step is admitting it. Can I give you a little more of my advice?"

"I have a feeling you'd do it anyway." Gunner shoved his hands in his pockets and looked at his boots.

"You know me well." Hawke laughed and eased in his chair. "You need to think about where you want things to go with her. You can't keep this up, and I suspect she can't either. Wrecks my gut too, she went off away from the team. Ask yourself this...do you want to be a part of her protection detail? Or do you want more?"

"Can't I do both?"

"That's where the lines get blurry." Hawke lifted his palms and raised each up and down like a weighted scale, then stood. "You're one of the smartest men I know. You'll figure it out. I'll support you, whatever you decide." He walked away, then turned, peering over his shoulder. "Hey. Both of you are worth the risk. Even better, you're right for each other. Hate to admit it, but I've seen this coming for a long time."

Gunner arched a brow. "Hawke, thanks man." Gunner shifted and anchored his elbows on his knees, staring at the multi-colored rug beneath his shit kickers. "Guess I had that one coming," he whispered to no one.

Jeffrey tramped in the room. "We need to go. We've arranged for a morning stroll with her sister on the property. Jax and Roman know you're coming and said they'd keep to themselves but will be close by, so you have a window. Her sister will distract her."

Gunner jumped up and smacked his hands together. "I'm ready."

"Gunner, you need to tread lightly. None of us know exactly what she's feeling."

~

CJ WALKED with Andrea on the property. She felt safe with her brother and Jax hanging closely behind. "Guess the guys don't much like picking flowers." CJ glanced at them. "I'm sorry I've been such a burden."

"Stop that kind of talk this instant." Her sister stomped her foot and it made her laugh. "The time you have been here, has been healing for all of us. Besides, you need to make up for the lost years. I'll take it in any form, but you are not a burden. I can't express this enough." Her sister grabbed her hand. "We've missed so many years and we'll never get them back, but we have today and hopefully more tomorrows. I know it has been for me." Her sister stopped and faced CJ, "It has been but it's not enough. You're here, but not 100 percent."

"You're right. I've hurt a lot of people over the years, and I'm trying to do the right thing. I don't know how to move forward. This isn't the life I imagined."

"It's in the past. All you can do is move forward."

"Some of it isn't that far in the past. I mentioned I almost killed one of my guards."

"Gunner, right? He was doing his job, protecting you." Andrea pulled her in tighter and put an arm around her, like they used to when they were younger.

CJ leaned her head to her sister's. "Protecting me and him getting hurt is my fault. The same thing will happen here. I can't risk your lives either."

"I think that's a decision for us to make. Many things in life are worth holding onto." Andrea released CJ and turned her around. "Move forward and hold tight."

"What?" CJ squinted, lifting her hand to her forehead. She turned her gaze to her sister, who pointed off in the distance. She had tears in her eyes.

CJ whipped around. "Move forward and hold on, sissy." Her sister said with emotion-quaked words.

Out of the corner of her eye, she saw him. CJ gasped.

Gunner stood off in the distance. She stumbled and he moved in her direction.

"Gunner!" she screamed at the top of her lungs. Each step was unsteady and filled with uncertainty, but her heart propelled her forward. She took off at a run and leaped into his arms. He stumbled a few steps and grunted. "Oh, my gosh, I'm sorry, I hurt you."

A grin creased his face. "Not a chance." He wrapped his arms around her. With them firmly secured around her, she knew she was home. She cupped her hands to the sides of his face. "I can't believe you're here. Are you okay?" She shivered.

"I'm better now. It may have taken me a while, but I'm here for something I lost. I'm not leaving without her." He kissed her softly on the lips. "If you will have me. Please say you will." His gaze penetrated her soul. "Your rules, I'll abide by them. CJ, my life makes no sense without you by my side." He rested his forehead to hers.

"I don't need you to protect me. Who am I? I don't even know who I am anymore."

"I can't promise you I won't protect my woman. I know exactly who you are and who've you've always been—the strongest, most beautiful woman I've ever been privileged to know. But I can promise you I won't be a bodyguard for hire. I'd throw it all away for you." He knelt on one knee. "Cinder Ashely Johnson, you have the most jaw-dropping energy. Being near you is where I must be. You make me strive to be a better man. You're the life force that runs through my veins. You saved me when I didn't know I needed saving. We can have it all, if we're together."

"Side by side?" she asked, running her hands over his shoulders. "It doesn't work any other way."

He pulled papers from his cargo pocket. "I have your new

identity if you want it. We can stay or go wherever you want. You choose."

CJ squinted her eyes, not one hundred percent convinced she was prepared for where the next stop was. She studied the first line and her heart fluttered. Tears filled her eyes as she stared at the passports and identification. Gunner Ward and Cinder A. Ward. "This has serious potential." she waved the papers to her face. "But how can we?"

"Taz is dead. The rest of them are behind bars."

CJ gasped. "Dead? Gone? For real. How?" She put her fingers to her lips and trembled. "I may get my life back?"

"We took care of it. They didn't know who they were messing with. You did it. It's always been your life, but now we have a chance to breathe a little and experience the years you've missed."

She wiped at her face and bubbled inside.

"I'd like to walk the journey with you. Please marry me for real this time." His eyes sparkled and his face beamed.

She lifted her shaky hand. "Can I keep this ring though?"

He laughed and nodded. "You can have whatever you want."

She cocked her head to the side and studied Gunner. "If I can choose whatever I want, I choose you." She leaned in, wrapping her arms around his waist. CJ kissed Gunner lightly on the lips and pressed her ear to his chest. "Do you feel that?"

"More than you can imagine." He inhaled deeply and exhaled.

"Good. I feel us too." She gazed into his hazel eyes. "We've waited long enough for our turn at a happily ever after. I say yes—yes, I'll marry you."

AFTERWORD

To my Readers,

Thank you so much for your support and interest in my books. Thank you for giving me this opportunity to share my stories. I can't thank you enough.

Stay tuned as the Noble Network Security and our favorite bodyguards fight against peril to defend a new chapter of hope.

So many heroes and heroines are waiting for their story to be told.

Do you want to join my street team?

Show me some love and join me on Facebook in my private readers group, Jodi's Hot Zone.

This group is a place of positivity and empowerment for strong women and the book boyfriends who light up their lives.

https://www.facebook.com/groups/JodiJamesHotZone

ACKNOWLEDGMENTS

I'm a family first kind of girl, and I'd like to thank my peeps for their unwavering support and love. Your strength and cheerleading pushed me when fear and doubt derailed the process.

Mom, I'm still making my heart sing. Thank you for being my biggest fan. I am blessed beyond measure.

To my husband Tim, you are my best friend, advocate, and supporter. You taught me the true meaning of love and respect. I hope you are proud of me.

To my fur baby's Romeo and Guinness, you are such patient, happy boys. Thank you for being my companions as I spend way too much time in my office, writing. I owe you more kisses and cuddles. You have taught me to see the beauty that surrounds us.

To my village...

I want to extend a colossal thank you to Kelly Johnson at Cornerstone Virtual Assistance for being my right-hand powerhouse through the years. I won the Mega-million with you. Thank you for holding my hand through many firsts. I can't imagine my life without you. I think we make a fabulous team and I'm in awe of your talents, which are too many to count.

Thank you to my editor, Karie Crawford, at CookieLynn Publishing Services, you have made such a difference in my writing journey.Thank you for bringing my story to new heights.

Kudos to Megan Parker Squires at Em Cat Designs, for the 'Noble Network' and 'Brothers of Solemn Creed' covers. I'm excited about the rest of the series. Thank you for making my visions come to life.

Sue Kraus, much love and thanks for the 'Noble Network Security,' crosshairs logo. You hit the mark.

A special applause to Nancy and David Moline for brainstorming names that encapsulated my honorable protective heroes and now known as the Noble Network. David, thank you for answering my random questions. You are so knowledgeable about everything.

Melody Calder, thank you for adding a little extra sizzle to one of my scenes. Thank you for your time and a fresh perspective. I look forward to working with you again.

Lisa O'Neil, thank you for being such a positive influence in my readers' group, Jodi's Hot Zone. You make waking up a pleasure, you bring happy into our little corner. I am beyond blessed to know such a beautiful soul. Thank you for your friendship.

To all the Hotties in the Hot Zone, thank you for supporting me and my writing. You are the genuine heroes. Your kindness makes this world a better place.

To the Dream Team, you are my tribe and my soul sisters. I've never met such loving, giving women, and it is truly an honor to walk this journey. I am stronger knowing you have my back. I'm privileged to be in your circle. Much love and admiration.

To the members of Romance Writers of The Rockies and Florida West Coast Writers, thank you for teaching me the value of community.

Thank you to all the branches of the military, and everyday heroes. Much respect to hospital workers, medical personnel, and first responders who inspire my series. Thank you for your sacrifice and service.

ABOUT THE AUTHOR

Jodi James was raised in the heartland of Iowa. She currently lives in sunny Florida with her husband and her two fur babies, Romeo, and Guinness. Blessed with a successful career in the hair and beauty industry spanning four decades.

She's fulfilling a passion of writing. Her journey has transcended and evolved from reading and being inspired by the authors that wrote the words, forever changing her path.

Reading gave her a soft place to land. Jodi writes about perseverance, positivity, and passion. She believes in the happily-ever-after. Writing makes her heart sing.

Jodi loves to connect with readers.
https://linktr.ee/jodijames
AuthorJodiJames.com
https://authorjodijames.com/newsletters/

ALSO BY JODI JAMES

If you like strong women, tormented heroes, and sizzling attractions, then you'll adore Jodi James's pulse-pounding novels in the Brothers of Solemn Creed romantic suspense series.

https://books2read.com/LegacyPrequel

https://books2read.com/InTheHeatOfItAll

https://books2read.com/ToTheCore

https://books2read.com/OneNightBook3

-

https://books2read.com/AtTheEndOfTheDay

Holiday novella with all the feels.

Merry Frickin' Christmas

https://books2read.com/MerryFrickinChristmas